A LITTLE MERMAID RETELLING

BOOK ONE

KITSUNE

NICOLETTE
ANDREWS

SECOND EDITION

Dedicated to all my Kickstarter backers who made this book possible!
Thanks for believing in me.

This Edition Made Possible By My Kickstarter Backers

Extra Special Thanks To:

Iris, Shireen Harrison, Rebekah Deats, Effie Hofer & Evelynn Hofer, Nathalie, Jas Z. Alicia T. Stoesser, & Bryan Zeitz

And Thanks To:

Brittnay King, Li Cai Haney, Ashley Tomlinson, Wendy Alvarez, Lilian, Kara Stogsdill, Kellie N., Megyn "Crimson" MacDougall, Lauren Armstrong, Sunny Side Up, T.L. Branson, Vera Soroka, Tessonja Odette, Kristen White, Allyson Lindt, Matthea W. Ross, Cassidy, Melissa Williams, Billye Herndon, Courtney G., Carlye Pierce, Jenna Leavitt, Foxz Bambina, Charis Lavoie, Taylor Lust, Michelle Huang, Emma Radovich, Michelle Badillo, Katherine Shipman, Hannah Schindler, Kayla Cotrell, Ariadna, Natasha McGrath, Crystal Christian, Oliver Gross, Mekomiya, Melanie Briggs, B. Sawyer, Renee Portnell, Dragondariu, Ursula Urrutia, Ashley Jean, Vixen Rue-Aurora, Alexandra Werhan, Kanyon Kiernan, Iris Pleitez, Melanie Karsak, Stephanie Meredith, Meredith Carstens, Heather Dianne, Catherine Banks, Nikole C., Alli Tambaoan, PunkARTchick *Ruthenia*, Zack Newcomb, Sherry Mock, Charity Chimni, Anna Sherles, Mike Dobey, Chris Munroe, Felicia MacLaren, Manon Lanzarotti, Christina Hecht, Reina Setsuna, Konvinna S., Christina B., Lauren Sarsby, Kris B., Sabrina Elizabeth Cline, Nicole Akeroyd-Slater, Alexandrea M, Myranda Haarman, Robert & Sierra Krusmark

ONE

The boar was covered in coarse black hair. The giant yellow tusks curved around his snout as he pawed at the ground. The young man stood transfixed in place, staring down the eyes of the beast. Rin watched him, wondering what he would do. From the trembling of his hands, he did not seem to be the type who could defend himself very well. His clothes were tattered and dirt stained but finely made. *He must be someone important in the human world. I wonder why he came into this forest.*

She did not meddle in human affairs as a matter of principle. They lived such brief uninteresting lives she could not be bothered by them. Then as she stared at the young man, he turned slowly to face her. His dark eyes looked at her and saw her not as a fox, as he should, but as a woman. She could see the spark of recognition, and the confusion, overlaid by his fear. The boar charged and the young man looked for his sword, just out of reach in a bush nearby. Not that it would have mattered either way—no human blade could kill that beast. She should not have cared what happened to him. But as if controlled by some outside force, she pushed the young man out of the way of the churning hooves of the monstrous boar.

The boar roared as he passed, the sheer weight of his body propelling him forward and crashing through the brush. It was a large clumsy beast. It collided with a tree twice as thick as Rin and snapped it in half. It tossed its massive head and focused gleaming yellow eyes on the pair of them. *Now I've done it. Akio will have my head for interfering.* She looked down at the young man as she straddled his waist and he stared up at her in a daze. His eyes glazed over her face and came to rest upon the pair of fox ears on top of her head. *No doubt about it now, he knows what I am.*

He opened and closed his mouth like a fish out of water. It was rather amusing. She grinned as she jumped off of him.

"We should get out of here; those trees will not hold him back for long." She jutted a thumb towards the trees that shielded them from the boar's wrath. The boar tore at bark with his tusks, grunting and snorting as he dug chunks of earth out of the ground. The space in between the branches was too narrow to allow for his massive body to pass. But judging from the growing pile of splinters, they would not remain an obstacle for much longer.

A wild animalistic panic threatened to overcome her. It screamed at her to transform into a fox and hide in the underbrush. She smothered the impulse; for some strange reason she felt she had to help this young man. *If Akio wants him this bad, then I cannot let him have this man.*

The young lord climbed to his feet, his hands shaking. His open mouth gaped at her ears; then slowly his gaze traveled downward to her foxtail, which she swished back and forth behind her. The boar roared again and the young man tore his gaze away from her and stared terrified back at the beast trying very hard to come and tear them apart.

"Run, my lady, I will defend you," the human said. He reached for a sword that was not there. So instead he put up his arms to shield her from the boar.

She laughed. She did not mean to, but he had all but wet himself out of fear. How could he hope to protect her when she had to save him first?

"You cannot hope to defeat him," she replied. "Follow me or die, those are your choices." She jogged away from the clearing and deeper into the forest, where the undergrowth grew to her thigh and the trees close together. It would be impossible for the boar to follow.

It was foolish to save him, even more foolish to talk to him, but sometimes it was the foolish things that brought the most entertainment.

What I want to know is how he can see me. A human should not be able to see my form without me revealing it to him. Any other Yokai in her position would leave him to the mercy of the boar, but he had piqued her curiosity. He fumbled in the undergrowth as he followed after her, whereas Rin moved about with grace, not so much as bending the grass underfoot. He broke branches and mumbled curses under his breath when his silken robes got caught on a thorny bush and tore a gaping hole. *He'll wake every bloodthirsty Yokai in the forest, stomping around like that.* She waited perched on a boulder as he mourned his ruined clothes.

He glanced up to see her watching him, dropped the fabric and continued onward. She flicked her tail and leapt down from the boulder, running ahead, checking to make sure there were no more nasty surprises waiting for them in the shadows. She spread out her senses, searching for other Yokai, and though she sensed others in the forest, none were close by. *That's a relief, at least.*

She led him through the twisted pathways through the forest known only to forest inhabitants. She felt the boar waiting on the edges of the forest, where the woods were sparse. He roared again but too far away to be any danger now. *He'll be returning to his master, I suspect.* She glanced over her shoulder to check on the young man, and found him bent over gasping for breath. *I forget how fragile these humans can be.* She waited for him to regain his composure. She wanted to question him further, but she had broken enough laws just by saving him. She dared not incriminate herself further, not in Akio's realm. She looked away from him lest he catch her staring and take it upon himself to ask his own questions. She had seen the sidelong looks he gave her, and she knew he had questions of his own.

When he stood upright once more, she said, "Keep going this

way and you'll be outside the forest." She pointed to a narrow animal track that twisted around the trees and led out onto a human road. He looked up at her, then past her to the path. When his eyes were off her, she cloaked herself. When he looked up again, he would see the forest behind her.

"Thank—" he started to say. He swiveled his head back and forth. He scratched his head as his eyes skimmed over her, unseeing. She could see the question in his eyes, wondering what she was, just as she was wondering why he could see her. After a few moments, he shrugged and turned to walk away. She watched him amble down the pathway she had indicated. He took a few steps before stopping to check for her over his shoulder. A part of her wanted to chase after him, but she knew no good could come of that. They lived in separate worlds. How he could see her would remain a mystery. After searching for her to no avail, he continued on the path and disappeared around the bend. She waited until he was out of sight before heading back into the forest.

Once again in fox form, she flew through the forest under-growth. She could smell blood in the air; the boar had not been completely unsuccessful. *I thought humans of this region knew to stay away from this forest. I wonder what madness drove them in here.* She leapt over a fallen tree. *It does not concern me, I suppose. Though I would have liked to learn more about that human. He was interesting.* She laughed at her own curiosity. *That is the first time I've ever thought that of a human.*

As she ran, she spread out her senses. She had felt nothing since the boar, and then as she approached her destination, she noticed an overhead shadow, which leapt from branch to branch, keeping pace with her. If it was a Yokai, they had cloaked their spiritual energy, making them invisible to her probes. And if it was a Yokai, it also meant they were more powerful than her. She reached a clearing in the woods; the trees circled a grassy area open on all sides. It was a convenient spot to confront her stalker, one where she could escape from if need be.

She transformed back into a woman and said, "Come out, I know you're there."

It dropped out of the tree to her right. She tilted her head to look at him, as if she were merely curious and not on the defensive. His tunic and split pants were black and he wore a white mask over his face. The mask had only two dark holes for the eyes, no space for a mouth or nose.

"Can I safely assume you are here to welcome me?" Rin asked.

The messenger did not appear to be amused. "What business do you have in the guardian's forest?" was his monotone reply.

"I am the Dragon's messenger."

The warrior's hand hovered over his sword. "And what message might the Dragon have for Akio?"

"Are you Akio?" Rin asked, though she already knew the answer.

"No."

She laughed. "Then I am not inclined to answer your questions, now am I?"

"You saved that human, why? You know I must report this to the guardian."

She shrugged. How could she explain such a whim when she did not even understand it herself?

"Do you plan on taking me as a prisoner to Akio, then?" She held out her hands as if she expected him to bind them together.

"No, but I will escort you to his palace."

She waved her hand. "Lead the way, then."

Rin followed after the warrior. He walked with an upright rigid air that one would expect from Akio's guard. He did not turn to make sure she followed. Not that it was necessary, he could stop her in an instant if she tried to flee. The guardian's palace was hidden in the middle of the forest, the entrance guarded by a long rope bridge over a canyon. They crossed the bridge, which swung back and forth. Rin glanced over the edge at the chasm below. Low-hanging clouds blocked the bottom from view. The palace building itself was hidden amongst the trees, some twined with the building, as if it had been here since the dawn of time and the trees merely grew through the structure. The verandas and covered walkways were shaded by the canopies of trees to the point where Rin could not see where the building started and the trees ended.

Once they crossed the bridge, they climbed up a narrow set of stairs, which ended at a double door. There were two guards; both of them had the head of deer and the body of men. They wore armor, painted red, over black gathered pants and tunic. They stared straight forward, ignoring the warrior who had come to fetch Rin. The warrior moved silent as a ghost into the courtyard beyond. It was slated in marble, twisted with black and gold flecks. The roots of a large tree grew in cracks of the marble, like veins. She followed after the warrior, who gave her no instruction but seemed to expect compliance.

They climbed a smaller set of steps into the main building. Here the floors were covered in tatami, bamboo mats, and at the far end of the room on a raised platform sat the forest guardian, Akio. He was a massive creature who dominated the space. He had the head of a boar and instead of hands he had hooves. He wore several layers of bright silk robes. The sleeves draped over his arms and pooled on the ground near his thick meaty thighs. Yokai attended him, all of them animal hybrids like the guards at the door, a few monkeys, and a few more deer women served him platters of dumplings and fish cooked in a thick dark sauce. The warrior who had come to fetch her knelt down before the boar and laid his head down to the ground.

"My lord, I found this Kitsune wandering the forest," he said in a formal clipped tone.

The boar ate messily; dark sauce dribbled off his snout and onto his bright yellow kimono. He glanced over at Rin like one does a buzzing fly. He had small beady eyes like the creature who had attacked the young lord. But unlike the dumb animal, there was cunning staring back at her.

"You are a messenger of the Dragon," he said. His voice rumbled and shook his massive gut.

"Is it that obvious?" Rin replied. She could not help but taunt him. Her position as a messenger gave her immunity.

Akio did not seem amused. "Does your master forget that I have forbidden any of his court in my domain?"

"Ah. As the Dragon has often reminded you, your domain is within his kingdom and therefore you are his subject."

The boar laughed. "You are brash for someone with such a low status."

He thinks to humiliate me. Well... "That jibe might sting more if it were not coming from a mouth full of food."

He jumped to his feet, knocking over platters and spilling a jug of sake in the process. Rin grinned, not backing down an inch.

"How dare you insult me in my own palace!" he roared.

"I would chastise you for being rude as well, but I feel it would be a futile effort."

"You insolent worm. I should have you locked away to rot."

"And then you would have a real war on your hands," Rin replied.

The boar narrowed his eyes. "Who are you really?"

"Just the Dragon's messenger, nothing more."

"I find that suspect." He sat back down on his cushion. And then he leaned forward, his hooves folded in front of him.

"The Dragon asks that you attend a feast," Rin said.

"Does he now? Is this his way of distracting us from his human lover?"

Human lover? She had expected tricks from Akio, but this was too farfetched even for her to imagine. The servants that sat beside him leaned in and whispered to one another, giving her furtive looks. A doe towards the front gave her a slow smile. Rin smiled back, full of honey laced with poison. *They cannot possibly know me. I am just being paranoid.*

The boar grinned, revealing crooked yellow teeth. "You know about it, I am sure. They say the Dragon has become ensorcelled by a human woman. There are rumors he has even abandoned his palace in favor of dancing to the human's whims."

She tried to picture the Dragon with a human. She had spent so much time avoiding him she could not recall where she had last seen him. *He leaves from time to time and he's been known to take human lovers but never for long and never serious.* "That's the problem with rumors, they are often misleading. Don't you agree?" she said.

The boar shook his head. He waved his hoof and the servants rose as one and filed out of the room. Rin watched them go with a growing sense of dread. She may have bitten off more than she could chew with Akio.

"I have no time for your games. I know the Dragon wants to

lure me out of my palace, but I am no fool. You thought to trick me, but you're not nearly clever enough to play this game."

"I never intended to enter a game of wits with you. There's no competition where you are involved." She examined her pointed nails.

He grinned at her, revealing yellow teeth. *Perhaps he missed the insult.* "You would have done better to come groveling if you wanted to play a spy, Rin."

Her mouth dropped open as her stomach sank. How could he possibly guess her motives? She had told no one of her intentions, not even Shin. "You—"

"Yes, I know who you are, and I know you are no mere messenger. You would have been better served to not break my laws as well; I might have let you go otherwise." He waved his hoof and guards approached from all sides. "Take her prisoner."

TWO

As usual, Lord Kaedemori delayed in meeting with Hikaru. Though the nature of their peace treaty was important, his father lived and breathed ceremony. Before he could see his father, Hikaru washed and dressed in a fresh kimono. A servant brushed his hair and tied it into a topknot, which gleamed with oil. Perfumed and swathed in silk, it was difficult to think he had been running for his life just earlier that day. *It all feels like a dream now.* Once he had dressed, his father summoned him to his audience chamber. A servant led the way, his footsteps quick and precise. Hikaru followed after, lagging behind as much as he dared. Perhaps if he took his time arriving, he could delay his own fate.

The servant opened the sliding doors to the audience hall. Hikaru inhaled; this was it. He stepped over the threshold, taking care to avoid touching the actual threshold. Though as a whole he avoided superstitious actions, some habits were too ingrained to discard. *I practice these domestic superstitions, yet I ignore the monsters? What sort of hypocrite am I?*

His father knelt at the far side of the room, flanked on each side by empty suits of armor. Their polished masks glared at Hikaru like menacing sentinels. When Hikaru was a child, the armor scared him until he realized that boiled leather and hardened plate could not hurt him. His father, on the other hand, never ceased to terrify him. Lord Kaedemori worked at a low table, bent over a sheath of parchment. In his hand, he held a brush with which he made small sweeping strokes. From Hikaru's vantage point across the room, it appeared as scrawling lines, like ants marching across the white parchment.

"Come closer," his father said without looking up as he made another mark on the parchment.

Hikaru padded across the floor, his footsteps muffled by the soft bamboo flooring and his socked feet. He knelt down in front of his father, head pressed to the ground and palms flat against the rough tatami mats. He waited for his father's signal, listening to the soft exhale of his own breath.

"Rise, my son," Lord Kaedemori said.

Hikaru sat up, folded his hands in his lap, and looked to his father. Lord Kaedemori did not look up but focused on his writing. Lord Kaedemori's once black hair had gone silver in recent years, with a few strands of black shot through it. The tight topknot flaunted his receding hair. Long and nimble fingers made intricate characters on the paper. Hikaru tried to read the document upside down but found it impossible. After finishing the final line, his father set aside his ink and brush and then looked down at his oldest son.

"How many men died in the forest?"

Hikaru swallowed past a lump in his throat. "One dead and three missing... Father."

"Why did you take the forest road?"

Hikaru fiddled with the hem of his sleeve. "I thought it would be quicker..."

His father stood up to loom over Hikaru. Hikaru tilted his head, meeting his father's severe expression, which pinned him in place.

Then Lord Kaedemori said, "You did not consider bandits that might be waiting or that your men would be unable to maneuver to protect you?"

"I did not." Hikaru bowed his head.

"Look at me."

Hikaru's head snapped up.

His father stared down at him with an expression made of ice. "If you are to lead this clan, you cannot make these sorts of mistakes. If you had died, the treaty would have suffered."

His casual dismissal of Hikaru's life was nothing new. He had a place, as the oldest son, to inherit the clan, to become the elder. That was all he mattered to his father. If Lord Kaedemori held any affection for Hikaru, he never showed it.

"I understand. I will do better next time." He bowed low, mostly as an excuse to avoid his father's penetrating gaze.

"If there is a next time. I could always disinherit you and put your brother in your place."

"If you wish it, Father." He felt his father's glare on the top of his skull, but he dared not meet his gaze.

His father took a seat once more. "I trust all the other arrangements went as planned?"

Now this was something Hikaru could take pride in. "It was just as I expected, the squabble about territory lines and compensation. But in the end we came to an agreement that we could both be satisfied with." He smiled, but his father's blank expression wiped the smile right off his face.

"You have done well, Hikaru."

He fought the smile that threatened to crack his features once more. His father so rarely gave praise, it was an unexpected delight to have him do so. It almost soothed the bitter sting of his father's earlier disappointment.

"You are excused." His father turned his attention back to his parchment.

Hikaru bowed to his father once more and hurried out of the room.

It was not until he was down the hall that he exhaled. His meeting with his father had gone better than expected. He had expected to be chastised for leading four of his father's warriors to their deaths. Deep in thought, Hikaru did not see his brother Hotaru approaching from the opposite way.

"Hikaru! Welcome home, brother," Hotaru said with a forced levity.

Hikaru plastered a smile on his face for his brother's benefit. "Brother."

"You're back from the Fujikawas' already? I thought these sorts of things took longer to manage," Hotaru said.

"Did you come to see if I had failed?" Hikaru replied, hard-pressed to hide his rancor.

Hotaru returned a false smile of his own. Like most of their interactions, this one was laced with barbs. Hotaru was often intent on tearing Hikaru down. It seemed to be his life goal. "Not at all. I heard there was some trouble on your way back. A few of the men in the yard are telling wild tales about an enormous boar that tore apart half of your guard." He laughed. "The more they drink, the wilder the tales get. I think upon the last telling they were saying that you ran away like a dog with your tail between your legs."

Hikaru flinched internally. He would not let his brother have the benefit of seeing how his words cut him. He would remember those men's names until he died. They had died in his service because of his mistake. "Three men are dead, brother, is that really something to laugh about?"

His brother's smile faltered but only a bit. It was a small

triumph. "I'm off to speak with father. He summoned me. The servant who relayed the message said it was urgent. Perhaps he already spoke with you?"

Hikaru bit his tongue to keep from spitting another ill-timed reply. His brother loved to flaunt their father's favor. Even though Hotaru was Lord Kaedemori's second oldest son and born to his second wife, Lord Kaedemori still gave Hotaru preferential treatment over Hikaru, his firstborn. Only age-old tradition had saved Hikaru from being passed up as the heir to the Kaedemori clan. Some days he wished his brother would inherit instead of him. Hotaru won the men's love with little effort, and he was an accomplished swordsman, everything a father looked for in a son. He had all the makings of a great leader, while Hikaru garnered disappointment and scorn from his men. *And got them killed.*

"I did not think so, why would he share such information with you?" Hotaru smiled as he brushed past Hikaru.

Hikaru watched his brother head for their father's chamber, his thoughts churning with anger and bitterness. A dozen too-late retorts came to mind but withered on the vine. As usual, his brother knew when to leave to inflict the most damage.

HOTARU SLID INTO THEIR FATHER'S CHAMBER AND WIPED THE SMILE off his face. Lord Kaedemori would not appreciate a cheeky grin. In the past, Hotaru had made the mistake of smiling in front of his father and earned a tongue-lashing for it—lords of good standing did not grin like a Tanuki. Lord Kaedemori glanced up as Hotaru crossed the room. His expression was unreadable but for the faint shade of disappointment that turned down the corners of his mouth just a bit more than usual. Once again, Hikaru had failed to meet their father's expectations and it was up to Hotaru to pick up the pieces. He knelt down in front of his father, hands arranged perfectly on the tatami as he bowed low. He pressed his head to the ground and then looked into his father's dark eyes. How many times had he looked there, searching for affection, a sign of favor or praise?

"Is something troubling you, Father?" he asked.

Lord Kaedemori stared down at his second son. He was made of ice and no amount of affection could melt him. Like a fool, Hotaru kept trying, no matter if his fingers turned black from frostbite and he froze his own heart in the process. Hotaru would keep on trying to win over his father until he saw what talent he was squandering in him.

"I heard about the deaths." Hotaru paused, thinking of the men he had trained and fought with, his brothers in arms. They had lost their lives due to his brother's ineptitude. "The men are telling some tall tales about Yokai. Perhaps I should speak with them, have them hold their tongues?"

"That will not be necessary." His father spoke at last, his voice as frigid as a winter storm.

Hotaru clamped his mouth shut and buried his feelings. But his father did not summon him on a whim. What could be more important than the death of their clansmen? "Why have you summoned me, Father?" His anger made his tone sharp, a mistake. Lord Kaedemori glared at him and Hotaru looked away. Speaking like a child would never earn Hotaru his father's respect.

Lord Kaedemori folded his hands on the table in front of him. "The signing of the treaty is unprecedented. Never before have two clans come together as we have with the Fujikawas. Now that all eyes are upon us, we must prepare for what comes next."

"What comes next?" Excitement bubbled up; had his time come at last to prove his worth? His father had been dangling a marriage in front of his nose for months. Had he chosen someone at last? Would he be married to some lord's daughter and thereby strengthen the clan?

"People fear what they do not understand. The other clans will seek to undermine us; they will plot and plan to topple our clan. The men's training should be increased and the guard doubled."

Hotaru deflated. "I thought perhaps now would be the time to send letters to other clans and inquire about my marriage."

"That will come in time."

The answer was unsatisfactory. Hotaru had been patient. He had waited for ages and obeyed all of his father's orders. He'd delayed marrying, focusing on increasing his talent with a blade and strategy. He let Hikaru pretend at being a lord, and watched him flounder time and time again. Now men had died, good men, young men who should have served the clan until they were old and gray. They were in a time of peace, for now. Signing the treaty had secured an ally in the Fujikawas, but it created half a dozen enemies among the other clans. Hikaru did not have the authority or the knowledge to defend their clan; surely his father could see that. "I do not mean to speak out of turn, Father," Hotaru said.

"Then halt your tongue."

He closed his mouth, but the words boiled inside him, writhing like a snake. Hikaru was not fit to rule; with no ambition and no skill with a sword, he was not the leader they needed. Hotaru had both and more. He alone of Lord Kaedemori's sons was the most fit to rule, and it was time his father saw it.

"Father, Hikaru is no leader. The men do not trust him. He is weak and—"

"You speak treason, son."

Hotaru clenched his jaw shut hard enough to crack his teeth. *Father is blinded by tradition. Why can't he see I am meant to rule?*

"There is an order to things. Hikaru is my firstborn by my first wife and so he shall inherit."

Unless he dies. The thought scared him and stole the breath from his lungs. What dark corner of his heart had such a vile thing been born from? He never wished harm on his brother, no matter how much he frustrated him. They verbally sparred often but only because he thought Hikaru unfit to rule, but wishing his brother's death, unthinkable, heinous, treasonous. Desperation was chasing his thoughts down dark corridors. He clenched his hands into fists to hide their shaking. *I will find another way to rule that does not create bloodshed.*

Out loud he said, "Yes, Father."

THREE

The warrior in the mask approached Rin. His movements were slow but deliberate.

Rin snarled at Akio, "You cannot do this, you will start a war with the Dragon!"

"I would only start a war if he had sent you himself. He will not risk war over one foolish girl." Akio grinned.

The warrior did not reach for his weapon. He thought she would come quietly. That was his first mistake. Rin unleashed her inner fox fire. Like taking the stopper out of a jar, she felt the energy flow to every part of her body, bones twisted and reformed, white hair burst from follicles, and she tripled in size, her head brushing against the ceiling. In her true form, she was nearly eye to eye with Akio, and the warriors were the size of dolls. Though size meant little if the masked warrior had a greater spiritual energy than her, as she suspected. Whatever form he hid beneath that mask must be terrifying.

"Oh, so you show your true colors, Kitsune." Akio laughed.

She responded by lunging at him, teeth bared and a ball of fire building in her throat, prepared to burst from behind her lips. Before she could so much as leap over the table between them, the warrior collided with her side, sending her careening across the room, and slammed her against a wall. She twisted and snapped at the warrior, unleashing the ball of fire, which whizzed past his shoulder and singed a nearby column. He swung a sword with liquid grace, both deadly and beautiful. She jumped backwards as the blade grazed against her underbelly, shearing a few hairs off. She landed with teeth bared and a second fireball billowing in her gut.

The masked guard stood between her and the guardian, but the door at the back of the chamber lay open. Rin knew better than to fight a battle she could not win, so she ran for the door instead. Akio shouted for her capture and guards ran to block the exit. Unlike the masked warrior, they were inferior in power. She unleashed her fox fire, setting them ablaze. They screamed as they beat upon their bodies, falling on the ground, rolling about to put out the flames. She leapt over them and out into the hallway.

The palace was a maze of twisted corridors. When she had arrived, the hallway had no doors; now there were ten different doors, at least, and three different hallways. Picking a door at random, she found a courtyard garden dominated by a jasmine bush the size of a tree. There were only two choices: one to the left and one to the right. When she looked over her shoulder to see if she was being pursued, the door she had come through disappeared. She took the pathway to the left and found another door-lined hallway. She ran down the corridor, chose a door at random again and found a covered walkway. She went through three more doors, down five halls, only to end up back at the same courtyard with the overlarge jasmine bush.

Rin turned to go to the right again. She must have made a wrong turn somewhere; she was certain she had seen the main courtyard at one point.

"You should turn left," said a monotone voice from behind her.

She spun in place, teeth bared and tails flickering with flame whipping behind her.

"The trick to escaping this palace is you must always choose the path to the left," the warrior in the mask said.

"Why would you help me?" Rin asked, her voice a rumble. Flames flickered at her feet, and the fire in her gut burned, itching to be unleashed.

"Go, before Akio realizes."

Rin eyed him for a moment. She had no reason to trust him, so she decided to turn right. He jumped in front of her, blocking her from going through the right-hand doorway.

"Go to the left, or I will fight you, and if I do, we both know you will lose."

She growled but did as she was told. She backed towards the left passageway, not taking her eyes off him. When she was certain he would not attack before she could get away safely, she turned and fled down the hall. When she came to two passageways side by side once more, she considered going to the right but decided against it. After a few more left turns, she emerged at the front entryway. She leapt across the bridge and into the forest and into the night.

FOUR

Hikaru went back to his private rooms, dismissed his servants and started to undress on his own. As he stripped off his outer robe, his brother's taunts gave him pause. That led to thoughts of his shameful actions in the forest. *I couldn't even protect myself. If that strange woman hadn't intervened, I would be dead.*

Hikaru turned to face his veranda. The sliding doors opened onto his garden. The manicured bushes were shaped and perfect, not a stray branch in sight and not a single leaf lingered on the ground. *I must have imagined the ears and tail, and surely that boar was not as big as I remember it.* He stood for a moment, gazing up at the sliver of moon in the sky, his memories playing in his mind's eye. He was never one for fanciful exaggerations; he was a man of learning and reason. *I cannot be sure until I go and look again.* He moved before he could change his mind. Urgency hurried his feet as he stormed down the hallway, through the inner rings of the palace and into the outer circle, where the stables were housed.

A group of warriors dallied about between rounds of guard duty as he approached. A few leaned against the side of the building.

One warrior, who had his back to Hikaru, was in the middle of a story. He spread his arms out wide as he said, "I'm telling you, it had tusks as big as me. And the noise it made turned your bowels to liquid."

A second warrior laughed. "This sounds like an old wives' tale."

"I'm telling the truth, it was massive," the first man protested.

The others spotted Hikaru watching them. They stood up straight but more out of obligation than any sense of respect for Hikaru.

"I wish to ride; bring my horse," Hikaru said.

They hesitated a moment, as if considering whether or not to obey his command. He could see the resentment bubbling beneath the surface. The accusation in their eyes that pinned their friends' deaths upon him. He wanted to apologize, but the words failed him. He was no good at speaking with others unless it was about books.

"Yes, my lord," said the man nearest to the stable doors.

Hikaru walked away to stand in the courtyard. When he turned his back, the men spoke in low tones to one another. The night air felt cool against his flushed cheeks. He fought the urge to shift from foot to foot. From the furtive glances in his direction, he knew they were talking about him. Just then the stable master emerged with his horse in tow. Hikaru swung into the saddle in a rush to make his departure to avoid any more uncomfortable stares. As he hurried through the palace gates, he did not notice the angry glares that followed him.

ROKURO WATCHED LORD HIKARU RIDE OUT THE GATES WITH A SCOWL. He grasped the hilt of his sword; if he did not value his life and that of his men, he would chase after him and run the arrogant lord through. These were dangerous thoughts, spoken aloud and his head would soon be parted from his shoulders. The others stared at him, his brothers in arms, four less than they had been that morning. They looked to him, as lieutenant, for guidance, and he should set an example. In their eyes, he saw his own thoughts. They wanted vengeance. Treason was like a weed, and as much as he'd like to see Lord Hikaru die as his brothers had—ripped apart, bloody, and broken—if he acted, his men would suffer. He already had the memories of his brothers' deaths on his conscience, he would not add the rest of them to the list. Or his soul would not rest, even after death. As it was, the violent ends of the four would haunt his dreams. No, Rokuro would not find his vengeance through rash acts.

"If it wasn't for him, Daiki, Jun, Hiro and Captain Sadao would be here." Masayoshi spat on the ground. He was a round barrel-chested man, squat and with a long mustache and goatee.

Masayoshi was a man you wanted beside you in a fight, but he had never learned the art of holding his tongue.

His companions nodded in agreement anyway. The men had no love for the young lord. Lord Hikaru thought he was better than them, and he mocked the Yokai. A foolish man did not fear Yokai; they were cruel, vicious and petty. If you did not pay the right favors and dishonor them, they might curse you and your family for three generations. Just thinking of those red gleaming eyes and the tusks as long as his arm, he felt lucky to have gotten away with his life. He pulled out his lucky talisman from beneath his shirt and gave it a rub. The men passed around a jug of warm sake and refilled their cups. The more they drank, the rosier their cheeks and the looser their tongues became.

"How can we serve him?" said Osamu. He tossed back his sake. "Now his brother, Lord Hotaru, is a man I would gladly die for."

Dangerous words. Rokuro took a drink, the liquid burning a trail of fire down his throat. It dulled the edges of his pain but did not take it away. His men, his brothers, nodded their heads in agreement with Osamu's drunken ramblings. He knew he needed to still their tongues. If the wrong ear heard them, they'd all be brought before Lord Kaedemori for treason. Then he thought of Jun. His younger brother in blood and recently by the blade. He had been all of seventeen, as green as they came. But talented with a sword, more talented than Rokuro, and loyal to a fault. He had been so proud when Jun had joined the royal guard.

When the boar had come charging at Rokuro, he had seen his death in those red eyes. Lord Hikaru had mocked the Yokai and they had come to teach him a lesson, but while that coward fled, Rokuro stayed to fight. It should have been Rokuro who took that tusk to the gut, but Jun jumped in front of him at the last minute. He could see his face clearly: young innocence shocked as the tusk went through him. The boar pulled back and tossed him like a rag doll, only to continue chasing the lord. Rokuro had held Jun in his arms as he died, too young to die in such an awful way, blood frothing on his lips as his insides filled up with it.

The jug came back around to him, and Rokuro took a swig straight from the source. Then he slammed down the jug and stood up. His men, his brothers, stared up at him, a mixture of shock and confusion on their faces.

"Lord Hotaru should inherit. Lord Hikaru is not fit to be elder."

Silence fell. It was one thing to grumble and complain, but he was skirting treason. One more toe and his life could be at stake. The men wanted this, but they feared to take it. They looked anywhere but at him. But how many more men would die? Could he with good conscious let Lord Hikaru lead them to ruin? He knew this was the right path as if divine intervention was guiding him. Jun. Daiki. Hiro. Sadao. They should not have died in vain. They had not even found Daiki's, Hiro's and Sadao's bodies; their spirits would never be able to rest until he got vengeance.

"If only!" Hisoka laughed, giving him a chance to back down and save face.

But he had made up his mind. "We have a chance to do what is right for the clan. Lord Hikaru has gone out in the night, when the Yokai reign. He has angered them, so we should leave him to their mercy."

Silence followed this proclamation, but this time they looked at him, hopeful but wary. *Turn back now, pretend you were drunk, stop this before it's too late.*

"Are you saying we should follow after him and..." said Takeshi.

Rokuro clenched his hands into fists. He would give anything to follow him and wring his neck, watch the light fade from his eyes. Perhaps he had drunk too much and gotten ahead of himself. It was not too late to laugh it off as a joke. Then he thought of Jun dying in his arms and he knew there was only one choice.

"Let the Kami judge him," he said, looking from man to man. "You saw how he disrespected the guardian's forest. How he laughed at the idea of the Yokai. They will not stand it, and he will learn what it means to mock the gods."

The men shifted in their seats, glancing from the corner of their eyes at one another.

"And if the Kami spare him?" asked Shinji.

"Did any of you see the young lord leave this evening?" Rokuro replied, arms folded over his chest as he let his message sink in. *He will never step foot within this palace again.*

They murmured insubstantial words to one another, filling the silence. Rokuro did not take his eyes off them, though their gazes flickered to the guards at the gate, to the men on the wall, fearing they'd heard their devious plotting.

"It's time to close the gates, the night is closing in."

Osamu opened his mouth, prepared to challenge or correct, but then realization dawned on his face and he lowered his head as he said, "If a man chooses to face down the monsters that lurk in the night, then that's no business of ours."

"And what do we tell those on duty?" Shinji asked. Of all the men, he still held reservations, Rokuro could see it in his eyes. If anyone broke their silence, it would be him.

A grin spread across Rokuro's face. "The guards will be changing soon. When the fresh guards come on duty, make sure to tell them that an impostor has been seen. Anyone coming to the gate claiming to be Lord Hikaru should be sent away. If he persists, they have leave to use all necessary force."

Shinji stared at him. An intelligent man, but faithful to the clan above all else. *If I am tried for treason, I bring you with me.* Slowly, Shinji bowed his head, conceding to his lieutenant's command. The others rose together, and one by one they went to do as they were bid, bound together by their secret. When Rokuro was alone once more, he pulled his lucky charm out and squeezed it hard enough to bite into his flesh.

HIKARU STARTED OUT AT A TROT, BUT ONCE HE WAS DOWN THE HILL A ways from the palace and the darkness swallowed him, he took off at a clipped pace. The hill on which the palace sat lent itself to panoramic views during the day. With the daylight dying, he could see little beyond the stars reflected in the paddy fields that surrounded the palace. He rode along fields, skirting farmhouses and avoiding the populated areas. He had no particular destination in mind, he just wanted to put space between himself and the palace. He needed room to think. His entire life had been planned out for him, from the moment of his birth, but now that everything was set in motion, he could not help but take what little rebellions he could manage.

He arrived at the forest edge. It was miles from the palace. The moon, a mere sliver against the inky black sky, gave poor light. He knew he had been gone too long, and his absence would be noted. *I should not let Hotaru's taunts goad me into recklessness.* But that wasn't all of it, not really. He was curious. Had the boar really been as big as he remembered? Did that woman really have fox ears and a tail? And where had she gone when she disappeared?

He dismounted and walked along the edge of the forest. He held onto the reins of his mount and his horse trailed after him.

The trees were spaced farther apart here. The pale sliver of light cast deep shadows between the trees. The woods creaked and moaned as the wind rustled through the branches. He dared not go further. He thought he had seen a pair of eyes gleaming in the shadows, but it may have been his imagination. *It's just a forest, I was foolish to even doubt it was anything other than that.*

He listened to the song of the night birds and the rustle of wind for a few more minutes. When he turned to leave, he found a fox sitting in the middle of the pathway, its tail wrapped around its lower half. *It cannot be.* He blinked, and when he opened his eyes again, the fox was gone and in its place a woman stood.

Hikaru rubbed his eyes in disbelief. But the image did not alter. The woman was young, close to his own age, wearing a golden kimono with a pattern of crimson maple leaves. The maple leaf pattern clustered on her shoulders and cascaded down her sleeves and along the front panels of her kimono. She stood absolutely still in the center of the road. Her entire body seemed clenched tight as if the slightest twitch of muscle would send her skittering away like a wild animal. She stared at Hikaru with a confused expression. Perhaps it was the moonlight, or maybe he was losing his mind. But she looked just like the woman with the fox ears.

FIVE

Rin traveled along a human road, her ears twisting to and fro and her senses spread out looking for other Yokai. The night was silent and no one pursued her. It seemed strange; knowing Akio, he should have sent an army after her. *Why did he let me go?* She hated using human roads because even those posed their own dangers. The stink of humans and the scent of earth and water invaded her nostrils, tugging at her animal instincts to run and hide, but the forest was no safer than the road. She disguised herself as a fox to travel. If she crossed paths with a human, they would see a fox unless they had spiritual powers, like that young man. *There was something different about him, though I cannot quite place what it was.*

Wet earth squished beneath her paws as she wandered. She glanced over her shoulder. Even with her defenses up, every shadow and chirp of the night insects made her jump. She had not thought Akio would know her. She was of minor standing in the Dragon's court. Well, she had been, but how could rumors have spread this far? *How can I return home now? My reputation may never recover.* A twig snapped behind her and Rin jumped, the hair on her back rising up. She peered into the dark, teeth bared. The trees swayed in the breeze, but apart from that, nothing else moved. Her spiritual powers were limited in this form, but if anyone was following her, she should have been able to sense them. Though her senses told her she was alone, she could not shake the feeling she was being followed.

She was better equipped to fight in her true form, but there were rules against doing so close to humans. Her muscles constricted, ready to spring. She sniffed the wind; the hundreds of human scents on the road had disguised a fresh scent. A quick probe indicated whoever was approaching was human. She relaxed. Along with the scent of human, there was another musk, one she could not place. Whoever it was, they were drawing closer. Rin's golden eyes pierced the darkness. In this shape, her vision was more acute and the dark did not hamper her vision. A bent figure shuffled in Rin's direction. The scent she had smelled before intensified and the musky smell disappeared, replaced by a rich tangy scent. The scent was intoxicating and her mouth watered.

An old woman hobbled over, leaning heavily on a cane. Her other hand, balled into a fist, clutched a parcel. Rin's eyes followed the parcel. The smell was coming from there. She knew that she should flee, but her feet would not listen to reason. Instead she crept closer to the old woman, who had stopped a few feet away from her. The old woman opened her crabbed hand and pulled back the covering on the parcel, revealing a brown square. It was food, Rin knew that much. Human food had never appealed to her, but this was different. She crawled closer, her belly nearly touching the ground. She sniffed the old woman's hand. *It does not smell like poison.* The old woman smiled; she seemed harmless enough. The wrinkles on her face reminded Rin of folds of fabric.

"Take it," the woman said. Her voice was thin and reedy. "I know you want it."

The spell the scent of the food had wound around her was irresistible. She snapped up the food. It was soft, almost creamy, with a crunchy exterior. It was divine. She had never tasted anything so good, even in the courts of the highest Kami.

Rin swallowed her food and looked to the old woman for more. The old woman was still smiling, but it was not the kindly expression from before, but a wicked, triumphant grin. *How could I trust a human?* She turned to run and collided with an invisible wall. Where her skin touched it, it prickled with energy and sparked as if she had brushed against a flame. *It's a barrier.* Panicked, she let her animal instincts take over and she turned, only to crash against another wall. The energy erupted from the barrier and singed her fur. It wasn't just a barrier but one made of spiritual energy. The old woman had penned Rin in on all sides; a barrier made of spiritual energy was one of the only things that could hold a Yokai. She looked down at the ground and a circle glowed a faint blue; unfamiliar markings had been traced in the soil. Rin growled at the old woman. *Now Akio is using humans?*

"There is no need to pretend any longer, Kitsune," the old woman said. "I saw you as you emerged from the forest. Show me your true face, I command it."

This woman was ignorant of her power if she thought a simple binding spell would force her to reveal her true form, so instead she shifted. Light flashed around Rin, a burning gold and orange. A flurry of leaves settled around Rin before they dissipated like raindrops on the ground. Hands on hips, Rin stood before the woman. Humans, she had found, were more willing to speak when faced with a humanlike face. Rin's coppery red hair fell down to her waist, and her head crowned by fox ears was anything but human. Rin twitched her foxtail back and forth as she regarded the human.

"You have captured me, human, and as a reward I will grant you one wish," she said. It was difficult not to snicker. Humans were too easy to manipulate. If she was working for Akio, she would be easy enough to bribe.

The old woman rubbed her hands together. "How fortunate am I to find a Kitsune wandering about at night. Why did you come here?"

"Is that your wish; to answer your question? I can only grant you one."

The old woman shook her head. In the dim moonlight Rin noticed a crescent-shaped scar on her right cheek. Her long white hair, tied in a single tail, draped down her back and swung back and forth as she shook her head. "No. No. It does not matter, I have won a great prize. I will not squander it." She paced in front of Rin with her hands folded behind her back.

"I can give you gold, power, or perhaps there is a man you desire?" Rin said. Humans, in Rin's experience, had basic wants. From time to time, she allowed herself to be captured just to play tricks on them. Their petty needs amused her. She had never cared about their well-being until that young man.

The woman turned to face Rin, her lips spread wide in a ghastly grin. Under the pale moonlight, her face was cast in shadow, exaggerating her smile and making it look too wide, her teeth too large for her mouth. And the crevices around her mouth and eyes looked like dark gashes, as if she had been carved out of darkness.

"I think it is you who desires the love of a man," the old woman said.

The hairs along the back of Rin's neck prickled. Rin laughed off the old woman's comments and tossed her head back. "I have no desire for mortal men."

"What about the Great Dragon? It is him that you desire, am I correct?"

Rin took an unconscious step backwards. Energy from the barrier leapt out at her, burning her skin. She shifted away and brushed a hand unconsciously against her tender flesh. "You finding me was no mere accident, was it?" Rin asked.

The old woman laughed again, throwing her head back in a parody of what Rin had just done. Her voice echoed and surrounded Rin inside her tiny prison, as if there were thousands of the woman closing in, their laughter cutting through her. "I know much about you, Rinmiyu."

Hearing her full name from a mortal's lips was like a bucket of ice dropped over her. A Yokai's name meant power over them, it meant she was bound to do this woman's bidding. How had she learned her name? The words swirled around her, choking her with invisible bonds.

"How do you know my name?" Rin choked out. Rin had not spoken her own given name in centuries. Even Akio would not have known it.

"I have been following you for a long time. I know much about you, Rinmiyu." She used Rin's name to taunt her.

Rin laughed; she would not show the old woman her fear. "I think you are bluffing, old woman."

The old woman continued. "You can believe what you will. As for me, I have been waiting a very long time for this moment and I wish to make a bargain with you."

"You should know never to make a bargain with a Yokai. Especially a Kitsune, we do not play by the rules." Rin stood up a little taller. She could not get a good sense of the woman. She should be able to feel this woman's spiritual energy, but all she felt was an empty void. *She is very powerful if she can suppress her spiritual energy that way.*

"I am willing to take the risk."

Rin had to fight the urge to rub her hands together in evil glee. The old woman may have trapped her, and knew her name, but humanity's critical flaw was that they were too arrogant for their own good. This woman was no different. She may have gotten Rin's name, but she must not know how to use it or she would not try to bargain.

"Then give me your terms, and I will see if I am willing to agree."

The old woman clapped her hands together. "You desire the Dragon, but as you are now, you cannot hope to win his favor. You are a minor Yokai, and without the power and strength of a greater Yokai, you cannot hope to compete on his level."

Rin rolled her eyes. *She may as well tell me to transform into a fish. That is not possible.* "Are you claiming to have the power to *make* me a greater Yokai?"

"I do not have that power, but I can lead you to a place where power runs like rivers and any creature can become as powerful as the first Eight Kami."

Rin laughed long and hard. There was no such place, nor any power on this earth that could do such a thing. This woman was mad and misguided. *I should transform into my true form and snap her in half like a twig. I am tired of playing games.*

"You doubt me, Rinmiyu? I have your name and I can bind you to my will."

43

Rin transformed; her hands grew into paws covered in white fur. Her tail extended and more burst from the base of her spine. Each one was tipped with licking flames. She loomed over the woman, though still confined within the barrier. Even trapped, Rin was an imposing sight.

"Mere mortal, you think to use me. The moment I break these seals, I will devour you." Her voice sounded like rolling thunder and she bared teeth the length of the woman's head. She would enjoy devouring her. Humans with spiritual energy were always delicious.

The woman sang an incantation Rin had never heard before. *She thinks to seal me, but this barrier will not hold me.* In her true form, her power was at its peak. She pressed against the walls of the barrier and they sparked and sizzled, but it felt like flies buzzing against her skin, a mere annoyance. Rin may be a lesser Yokai, but she was more powerful than this human. But the walls did not budge, no matter how she focused her own energy into destroying them. They did not shrink either, as they should if the old woman was attempting a sealing. A warmth enveloped Rin. Like a blanket wrapped around her, it forced the hair back into the follicles and her strength waned. She threw herself against the barrier walls again and again, but it made no difference. She changed, returning to her humanlike form. She fell to the ground, heaving for breath. She looked up at the old woman through a curtain of ebony hair.

It was dark out, darker than she remembered. She opened her mouth to speak, but nothing would come out. She glared at the woman.

"I have made you mortal, a form you despise. I will return you to your real form once you complete a task for me. I need you to break the treaty between the Kaedemori clan and Fujikawa clan. End their pact by the next full moon or I will turn you into a real fox."

WHEN NAOKI REACHED THE BORDER OF THE FOREST, HE FELT THE residue of magic; it clung to his skin as it hung over the countryside like a shroud. Stretching out his senses, he felt an Okami hunting in the night; small, ignorant Yokai watched him fearfully from the shadows. Intertwined among the other energies, very faintly, he felt the presence of a priestess. Intrigued, he stretched out his senses and touched the edges of her power, like a vine reaching toward the sun. She had masked her energy or else he would have felt her straight away, which meant she was powerful. He probed her energy, analyzing it—confident his own greater spiritual power would hide him. Even at a distance, he could often learn all about a Yokai or priestess without them ever knowing he had brushed against them, reading their emotions and sometimes their memories. But she fought him; like a breeze blowing against a tree branch, she tried to repel him. He focused his energy into a single beam. Now he was truly curious.

He skimmed through her energy, reading it, but he only got vague impressions and flashes of emotions. This wasn't a priestess, a human priestess' energy was pure. This human's spiritual energy was clouded with darkness, and familiar. As he tried to pinpoint her location, she disappeared entirely. *This is dangerous.* Few could fight against him, and if a human could hide from his probes, then she was equal in power to him. He searched in vain for her—he was certain he recognized that energy. As he searched, he found traces of the Kitsune as well. He hoped she would leave this region straight away. But he could feel her all around; he could see her progress in his mind's eye, running along the human road disguised as a fox, until her energy disappeared as well. Something was not right.

Then like a flash of light, he felt the priestess' spiritual energy unmasked. She had revealed herself to give him a taste of her real power. He knew this energy, though it had been centuries since he'd last experienced it; she was no mere priestess. *What is she doing back here?* He stopped, pretending to straighten his sandal. He would rather go on his way without a fight, but the priestess was drawing closer—there was no way to avoid a confrontation now. He drew up and reached for his sword.

"He has let you off your leash, then?" she said from behind him.

Naoki rested his palm on the end of his sword but did not draw. "It is you. I did not think to see you here after all you have done."

The witch came out from around a tree. She bowed low to Naoki, mocking him most likely. She had not changed much over the years; everything about her was the same from her white hair to the crescent-shaped scar on her face. His hand itched to draw his blade, but he would be dead before he pulled it free.

"Have you visited Akio? I am sure he would like to see you."

The witch cackled. "I am sure he would love to see me. Have you come for me, then?" She looked him up and down. "Perhaps not. You wear a human's skin."

"Why are you here?"

"I had some work to take care of in the area." She looked him up and down and a slow smile spread across her wrinkled features. It had been a long time since they had crossed paths. He still remembered that look and it still set his teeth on edge even after all this time. "I am glad I ran into you," she said slowly, enunciating each word. "You can assist me."

He never showed his emotion, but a scornful smile flitted across his face. "Why would I help you?"

"You want free of the guardian, and I can help you."

He ran his thumb across the hilt of his blade. This must be a trick. With her it was never this simple. If he helped her, he was likely to incur some other favor and be beholden to her instead of Akio. But he could not say it was not an enticing offer. "How can I trust you?"

"Do not mistake me for Akio. He made his own choices. I never wished you any ill will."

He crossed his hands over his chest, to defeat the urge to draw his blade and take her head as a prize. "What business do you have here?" he asked.

"Human business. Nothing that would interest you." She waved her hand. That was as much as he would get from her, he expected. "Do you want to hear how I can free you of Akio or not?" Her gloating hung over her like a cloud; she loved to be in control.

He did not respond, but he was curious. He did not trust her. He had once, but that was when he was a different man.

She took his silence as assent. "There is a clan near here who I have some interest in. I sent my own spy, but another would not go amiss."

"And what exactly are you spying for?"

"I am making war." She smiled with an almost childlike glee.

A shiver went down his spine. Only she would find joy in carnage. "And what could I do to that end?"

"Watch, listen, and report, nothing more."

"And in exchange you will free me from Akio?" He was skeptical. "I know you are powerful, but even you cannot break his pact."

"Hmm. Perhaps, but I know where she sleeps, and if you wake her, she will be able to."

Where is she, where is she! he wanted to shout. He had been searching for five hundred years and not been able to find Tsukiko. How could this witch know? He knew the witch was powerful, and her power had only grown over the centuries. It should have been expected from a priestess who did not fear black magic. But to know where Tsukiko slept, when even the Eight could not tell him, it was impossible.

"You lie."

The witch reached into her billowing sleeve and removed something from it. She tossed it onto the ground. He slowly knelt down to pick it up off the ground, not taking his eyes off the witch. His hand closed around the cold stone. He unfurled his hand, revealing a comb—inconsequential, uninteresting, made of jade with a carved rose on the front entwined with thorns. It was his last gift to Tsukiko before they had been separated.

"Where did you get this?" *How could she have known? It could not be hers...*

"If you want to find her, then perhaps you would be willing to do me a favor?"

He stared back down at the comb. After centuries of waiting, how could he say no? He could try to overpower the witch and demand the answers, but he knew the witch well enough to know she would die before telling him. And then he would never find Tsukiko.

Six

"My lady, what are you doing out here this late?" Hikaru asked.

She shook her head back and forth slowly, then returned to an eerie, still state.

He took a step closer to her. She did not move. Her shoulders were taut as a bowstring and her eyes followed him. She threaded her fingers together in front of her. He held up his hands, showing that he meant her no harm.

"Are you hurt?"

She only shook her head once again. He could see her clearer as he drew closer. Her hair, a dark ebony, was piled on top of her head in a messy bun. Despite her fine clothes, there was no care or artifice done to her appearance. Yet her raw beauty shone through. Her round face, almond eyes and rosebud mouth were well formed. On closer inspection, she could not be the fox woman. She did not have ears and a tail, for one thing, and for another, the fox woman had coppery hair. He wanted to shake himself. There was no such thing as Kitsune! It had all been a hallucination brought on by a panicked mind. He must have imagined the woman. The resemblance was uncanny, however.

I jumped to the wrong conclusion because I found her alone in the dark. Where did she come from? He looked around; there wasn't anyone around for miles. How did a woman so well dressed end up at the edge of a forest? *They tell stories about women appearing to travelers. They seduce men and drain them of their life force.*

When he looked back at her, she had moved closer to him. She looked at him with her head cocked to the side. She regarded him for a moment. He may have imagined it, but it seemed she recognized him as well.

"I'm sorry, do I know you?" he asked.

She looked past him to the forest. He turned to look over his shoulder. *This is the part in stories where the woman would transform into a monster and eat me.* He shivered. When did he start believing in such superstitious nonsense?

"Are you hurt, is that why you do not speak?" Hikaru asked, trying to coax something out of her. Anything to offset this twisting feeling of dread coiling in his stomach.

She stared at him for a moment; then she raised her hands. Bringing them close to her face, she examined her flesh as if seeing it for the first time. After she had scanned both hands, she shook her head.

He frowned. *She is very strange.* "Are you unable to speak?"

She touched her throat and nodded.

He sighed. "Well, this could prove difficult." He looked around as if the night would offer up the answers he sought. "Are you from around here?"

She smiled, a coy sort of smile. It was different than the smile of court ladies, it was playful and secretive. It caught him off guard. Though her clothes indicated she was, he wondered if she was a noble lady. What noble lady would be traveling alone and in the dark?

"Well, I suppose there is no use in standing out here in the cold. I'll take you back to the palace and we can try to figure this out." He held out his hand to her. She stared at it for a moment, hesitant to take it. He got the impression once more of a wild animal, but the thought passed quickly.

He helped her into the saddle of his horse and swung up behind her. He held his hands up, unsure where to rest them. It was not often that he was this close to a woman. He decided to rest one hand on his thigh and the other grasped the reins. She brushed against him by accident, and he could not help but notice how soft her skin was or how she smelled sweet like a blooming flower.

She leaned forward and pressed her nose against his arm. He jerked his hand back. *Did she just smell me?*

"Is anything the matter?" he asked. He looked at the back of her head, wondering if this was the right thing to do. Perhaps she was addled in the mind. It would certainly explain a few things.

She shook her head in response.

He shifted uncomfortably in his seat. She did not seem simple-minded. One of his father's tenant farmers had a son that was born simple. He often smiled at Hikaru when he rode through the countryside. He was harmless enough, but one could tell upon meeting him that he was not in full control of his mind. This woman was different. Though strange, to be certain, she seemed to be aware of her surroundings. Maybe she was confused.

She touched his arm with her fingertips, and just the innocent brush of her skin against his ignited his flesh in a way he had never felt before. He wanted to pull away, as was proper, but could not bring himself to do so. His arm brushed against hers when he twitched the reins, closing her into a tight embrace. She flinched and he snapped it back, bowing out his arm to avoid any further unintentional touches. She glanced at him over her shoulder.

He avoided her gaze by looking over the dark countryside. "It's not much farther," he said, his voice cracking.

She turned back around, a smile ghosting along her lips. *She's laughing at me, I am sure of it. If only I could share in the joke.*

"I'm sure it seems strange that I keep talking. I know you cannot speak—or at least I hope this is not a cruel joke." He paused. The plodding sound of the horse's hooves filled the silence for a moment.

"You're not tricking me, right?" He hated how vulnerable he sounded.

She shook her head and her shoulders shook as if she were laughing silently. His neck burned and he was thankful she was facing the other way so she could not see his mortification. *Perhaps Hotaru paid her to humiliate me.* He looked about, expecting to find his younger brother and his men hiding in the rice paddies. Hikaru and the strange woman were alone but for the moon's reflection on the water of the rice paddies. He eased back in the saddle.

"Of course not," he sighed, more to convince himself than her. Her secrets were locked tight within her silence. Which he had to believe was genuine. *Unless her voice will reveal she is some terrifying Yokai intent on eating me.* As much as he wanted to discard the terrifying notion, after the events earlier today, his long-held beliefs were shaken. The night birds called to one another in the dark and the wind brushed over them. He studied the back of her head, expecting a mouth to appear there.

The palace was in sight when he found the courage to ask, "This is going to sound insane, but you're not an evil spirit, are you?"

Her body vibrated.

"I'm sorry, I did not mean to offend."

Then she snorted.

Hikaru laughed, he could not hold it back. It was a rolling sound that erupted deep within him and shook his entire frame. She touched his hand and he stiffened all over. When she peeked at him from over her shoulder with a grin, whatever fear he had before dissipated. The stress of the treaty had been playing tricks with his mind. Evil spirits, Kitsune, and Yokai were all just myths. Nothing he had to worry about.

LORD KAEDEMORI STARED AT THE DOCUMENTS IN FRONT OF HIM. HIS vision blurred as the characters ran together. There was more work to be done, compensation to be sent to the families of the deceased warriors, and more letters to write to their neighboring clans to placate their likely anger at his treaty with the Fujikawas. Just imagining their reactions made his head throb. He massaged his temple and closed his eyes.

With the Fujikawas' backing, the Kaedemoris would be the most powerful clan in the region. Hikaru had laid the groundwork, but there was still more to be done. Just the rumor of a treaty had flooded his chamber with letters from the other clans sniffing for confirmation. Well, they would have it soon enough and then the real work would begin. If only this damn headache would desist. He glanced up, prepared to call for the servant to bring him a headache remedy, when he heard the tinkling of a bell.

He looked around the room. He was alone but for the shadows.

"Yoshirou..." The wind whispered his name, like a caress.

The hairs on the back of his neck prickled. The fire in the braziers flickered and then died down to mere embers. *It is my imagination; she has been dead for years.*

Then he heard it again. "Yoshirou."

The prickling sensation raced down his arms. He stood and went behind a screen to a secret exit at the back of his room. He would take a quick look, to sate his curiosity. Down wooden steps and onto a narrow pathway between buildings, he followed the track as he had done hundreds of times, the ground worn flat by his footsteps.

The shrine was empty, lit only by moonlight, which illuminated the idol in its alcove. He stood before the idol, the voice that had called out to him a figment of his imagination. But this time he swore he had heard her calling his name. He pinched the bridge of his nose. *This is madness. When will she cease to haunt me?* She had been gone for nearly twenty years. He looked up at the moon, a mere sliver in the cloudless sky. There would be no moon come tomorrow night, leaving the world in darkness. He touched the feet of the idol, an old habit. He turned to leave, back to his work. *I may as well work through the night, I won't be able to sleep either way.* Then he heard it again, the tinkling of bells. He spun around and the space in the center of the shrine was occupied.

Wiping away his shock, he greeted his visitor. "What brings you here, priestess?"

The old woman smiled, a wicked smile that he never knew if it meant him good or ill. She wore rough-spun traveling clothes, a brown haori over dark brown hakama, white hair in a braid down her back. She looked ancient, deep creases carved around her mouth and eyes. A crescent-shaped scar on her face gleamed in the moonlight. How she moved silently and appeared without warning, he never knew. She had seemed ancient when he was a young man, and she looked the same now. He was surprised she lived still. Even when she was not dressed as a priestess, she exuded a spiritual aura that even he could see. It was why he had trusted her, once upon a time, but he had second-guessed his actions every day since. He turned his back to the shrine, blocking the priestess from seeing it. Even after all these years, he felt protective of this space. As if guarding it would preserve a piece of Sayuri from others. But the priestess never came to play games, not in all the years he knew her.

"I felt a disturbance in the energy and I thought I would come and visit, old friend."

"Then you were in the area, for what reason?" he asked directly. If not, she would only answer in riddles, as was her way.

She tilted her head to the side and regarded him. "You have aged since the last time I saw you." Her long white braid fell forward over her shoulder.

He folded his hands over his chest. *And you have not. Do the*

Kami preserve you? "Did you come to mock me? Surely someone with your ability has better things to do."

"You're right, I do." She smiled. She had a secret that she wanted him to fish for, but he was not the young man taken in by those smiles and secrets any longer. She had brought him danger before but saved him as well. It was what kept him from sending her away—he was just as guilty as she.

"If you have nothing of import to say." He turned to walk away.

"Wait," she called out to him, stopping him in his tracks. "There is something."

He turned back around. "Yes?"

"I was walking along in the forest and came upon a Kitsune."

He clutched at his chest. It felt for a moment as if a knife had been stabbed there. An old wound bled anew. "You cannot mean to say she has returned from the dead?"

She shook her head. "Don't be a fool. What is gone is gone. This Kitsune is new to this region. I caught her and questioned her, but as you know, their kind can be tricky. I got no real answer as to why she came here."

"Then why are you telling me this?"

"Because I thought you deserved a warning. The Yokai have long memories, and if one came for vengeance..." She shrugged her thin shoulder.

He kept his expression mild while his mind reeled. *It means naught. Just a coincidence, perhaps the creature was passing through.* But he said through dry lips, "What did you do with her?"

"She escaped, unfortunately. If you see any of suspicion, let me know."

He held his breath. It was nothing but the witch's taunting. But still he had to ask, "You don't think she will come here, do you?"

"When it comes to a Kitsune, anything is possible."

She bowed, and then with another tinkling of bells, she disappeared. He stayed in the shrine room for some time, staring at the shrine. A string of ofuda danced on the wind, but other than that, everything was still. Then very slowly he went and knelt before the idol, a fox—a Kitsune. He pressed his forehead against the feet of the idol.

"Will you ever forgive me? Perhaps in the next life I can make amends for my crimes against you."

THEY ARRIVED AT THE PALACE LATE AT NIGHT; THE MOON HAD ALREADY reached its apex. The palace doors were slammed shut. *I didn't count on them locking me out.* Hikaru slid down from the saddle and approached the gate.

"Hello?" he called. His voice bounced off the walls and rolled over the farmland behind him.

He waited for a response. He looked back at the woman; she watched him curiously. *I must look like a fool, locked out of my own palace.* He turned back to the doors. He knocked upon the wood. The sound was quickly swallowed by the night. Even the night birds had ceased their singing to witness his embarrassment. *What if my father uses this as an excuse to disinherit me? They must think I ran away.* He held his breath, waiting. Surely someone had heard and would come open the doors. He craned his neck back; there should be guards walking the walls. He turned to walk over to Rin and explain when he saw the glow of yellow light over the top of the wall. *Finally.*

A slot in the door slid open and Hikaru approached it. The yellow light spilled through the opening and made a square of light on the ground beyond. Hikaru stepped into the shaft of light.

"Who's there?" a gravelly voice said.

"It is Hikaru, first son of Lord Kaedemori."

The guard peered at him through the hole. He recognized him as one of the men who had come with him to the Fujikawas. One of the survivors. He swallowed.

"Lord Kaedemori's son?" the man asked.

"Yes. I went out for a ride and was delayed. Please let me in, we are cold and weary."

The man's face disappeared from the hole for a moment and Hikaru heard the man conferring with another. He clenched his fists and waited.

"Master Hikaru is asleep in his chamber. I think you're an impostor."

Hikaru clenched his jaw down on his anger. He took a deep breath and then replied, "That is not true. You saw me when I rode out earlier this evening. Let me in—"

"Get out of here or we'll be forced to open fire on you," the man replied.

Hikaru glanced up as half a dozen men armed with bows and arrows arrayed themselves on the wall. They trained their bows on Hikaru. He looked each one over; he knew them all by name. They had been in his father's employ for years. They stared back at him with hatred and anger. They spared him no loyalty, and after he had mocked them and led their friends to their deaths, they wanted revenge.

Hikaru returned his gaze to the man who grinned through the square hole in the door.

He wanted to look back at the woman to gauge her reaction, but he feared he would see pity or revulsion there.

He mustered up all the authority he could manage and said, "I demand you let us in."

"Demand all you like," the man said. His face disappeared and in its place a notched arrow appeared.

Hikaru took a few steps backwards. *What will my father think when they find my body? Will he weep, or will he blame me for my lack of leadership?*

The woman jumped down from the saddle and approached the door. Her footsteps were so light she hardly disturbed the gravel beneath her feet. Hikaru held up his hand to stop her.

"Don't, these men are mad." Then to the men beyond the gate he said, "When my father hears of this, you will be flogged or worse."

The man did not respond. The woman frowned and looked between Hikaru and the warriors on the wall. She gave him a questioning look that he could not answer. The arrow in the door disappeared. The men on the wall did not move from their spots, though a few tilted their heads towards the courtyard. Raised voices drifted over the wall, and a few of the warriors dropped their arrows. He looked at the woman. She shrugged. Hikaru approached the door, but as he did, it cracked open. Then with a groan it swung open. A man stood in the doorway. He was of average height, unassuming, his expression blank.

"My lord, I apologize for my men's insubordination," Captain Sadao said. He bowed to Hikaru. When he stood up, his eyes drifted to the woman and that was where they rested. They stared at one another, giving each other measured looks. Hikaru felt the urge to protect her. Something about the captain's expression was honed and deadly. She seemed to recognize him as well.

"I'm glad to see you've returned, Captain Sadao. I was afraid we had lost you." At least he had one less death on his conscience.

"I only just made my way back, my lord." The captain nodded. "It was difficult to get inside. The men are a bit on edge after this afternoon, it seems."

Hikaru avoided his gaze. He was not sure if that was meant as a dig at his poor decision making. Hikaru cleared his throat and said, "I found this woman along the road. Summon the head servant and have a room prepared for her."

The captain bowed, and with a few quick words to one of his men, his orders were carried out.

The woman grabbed onto Hikaru's sleeve. He glanced at her. The captain strode off, his men in tow looking sullen, and when he was out of sight, the tension melted off of her and left behind a childlike glee that sparkled in her eyes as she looked around the courtyard. She skimmed over objects, her gaze bouncing about like a ball.

Just then the elderly head servant arrived. His kimono was falling off his shoulder, and his hair was half down as if he had intended to brush his hair but decided against it at the last second.

"My lord, you have returned!" he gasped.

"Yes, I found this young lady wandering alone in the dark. I would have her fed and taken care of."

"That is your father's decision." The servant wrung his hands. "He gave orders that you be brought to him the moment you returned." His beady eyes flickered from Hikaru to the woman for just a moment before fixing on the floor.

"Very well, I will see him in a moment, but first I would have the lady's comfort seen to."

"He will want to see her as well," the servant said while looking at the ground.

Hikaru clenched his jaw. He ground out, "Then we shall present ourselves to him."

SEVEN

Shin sniffed the air. This was where Rin's trail ran cold. He had chased her from the Dragon's palace to this far corner of his kingdom only to find she had disappeared. The forest buzzed, the residents all talking about the guardian, who was in an uproar. And he suspected a certain Kitsune he knew had something to do with it. Disguised as a wolf, he could walk along the human roads. He did that now, his Yokai senses spread out to find her. He knew her signature like his own beating heart, but apart from the broken branches with tufts of coppery hair and fox prints on the ground, he did not notice anything that belonged to her.

He stopped when he felt a strange energy coming from nearby; it raised the hairs on his back. *That is human energy but tainted somehow.* He ran forward and came to a skidding halt when he found the markings on the ground. He brushed his nose against it. And recoiled. A human had trapped a Yokai here. He could taste the spell on the air, acrid and foul. Beneath it, he noticed it faintly but still her scent. Rin.

What have you done now? She would be the death of him, he was sure of it. He never should have chased after her. What would the Dragon do when he found out he had abandoned his post? The Dragon had left him in charge while he went on one of his infamous trips. But he had seen Rin's face the day she disappeared. He thought she needed time to cool off, as usual, but when she had not returned, he realized he had underestimated her. And so here he was on a madcap search for her. He growled in his throat.

He ran along the path, smelling her faintly corrupted scent. He followed the trail along the human road, growing more confused all the while. Then her scent mixed with that of a human, at least he thought it was human. This scent also had a strange note to it. He looked through the dark, his advanced vision showing the road ahead of him, and in the distance he saw a human palace. He sighed. Something told him that was where he would find her.

THE SERVANT JUMPED AS IF HE HAD BEEN PRODDED WITH A KNIFE, AND scurried ahead of them down the hall. They followed after. Rin was curious as to what all the fuss was about. What was it about his father that caused this sudden change in the young man? She had only been in the palace for a few moments and she already had a billion questions buzzing around inside her skull. *Was my meeting him in the forest earlier today by chance or by design? How does the witch expect me to stop anything without my powers?* They stopped outside a set of double doors. The servant knelt down outside the doors and slid them open.

The young man turned to Rin. "I am going to speak with my father first, just wait here a moment."

She tried to peer past him into the chamber beyond, but she could not see much beyond the bamboo flooring. He disappeared inside and the servant slammed the doors shut with a sideways glance at Rin. She smiled back at him. The servant did not lift his gaze to her. He kept his palms pressed flat against his thighs. *They're not very friendly. I guess I should have known that. Humans seem to be a prickly lot.*

She had never realized how limited human vision was. It was difficult to see much beyond the darkness that cloaked the veranda on which she waited. She took a few steps towards the garden that ran parallel to the veranda. The servant cleared his throat. She looked at him and the servant straightened up. His eyes were wide and fixed on Rin. He reached to clutch his robe closed. *What, does he expect me to sprout another head and devour him?* She could not imagine she was very intimidating in this weak human form.

The young man opened the door. His frown carved deep creases into his handsome face.

"Come in." He motioned.

She stepped inside the room; it was larger than she had thought. The room was square and mostly bare but for a couple of empty armor suits and a table. At the far end there was a platform on which an imposing middle-aged man sat. He watched her approach with a frown on his face. Her bare feet slapped against the bamboo flooring. The lord's back was straight, his posture regal. His tousled white hair fell over his shoulders and he wore a loosely tied robe. The young lord took the lead and knelt down in front of his father. His every movement was precise down to the angle of his hands upon the bamboo mats. Rin followed his lead. She could not help but sneak a peek at the lord, however. She grinned up at him. He stared at her as if the force of his eyes could pierce her. Rin shivered. She had never had cause to consider a human intimidating, but this man exuded power and a faintly disguised fear just beneath the surface of his cold mask. The two mixed together were a deadly combination.

"How dare you bring her into this place," the lord said.

"Father!" the young man interjected.

The lord glared at him and the young man clamped his mouth shut. Rin looked between him and the lord.

"Who are you, and what do you want from us?" the lord asked Rin in a firm voice.

She met his dark penetrating gaze.

"She is mute, Father," the young man said in an apologetic tone.

"Don't be so easily deceived. Her kind play tricks; it is their way."

The lord stood and strode over to Rin. He stopped in front of her and she tilted her head back to maintain her eye contact. If she showed this man she feared him, he would push until she broke. She had no intention of failing even if the witch had stacked the odds against her. From the corner of her eye, she saw the young man half rise up to try to stop his father, but the lord held up a hand to halt him.

"I command you to speak," the lord said.

She opened her mouth, displaying her tongue, and then with a shrug of her shoulders closed it again.

"She appears to be a woman of noble birth," the young man said, though a bit hesitantly. "Were you separated from your clan?" This question he directed at Rin.

She did not want to take her eyes off the lord. He reminded her of a rabid beast. The moment you turned your back, he would strike for the kill. But just like taming a savage beast, she would stand her ground. Once she defeated him, nothing else would stand in her way of doing as the witch bid. She turned to the young man, keeping the lord in her peripheral vision, and nodded slowly.

The lord scrutinized her. His dark sharp eyes skimmed over her from top to bottom. There was challenge in his expression. If she had her fox fire, she would have used some of her magic to transform him into a salamander just to knock him down a size. As it was, she felt the loss of her connection with her powers as if she'd had a limb cut off.

"What clan do you hail from?" the lord asked again.

"Are you from the Torihara clan?" the young man asked.

She shook her head. *If I answer too quickly, they will think I am lying.*

"Perhaps the Akahana family?" Hikaru asked again eagerly.

She shook her head again.

"Fujikawa? Saruyama? The Nishimoris?"

The last name struck her; the meaning, though lost on the humans, was perfect. The west forest. She nodded her head and clapped.

"You're a Nishimori?" Hikaru confirmed.

She nodded again, smiling.

The lord narrowed his eyes. "Lord Nishimori has three daughters, though I do not know their names. I never heard any of them were mute."

Rin shrugged as if to say *What can I tell you?* She was fortunate the clan had any daughters at all. With her luck, he would only have sons and then she'd really be up a creek.

The lord turned and walked back to his seat on the platform. He planted himself on his cushion and folded his hands in front of him. "Lord Nishimori is a cousin of mine. I will send word to him that we have happened to discover you." He had yet to take his eyes off of Rin. She felt as if they were locked in a battle of wills. The first one to look away would lose.

"I'll show you to your room." The young lord jumped up.

Rin rose as gracefully as possible. If she was to pretend at being a human, she would need to work harder to convince the lord. The lord's gaze flickered to his son. A mild look of disgust crossed his features, but when he realized Rin had noticed, he wiped it away.

She bowed to him before following Hikaru out into the hall.

The servant was waiting for them in the hall. He had straightened his clothes and hair. The young man dismissed him, and the servant nodded stiffly before scurrying away. When they were alone once more, the tension from the audience chamber melted off of the young man. He smiled at her.

"I must apologize for my father's behavior. He has been under a lot of pressure lately."

Rin moved closer to him and touched him on the shoulder. *Tell me more,* she wanted to say. She had been given a gift when he found her in the forest. She knew he recognized her, but he had yet to mention it. He was the son of the lord, which meant getting closer to him would help her in her task. Who better to teach her human ways and with it how to exploit them to ruin their treaty. And if she was lucky, she might have a bit of fun along the way. Her sisters had told her stories about the humans they had seduced over the years. She had never done it before, but with someone as handsome as the young lord, it might not be so bad.

He tensed when she touched him, however, and sidestepped away. *I get the impression the humans do not welcome casual touches. Every time I brush against him, he acts that way. That will make my job more difficult.*

He led her down a series of hallways and the easy atmosphere they had shared before suddenly became charged. She suspected this was normally a servant's duty, to show guests to their chambers. *Is he expecting me to invite him into my bed?* She looked him up and down. He was handsome, tall and well formed. She would not mind seeing what lay beneath those layers of silk. They stopped along a veranda; a few rolling doors had been pushed back. Beyond was a sitting area and, partitioned off in the back, a sleeping area obscured from view by a reed curtain. He stopped with his back to the sitting area and faced Rin.

"We've prepared this room for you. If you need anything, the servants are on hand." He leaned against one of the sliding doors.

She smiled and arched a brow.

He waited a few more moments, not meeting her gaze but lightly gripping the door frame.

She tilted her head and nodded backwards, trying without words to invite him in.

"I failed to mention before, my name is Hikaru."

She smiled.

He picked at the wood and did not meet her gaze. "I suppose you cannot tell me your name."

That is what got me into this mess in the first place. But she supposed she could tell him; it would make things easier.

She waved her hand in front of him so he would look up. She crossed her arms over her chest and scowled.

He frowned back at her. "Is anything the matter?"

She shook her head and tried something different. She wrapped her arms around herself and pretended to shiver.

"You're trying to tell me your name?"

She nodded.

A smile transformed his face and lit up his eyes. "Let's see, cold... and angry?"

She shook her head. Next she tilted her chin upwards in a snooty pose.

He tapped his chin in thought. "Cold, arrogant?"

She shrugged, close enough. She nodded and waved her hand for him to keep guessing.

He thought for a moment, staring past her down the hall. She wished she knew the human character so she could write it down for him. Then he gasped. "Is it Rin?"

She clapped her hands together, delighted he had got it in one guess.

"Rin." He said it again, rolling the syllable around on his tongue. "It's pretty."

She touched his sleeve, tugging on it. Now that they had been introduced perhaps they could get to know one another better.

He opened his mouth as if he were going to speak before he snapped his mouth shut.

"I must be going, good night." He pulled loose from her grasp, turned and left.

She crossed her arms over her chest. Perhaps she had been a little too forward. But the sooner she got him into her bed, the sooner she would be back to her old self. She shook her head. *This may take all my charm and wits.*

She must be playing a trick on the humans. That is the only explanation. He followed Rin's muted scent all the way to the palace. When he reached the entryway, he considered turning back. But her scent went through the gates. He had come too far to let a few humans deter him. Waiting until the humans were on the opposite end of the wall with their backs turned, he leapt over the wall. He landed on the other side, in a dark courtyard. The stink of humans was overwhelming. The wolf in him rebelled, demanding he return to the forest. The energy here was foul and dragged against his other senses. He shook off his concerns and slunk through the shadows, searching out Rin's scent. The competing scents mixed together, making it difficult to pick one out from the gloom. Then he heard someone approaching from the opposite direction. He crouched in the shadows, sitting on his haunches.

"The young lord asked a room be prepared for the lady," said an older man.

"I'll see it done, then," replied a middle-aged woman.

He suspected Rin was said lady and followed the middle-aged woman to a chamber. She laid out bedding, lit the braziers and hung screens. He crept behind her while she worked and waited in the garden beyond. When she exited, he snuck in to investigate. The room was small but well furnished, the futon made of silk and the pillows filled with feathers. *This is a fine place but nothing compared to the palace.* He inspected the place but found nothing out of the ordinary. There were wooden drawers to keep possessions, a window at one end, and a garden facing the inner chamber. Reeds hung around the main sleeping area, blocking it from view.

She cannot avoid me forever. I'll just wait. He plopped down and waited for her arrival. It was some minutes before he heard voices outside the door.

The door slid open and he saw her profile. Her hair was long and black, and tied hastily. She looked like herself, but there was something not right about her appearance. Her energy was diminished and her glow gone.

She turned into the room and her gaze swept over the furnishings with an indifferent expression. Nothing out of the ordinary, he imagined her thinking. Then she saw him laid out on the futon. He had opened the front of his kimono so his flat stomach and defined chest were exposed. Had he been trying to seduce any other woman, it would have worked.

"I have been waiting for you, Rin," he said in a low rumbling voice.

She rolled her eyes and plopped down beside him.

He grinned, revealing pointed canines. That was his Rin, unimpressed. Maybe that was what had drawn him to her for so long. She did not fall prey to his charm like the other women. "What have you done?" He reached for her soft ebony hair and grabbed a few strands, tangling them around his long fingers.

She batted his hand away. She crossed her hands over her throat to indicate she could not speak.

He tutted. He should have known straight away. "You've been bewitched, I can see it now. What is the price to break the spell? Should I summon the Dragon?"

She shook her head furiously. Then things must have ended badly with the Dragon. Perhaps now was his chance. After waiting so long, he did not want to waste his opportunity to tell her how he felt. He should wait until he knew her heart was healed. Besides, she was under some spell. Now was not the right time.

Shin folded his arms over his chest. "You can't keep avoiding him for eternity. In fact, I came here to bring you back. I thought you were playing a trick on the humans, and now I can see this is much more complicated than that."

She sighed.

"You probably did it to yourself," he mused aloud.

Rin scowled at him in return.

He laughed, a rich husky sound.

She spread out her hands in a gesture that said, *Well, can you help me break this spell?*

He lay back on the futon and cradled his head on his forearms. "I don't know if I should help you this time. Maybe I'm done cleaning up your messes." He glanced at her from the corner of his eye. He loved the way her face flushed when she did not know what to do with him. Teasing her was the best way to elicit that reaction, but he'd much rather have her cheeks flushed for a different reason. He squashed down the thought. Now was not the time. He needed to focus on fixing this problem first.

She placed a hand on his shoulder and he flickered dark brown eyes towards her. She gave him a quivering bottom lip. She knew he could not resist. *She's good, I'll give her that.*

He sighed. "Fine, I'll look into it. For now you stay here. It's safer if you are among humans while you are one."

She clapped her hands. He grinned at her in return. It felt like old times before the Dragon. *I never should have separated myself from her. This is my fault if it's anyone's. I have to protect her.*

She threw her arms around Shin's shoulders. He toppled backwards and she pinned him to the ground. She leaned over him. Her now dark hair fell between them and tickled his nose. Her lips were slightly parted. It took all his self-control to not lean forward and kiss her. Did she not know how she drove him mad? How every casual touch, every movement drew him to her? He had held back these feelings for so long, but damn it, he was tired of waiting. He needed her. No amount of liaisons was worth even a tenth of just seeing her smile. His breathing was deep and shallow. Their faces were close together. He closed his eyes and inhaled deeply. No matter how brave or how powerful he was, she always brought him to his knees. He couldn't face the rejection if she still loved the Dragon. He sighed and then very gently pushed her off. She sat back and gave him a puzzled look.

"I'll be back tomorrow. Stay out of trouble until then," he said with his back to her.

She reached out for him, but before she could grab onto him, he transformed. He did not want her to convince him to stay and have him make a mistake he would later regret. A second later, the man disappeared and in his place was a wolf. The wolf bounded out of the room and down through the garden. *I'll be back with a way to break her spell, and maybe then I'll have the courage to say what I really feel.*

EIGHT

Hikaru hurried down the hall. His servant, Yori, chased after him, tugging at his sleeves and trying to straighten Hikaru's crooked outer robe. He spotted Rin across the veranda. She did not see him at first; she was looking around the palace with interest, her neck craned, and her pale skin contrasted against crimson leaves on her robe. Yori collided with him from behind.

"Pardon me, my lord," Yori said.

Hikaru waved his hand in a dismissive gesture. A jade comb in Rin's hair sparkled and winked at him as she moved under shafts of sunlight falling onto the landing. She turned and their eyes met.

Yori cleared his throat. Hikaru had forgotten he was there. "There's no need for you to apologize; I stopped too suddenly. I thought I felt something in my sock."

"Should I take you back to your chamber and switch them out, my lord?" Yori asked, with a hardly stifled laugh, which he poorly disguised as a cough.

As Rin drew closer, he suddenly felt very aware of his attire. He ran his hands over his hair to make sure it was smooth and then discreetly turned to Yori. "How do I look?"

Yori smiled, like a fond uncle would. "Very handsome, my lord."

"You know how to please your lord. I will call for you later."

Yori bowed, but the grin did not leave his face as he backed away. "As you say, my lord."

Rin was close enough now that he could touch her if he were so bold. Her smile flashed across her face. Unlike so many noble ladies he met, her smile was broad and reached her eyes. *Can the sun even shine as bright as that smile?*

He bowed to her in greeting. She stared back at him. *Did I do something wrong? Why did she not bow as well?*

The handmaiden who accompanied Rin gasped. When Hikaru glanced at the maid, she turned her head away, a blush staining her cheeks. He was not the only one who had noticed Rin's bad manners. It was her eccentric behavior that fascinated him and it endeared him to her more than anything.

"Lady Nishimori, I am glad to see you. I hope you slept well."

The smirk did not leave her ruby lips, but it curved the corners of her mouth in a way that was both enticing and mysterious.

The night before he had been sure he misunderstood her intentions. What noble lady would invite a man she just met into her chamber? But judging from the secretive way she smiled and how she looked at him through her lashes, that may have indeed been her intention. He tugged at his collar; he felt very hot all of a sudden. *I'm turning into a lecher. I must be misreading her signals.*

"I thought perhaps we might break our fast together." He motioned towards the room beyond. The sliding doors had been pulled back on all sides. The sun filtered into the room, giving it natural light. On the opposite end of the room, it overlooked a courtyard garden, one of many sprinkled across the palace. The maple tree in the center of the courtyard burst with crimson leaves, which brightened an otherwise bleak garden.

Rin walked through the room, and instead of seating herself on one of the pillows on the floor, she went into the garden. It was a small space and Rin, wearing the same kimono he had found her in, seemed to fill the bleak space with light. She stepped down from the landing and revealed dainty bare feet as she lifted up the hem of her kimono. She stepped onto the cobblestones that made a path through the small garden. She stood beneath the maple tree and tilted her head back. It revealed the column of her throat and the nape of her neck; it was oddly erotic. He had seen such few glimpses of her flesh, but each time it stirred something within him. He followed her out as if in a trance.

He did not take off his own socks, but he did find a pair of sandals by the door and slid them on so he could join her in the garden. He followed her same path, his sandals clicking on the stones. She turned to him. Her eyes reflected the gold of her kimono, and her hair in the light looked almost coppery. He stared for a moment, thinking once more of the strange woman who had saved him in the woods. But when he blinked, she returned to as she was, dark hair and eyes, a noble lady. She was an odd woman, but that was what drew him to her.

"Do you like the tree?" he asked. *How simple I must sound.*

She smiled and moved closer. She pressed her hand to the bark and then to her heart.

"You seem to have a strong attachment to nature." He hesitated, then under his breath said, "I wish you could tell me what you were thinking."

She did not look at him, but he could feel her smirk somehow. *She has secrets that I would drain the ocean to learn. She makes me want to write bad poetry. I may be more adept with a brush than a sword, but I do not think anything I could pen would do justice to her innocence and beauty.*

"I've heard that the Nishimoris have strong ties to the forest. They say it is because of your patron Kami, but I do not put much stock in those sorts of things."

She turned to look at him. Her eyes traced his face and then slowly went down to his throat and over his shoulders. It was an intimate feeling having her eyes travel over him like that. It felt as if she could see through him. Did she find him wanting? Did she like what she saw? She looked at his face again and then shrugged. The sting of her dismissal nearly staggered him. He was left with his mouth agape as she turned and ran back up the stairs. *She must be teasing me.* He followed her back into the room. The servants had laid out a meal of miso soup, broiled fish, rice, and an assortment of side dishes, including fried tofu.

Rin knelt down on one of the pillows and she leaned forward, smelling the food in front of her. Her expression was blissful. He could not help but drink in her appearance. She seemed to experience the world as if for the first time, like she had been born just the day before.

"Is everything to your liking?" he asked.

She picked up a bowl of fried tofu and had pressed it nearly to her nose. She closed her eyes and exhaled. When she opened them, she looked at him rather sheepishly. He laughed and she smiled before diving into the tofu with gusto. He watched her eat for a few more moments before taking a few bites of his own food. *I cannot keep staring, it's rude.*

When she finished the tofu, she tried the fish, which seemed to her liking, as did the rice and the soup. She ate heartily, which was a refreshing change. So many of the women he encountered nibbled and hardly ate. Rin was different from them in so many ways.

When they finished their meal, he offered her a tour of the palace. He started at the outer ring of the palace. This area was populated by the servants and lower-ranking clan members. A young woman walked with her head down, carrying empty dishes back to the kitchen. Hikaru did not notice the woman approaching them until she collided with Rin. Hikaru caught Rin about the waist and she fell against his chest, clutching onto his outer robe. He stared down into her large dark eyes. She smiled at him before very gently pushing away. Her hand seemed to linger on his chest a moment longer than necessary, but he might have imagined it. The servant who fell knelt over the broken dishes, which she picked up and placed in her upturned apron. Hikaru noticed and bent down to help her up.

"My apologies, my lord, I was not watching where I was going." She did not look at Hikaru, but he could see her eyes darting towards Rin.

"We should have watched where we were going. You are the one who was doing her duty." He smiled at her, but the young woman did not return it.

She gathered the dishes and fragments, refusing Hikaru's help. When she was finished, she gave him a low bow, scurried backwards and hurried away from them. When she disappeared around the corner, Hikaru returned his attention to Rin. They walked side by side through the palace grounds. He wanted to reach out to touch her hand or brush against her arm, though he knew it would be inappropriate. No matter where they went, the servants watched them go; their expressions were mixed fear and apprehension. At first he paid it no heed; then he heard their whispers and could feel the tension in the air like a blanket covering them. The servants would never openly stare, but they all but did. One man ran in the opposite direction as they approached. He looked at Rin, who grinned back at him. She did not seem to notice. *Rumors have already begun to spread. I must stop this now, or she may suffer the same fate.*

"Let's go to the practice yard. I can show you the men at work."

She inclined her head and they walked off together. The practice area was full of activity as they approached. A ring of men surrounded two who sparred. Swords rang as they collided, followed by the shouts of the watchers in support of their champion. Hikaru and Rin took a spot in the shade of a veranda that overlooked the yard. Rin scooted very close to the edge, her eyes glued to the fight.

The men were shirtless and glistened with sweat. The man to the right breathed heavily, his practice wooden sword held at the ready. Hotaru, on the opposite side, eyed his challenger with a grim look of determination. Hikaru had seen that look in his brother's eye before and he was glad not to be on the receiving end of it. Hotaru's opponent had his back to them and did not appear to even have broken a sweat. The two charged one another, swords slashing and jabbing.

Rin touched Hikaru's elbow, and he flinched involuntarily. Her casual touches inflamed him and filled his thoughts with images of what could have happened had he acknowledged her invitation from the night before. *Damn my honor. If I were a different man, I might consider it.* As it was, he was hard-pressed to push aside such selfish thoughts. She did not withdraw her hand, however. When he looked at her, it seemed there was a question she wanted to ask.

"Are you wondering what they are doing?" he asked.

She shook her head.

"Then perhaps you want to know why they are practicing?"

She nodded.

He looked back to the men. The man who had his back turned to them before was facing them now. Hikaru recognized Captain Sadao. He had his brother cornered and the strain of keeping his cool was visible in Hotaru's face. It gave Hikaru a jolt to see his brother with his back against the wall for once, but he knew it wouldn't last. Hotaru never lost. Hikaru held his breath, expecting his brother to turn the tables at the last moment. Captain Sadao jabbed again, the practice sword grazing against Hotaru's unprotected midriff. A killing blow. Hotaru threw up his hands in surrender. The fight was over. The captain and Hotaru bowed to one another. Rin stepped in front of him, her brow raised. She was waiting for an answer.

Hikaru hesitated to reply; his family's business was private. It had not occurred to him until this moment that she may very well be a spy sent by their enemies. "It is not right for me to speak of war in a lady's presence."

She crossed her arms in front of her in a most unladylike fashion.

He sighed. "We are preparing for war. There has been tension between the clans."

She looked back to the men fighting, her expression thoughtful.

"There is no need to worry, your father and mine are allies. You are safe here." He dearly hoped she was not a spy and he was just being paranoid.

She smiled, but it lacked the conviction of her previous smiles. Her eyes seemed troubled.

"Hikaru, have you decided to take up swordplay?"

His brother Hotaru approached them. Rin perked up as he approached. His brother's hair was down and he dabbed at his face with a towel. He had hoped his brother would be distracted by his loss and not notice them. *I've never seen anyone beat Hotaru before.*

"I was showing Lady Nishimori around," Hikaru replied. It was difficult to keep the ice from his tone when Rin looked at Hotaru like a woman dying of thirst.

His brother looked Rin up and down, his gaze slow and languid. Hikaru's hands balled into fists at his sides. Hotaru had a reputation with women; his natural magnetism and position made it easy. Hikaru stepped discreetly in front of Rin, drawing his brother's attention to him.

"I see you have met your match, brother." Hikaru nodded towards Captain Sadao.

Hotaru laughed. "I have to let them win from time to time. It keeps up morale."

Hikaru rolled his eyes, but his brother did not notice. While the captain did not appear taxed at all, Hotaru's brow glistened with sweat and his breathing remained labored. Hotaru stepped around Hikaru to approach Lady Rin. "I have heard much about you, my lady. The rumors of your beauty do not do you justice."

Rin batted her eyes at Hotaru.

"We should be going. This is not a place for a woman to linger," Hikaru said and grabbed onto Rin's wrist without thinking. He pulled Rin along after him. She came, but when they were alone again, she wrenched her hand from his.

She glared at him and he could see the accusation in her eyes.

"Don't be angry, Lady Nishimori, my brother has a reputation —" He choked on the rest of his words. He dared not offend her further.

She tossed her head and stomped away from him. He went to chase after her when he was intercepted by a servant, who stepped into his path, blocking him from following after Rin.

"My lord, your father bid me give you a message."

"What is it?" Hikaru snarled. He looked past the servant to Rin, who was about to turn the corner and out of sight.

"He has sent me to remind you that your wife is to come soon, and it would not be appropriate to be seen paying any special attention to our guest."

Hikaru looked at the servant. His eyes were lowered, but he knew how his father's men reveled in delivering his decrees.

"Tell my father I do not forget my place." He clenched his jaw, biting back what he would rather say.

"Lady Nishimori!" Hotaru called out to her. Though he was not one to shout, he did not want her to get away. He was fortunate his brother was stupid enough to fall for a fake message. She did not turn around, so he called out again, "Lady Nishimori."

Again she ignored him. Perhaps he had offended her? He jogged to catch up with her. A few servants saw him and gave him an indulgent smile. He grinned back. They turned their heads away, pretending not to see his uncouth manner. His father would be furious if he saw him chasing after a woman in broad daylight, shouting like a child at play. But because he had the hearts of the servants, he could do as he wished and his father would be none the wiser. His people loved him. He was more like them than his brother, who looked down upon them.

She turned suddenly and saw him jogging towards her. A slow smile spread over her features and he saw that glint in her eye that he had spotted before. Hikaru had all but dropped the perfect prize in his lap. He might not be able to take his brother's spot as future elder, but a good marriage could make all the difference. He caught up to Lady Nishimori and bowed. She tilted her head, looking him up and down, but did not bow in return. *Does she think herself better than me?*

The sudden flash of temper was quickly squashed. He replaced his frown with a charming grin. He needed her. The Nishimoris were wealthy, if not a bit eccentric, something he was willing to deal with if he could win her.

"My lady, I am sorry to chase after you in this way. I had to speak with you."

She raised an elegant brow, curiosity plain on her features.

"Do not think me forward, but I wanted to know if you would walk with me?"

She nodded her head and they fell into step together easily enough. Hotaru pointed out the different buildings and spoke of the founders of their clan, one of the first in the region to build a palace. He showed her his father's additions to the sprawling palace grounds, gardens and a temple to their patron Kami.

"This was built by my father some fifteen years ago." He pointed to the freestanding structure; it was surrounded by decorative plants and painted bright red. The roof was made of black tile, and strings of ofuda hung along a tori arch that separated the temple from the courtyard beyond. Inside they could see screens made of wooden squares. "The original shrine is sealed away and in disrepair. I used to play there when I was a boy until I heard about the ghost that haunts it."

He smirked at her, hoping to get a rise out of her. She blinked at him without fear.

"Do you not fear ghosts, my lady?"

She smirked in return.

He liked her fire. She was not a demure flower like the other women he met. She had a pretty smile and a comely expression; a pity she was mute, she would have been a perfect bride. But second sons never got perfect brides. He was sure if he presented the match to Lord Kaedemori, he would be sure to agree. *At last you do something right, Hikaru. This girl will be a great asset to me.*

"Perhaps my lady would like to see the haunted shrine?"

She nodded. He looked over his shoulder. One of the maids trailed after them, most likely charged with keeping Lady Nishimori's virtue intact. But for what he planned, that would never do. He grabbed her wrist and pulled.

"Run," he said and they ran down the hallways, the maid shouting after them. He tugged her down a corridor and then threw open a door to hide in the chamber beyond. They listened breathless as the maid ran past. Then laughing, they ran out the door and down the hall towards the hidden shrine. When they got close, he slowed his pace but did not let go of her hand. She looked around with interest, unaffected by the ominous aura that clung to this space. He had not been there in years, but something about the shrine gave him chills. They said Lord Kaedemori's first wife haunted this place—he thought it must be true. The servants swore they heard wailing here late at night.

"We're almost there."

Just as they were about to round the corner and reach the shrine, they were stopped by an unwelcome intruder.

"My lord, you should not go there. It is off-limits."

Hotaru straightened up. He winked at Rin, but she was staring at Captain Sadao. She scrutinized his face as if trying to solve a riddle. He held back a scowl; he did not want the captain to think he was a sore loser. He would be sore tomorrow, he was certain. That was the first time Captain Sadao had given him his all. He usually held back when they sparred, but there was something different about the captain since he returned from the forest. All the men had been altered by what they had seen. But did that mean he had to ruin his chance to woo Lady Nishimori?

"I was giving Lady Nishimori a tour. She wanted to see the haunted shrine."

The captain's gaze flickered over Hotaru and then to Rin. "I think you should leave this place, it's not safe." He looked at them both when he spoke, but his words seemed like they were directed at Rin.

Hotaru opened his mouth to argue, but Rin rested a hand on his shoulder and he desisted.

"Very well, we will go and find amusement elsewhere."

Disappointed and angry at being shamed by the captain twice in one day, he turned and grabbed Rin, urging her to follow. The men might love him and the servants might worship him, but when it came down to it, he had no real power. And that fact chafed. He gripped her wrist tighter than he intended, and after a few moments she wrenched her hand away from him. He replaced his smile, smothering his anger beneath a friendly mask.

She looked at him warily, her eyes scrutinizing him. He had not meant to show his anger. He was usually good about hiding that behind a carefully crafted facade. "There are many places to see around the palace. The moon-viewing pool is beautiful at night. Perhaps you'd like to meet me there tonight?"

She looked him up and down as if assessing him. It did not sit well; his temper, already rubbed raw, could not stand her judgment as well. He did not need another person to find him wanting. He had to take control of the situation, just as he would make his own destiny. He rested his hand on her shoulder.

"Excuse me for being direct, but perhaps your coming here was not an accident?"

Her eyes grew wide and panic fluttered across her expression. That was not what he was expecting. It was not unheard of for a nobleman to send an eligible daughter to entice a lord into marriage. But Lady Nishimori was like no noble lady he had ever met. She should know this game. They all danced this dance: flirt, negotiate, and marry. But she looked frightened of him as if he had uncovered a deeper secret. *Perhaps she did not come here looking for a husband. Could it be she is not a lady at all?*

He had to be sure. "Let me speak plainly. I know why you are here."

She met his gaze unblinking, chin lifted and defiant. She did not demure like other noble ladies. *She is very strange.*

"I am looking for supporters, and I think your father could be one of those. Perhaps a marriage could even be arranged between our houses."

She took a step back, relief on her face. *She is hiding something.*

"Forgive me, that is not something I should address to you. I should write to your father."

She shook her head and then rested her hand on his arm and squeezed as she drew closer to him, and her breast brushed against his chest. *She does not act like a lady, and she's wanton. She is no noble lady. I would bet my life on it.*

He tore his hand away. "Who are you? Are you a spy?"

She recoiled and shook her head. Before he could question her further, her breathless maid caught up with them at last. He dared not interrogate the lady in front of a servant. If he had misread her, it could cause a scandal, one he could not afford. He would wait and watch to find out more.

"My lady! This is highly inappropriate." Then seeing Hotaru, she bowed with a blush and led Lady Nishimori away with a quick apology. He watched them retreat, his mind whirling. *What has my brother brought into this place?*

NINE

ould the witch have given me a more difficult task? I simply have to break their treaty, without magic and without a way to talk to people. It's as if she set me up to fail. Rin tossed a few pebbles into the well. The water rippled, spreading outward. *I could do with a bit of chaos. That's what Kitsune are best at anyway.* She did not move right away and stood staring at the water's surface. *Why did Hikaru have to be such a bore? I liked him; I thought he might help me in my plot. He seemed discontent when we spoke with his father. But failing him, Hotaru would suit.* She sighed. *But then again, he knows I am a spy —or at least he suspects.*

She walked down the stairs away from the well. The maid, Yuri, who had been assigned to Rin's care, stood a few feet away. She trembled whenever Rin looked in her direction. And right now she was shaking. Rin pursed her lips. *I'd rather be alone. It makes spying easier if she is not hovering over me.*

The garden where Rin had been lingering most of the morning was at the center of the palace. Hallways radiated out from it; she had watched as minor clansmen bustled about. They all quickened their pace when they came close to her. They all feared her, she suspected. Which was almost laughable, she could do nothing to them in this form. After a careful study of the landscape, it seemed the most traffic went down the center hallway. She brushed past the handmaiden and went towards the hall.

"My lady, you cannot go that way," Yuri said, her voice as tiny as a mouse.

Rin gave her the most imperious look she could manage. The girl took a step back. Rin shook her head and walked in that direction. The young woman ran in front of her.

"That area is forbidden to women. It is a man's place," she said. Her bottom lip quivered. It would not be hard to knock the girl over and go anyway. But Rin knew she would not get far. The humans loved their rules and ceremony.

Rin bowed, pretending to be the obedient lady. But the young girl only scrunched her nose in confusion. The bowing seemed important to the humans, but she could not get the timing right. Rin turned to head towards her chamber, Yuri trailing after her. Back at her chamber, Rin pointed to the veranda that overlooked her private garden and with a slashing motion indicated the handmaiden should leave.

"Will you be needing anything?" Yuri asked.

Rin replied with a quick shake of her head. The girl all but ran from the room. She waited, listening to the sound of her receding footsteps, and when she was sure she was gone, she smiled to herself.

Rin shed her outer robes, down to the shift beneath. The copious layers of silk the humans favored kept her from moving freely. She wriggled her toes free of the socks the handmaiden had insisted she wear. She could feel the air against her skin, and she peeled the fabric from her sweaty skin. Standing in the center of the symmetrical, orderly garden, she longed for the forest, the open places, and the disorganized beauty of the wild. She wished she had her proper sense of smell and all the other little things she had taken for granted before. All these humans said one thing and their body language indicated another. Take Hikaru and his brother, though they used polite words with one another, the air practically crackled between them. *I think I have something there, if I can use their animosity for my own devices.*

At the opposite end of the garden a vine grew up the wall nearly to the roof. Rin stood at the base of the plant and looked up. She flexed her fingers and then tugged on the vines, testing their hold on the trellis. When she was certain they would hold, she proceeded to climb up. At the top the vines were thinner and they pulled away from the wall. One broke loose and she leaned backwards, the ground spinning beneath her. Blindly, she swung her arm out to grab at the edge of the roof. With the tips of her fingers, she clawed her way up onto the top of the roof. She lay face down on the warm tiles for a moment as she panted. *I do not have the same strength in this form. I must remember that. One misstep and I will snap my neck.*

When she had caught her breath, she crouched on the roof and surveyed the palace from above. Much of it was connected by covered walkways. From up above, she could see the wider pathways leading to the center and the hidden parts of the palace, including the allegedly haunted shrine. A part of her wanted to investigate, but she knew she had to focus on the task at hand. Once she had her bearings, she set out, hunched over in a slow waddle, towards her destination. She needed to learn more about the palace. Who was an enemy of whom, and what were their desires and goals. In that respect the palace was not much different than the Dragon's kingdom.

The palace occupants scurried just beneath her feet. She heard murmured conversations, servants greeting one another in the halls. They gossiped with one another about nothing of consequence to her. Her name came up more than once; the servants whispered it as if saying it would bring her down upon their heads. She considered doing just that, but as amusing as that would be, it would ruin all her spying efforts. She stopped on the rooftop closest to the center, where the family resided.

"You won't win with that tactic," said a grizzled voice.

"War is won with wit, don't you know that, you old fool?" replied a thin reedy voice.

Rin crept closer to the edge of the roof. She tilted her head to hear better. She was surprised she had heard them at all. Human hearing was sadly lacking.

"There, take that," said the grizzled voice.

"You're a cheat. This is why no one wants to play with you, Arata," said the reedy voice.

What are they arguing about? Holding onto the edge of the roof, she lowered her head over. All the blood rushed downward and her arms shook as she peeked upside down at the room beneath her. Two old men sat at a board covered in square tiles. The first old man, with wisps of white hair tied into a topknot on top of his head, stroked his beard as he regarded the board. The second old man, who was completely bald, crossed his arms over his chest and scowled.

"Taking longer will not win you the game," he taunted his opponent.

Just then the doors at the opposite end of the room slid open. A woman knelt by the door and was focused on picking up a platter. When she looked up, her eyes met Rin's. She screamed and the two men jumped, nearly toppling over the board. Rin yanked her head back and ran over the rooftops and away. But not fast enough, it seemed.

"It was an evil spirit, I saw it!" the woman screamed.

The shouts seemed to ripple out from there. *I must run or I will be caught.* The rooftop ended at a gap. Footsteps hammered behind her, and at the far end of the roof, soldiers climbed up and closed the gap between them. If they found her sneaking about, Lord Kaedemori was sure to lock her up or worse. She looked down at the ground below. There was a small garden, with a pond in the center. The space was not so far that she felt she could not jump it. But she was judging it based on her fox abilities. As a woman, she might fall and break her fragile neck.

"You there, stop!" a soldier called out.

She had no choice now. She backed up a few feet and then ran. Her bare feet pounded on the roof tiles. One slipped beneath her foot and she stumbled. It slowed her down, but she kept going, gaining as much momentum as she could. The edge came up faster than she expected and she leapt, a prayer on her lips. She sailed through the air in slow motion. Beneath her, she saw a pair of servants pointing up at her, one covering his mouth with his hand. She collided with the edge of the roof. She hung there for a moment, her legs kicking, searching for purchase. Then with trembling arms, she pulled herself up onto the roof. She ran over the top to the other side and crouched down out of sight. The space below was deserted. She lowered herself down, but her hands shook and her fingers could not hold her weight. She fell onto a veranda. Her legs jarred and pain ran up her limbs like sparks of flame. Fueled by fear, she kept moving. After a quick glance, she found an empty room, the doors opened onto the veranda.

Footsteps rained on the roof overhead and shouts rang out from beyond the garden. She scurried into the room and hid herself behind a screen at the back. Just as she slipped behind it, the door opposite the veranda opened and she heard footsteps.

"What is this commotion?" Hotaru asked.

She held her breath. It was just her luck. If Hotaru found her hiding from the guards, her cover would be blown.

"Sounds like the men are practicing in the halls," said a second man, who laughed at his own joke.

"This is serious, Kichirou," Hikaru said.

Rin moved closer to the screen to better hear what they were saying. It was a risky move, but she dared not let a golden opportunity pass her by.

"Are you afraid you will have to fight after all, brother?" Hotaru taunted.

"I fear our staff have run mad with stories of spirits, and they are jumping at their own shadows," Hikaru replied.

"But if it is an attack, then you will not be able to hide behind your wife's army as you hoped."

"Now, now, brothers, I am sure it is just a misunderstanding," said Kichirou.

A tense silence followed. Though Rin could not see them, she imagined Hikaru and Hotaru glaring at one another while the third brother grinned at their discomfort.

Hotaru broke the silence. "I will not stay locked away like a cowering old woman. You two can join me or wait, the decision is yours."

He stomped out of the room and slammed the door after him as he left.

"Do not let him get to you, Hikaru. He does not mean anything by it," Kichirou said.

"You do not have to defend him."

Rin fought the urge to reveal herself and comfort Hikaru. The defeat in his voice spoke to her. She knew what it meant to live in the shadow of someone who eclipsed you in all things. Her entire life had been spent attending to Yokai that were more powerful than her, better connected and knew it. Why the Dragon had chosen her out of all the other options, she would never know, but she knew she had to prove her worth. *I never realized how similar humans are to us.* It was a revealing thought.

"Will you come and lead the men?" Kichirou asked.

"No, go and join our brother. I will be out in a moment." Hikaru's voice sounded close by. He must have crept over without her realizing it. *Damn this inferior hearing.*

The door opened and closed. Rin held her breath for a moment. Now was her chance. Of all the brothers, Hikaru was the most likely to help her get back to her room unseen and without questions. She stepped out from behind the screen.

"Rin!" he shouted.

She rushed forward to cover his mouth from screaming further.

She looked to the door, listening for approaching footsteps, but it seemed they were looking for her elsewhere. When she looked back to Hikaru, he was staring at her. She was wearing nothing more than her white undershift. His eyes grazed over the swell of her hips and skimmed along the tops of her breasts. She flushed unexpectedly. She took her hand from his mouth. She brushed her fingertips against her palm; it was warm from his breath.

"What are you doing here, and dressed like—" He coughed.

She smiled at him. She regretted her temper from the day before. She had a hunch that Hikaru's wife had something to do with this treaty the witch was intent on destroying.

He shook his head. His eyes drifted downward only to snap back to her face suddenly. "You were the one on the roof, weren't you?"

She lowered her lashes in mock shame.

"It does not matter. I should take you back to your room. My father will be furious if he finds you here... especially in your underclothes." He cleared his throat and then turned his back to her. He shed his overcoat and handed it to her.

She took it and slipped into it. His scent clung to it. She inhaled deeply. Even as a human she found his scent pleasant.

"Follow me, I know a secret way." He held out his hand for her to take. He did not grab her as he had done before. *He can be taught.*

They went down the back steps through the garden and into a hallway. Hikaru led the way, not letting go of her hand. She found the pressure of his pulse against hers comforting. He opened a chamber door, poked his head inside and then motioned for her to follow with a jerk of his head. She went after him. They moved through the room, the only sound was their footsteps on the floor. Then through the transparent paper doors, she saw a shadow just beyond. Hikaru stepped in front of her, blocking her from view. The figure stopped outside the door and seemed to be considering opening the door, then after a few tense moments, turned and walked down the hall. Hikaru exhaled. He opened the door, checked to make sure the coast was clear, and then they ran down the hallway together.

When they reached her chamber, they burst through the doors and slammed them shut. They were both breathless as Hikaru laughed. "I cannot believe you were sneaking about in your underclothes. What madness drove you to do such a thing?"

She tilted her head and regarded him. He was very handsome, especially when he smiled. She pulled him close, and when their faces were inches apart, she leaned forward. He pulled back suddenly and dropped her hand.

"I'm sorry, you're beautiful and..." He shook his head. "I am a married man. I cannot betray my wife."

That doesn't matter. I only need you for one night, just enough time to learn your secrets. She moved closer to him despite his protests.

He stepped back. "I am sorry. If even a whisper of my infidelity reached my wife's father, it would destroy the treaty."

Rin stepped back, her hand pressed to her chest. She looked at him with new eyes. This was it. The answer to breaking the spell. *I will have you, then. You do not know it yet, but no mortal can resist a Kitsune's charms. Even one without her powers.*

TEN

His false skin chafed. As if the original owner fought him from beyond the grave, it grew tighter around him each day. His true energy needed release. He needed to return to the forest and purge himself of this evil energy. A dark aura clouded the palace. If he had known, he would have fought Akio on sending him here. Each day he felt his strength waning. The aura polluted the very air he breathed. The humans here were fearful and suspicious, and he was not sure how much longer he could hold his disguise.

Akio had ordered him to watch the young lord, and he had. Hikaru was peculiar, the others mistrusted him, and he had to wonder if this aura was the cause. Of the residents in the palace, Hikaru was one of the few who seemed unaffected by the evil that tainted the palace. As much as he wanted to spare Hikaru, he would need to report this to Akio. As he had suspected, Hikaru was not human, but once Akio found out, he feared for the young lord.

He paced the length of the halls. Going about the mundane human tasks helped him organize his thoughts. He spread out his senses like a blanket over the palace. In this way he could survey the entirety of the palace. Most nights it was quiet, but more than once he had sensed the Okami visiting Rin's chamber. It was a gamble allowing him into the palace, but because they were the Dragon's servants, he let them do as they pleased. After all, as far as Akio knew, Rin was long gone. And he planned to keep that secret from his master at least.

As he turned a corner, he felt a spark along the palace wall. The witch had returned. He let her enter without challenge—it would be futile anyway. He had underestimated her power. How could he have known she could turn a Kitsune to a human? No human should have that sort of power. *Perhaps I made a mistake agreeing to help her.* He traced her progress through the palace. She knew where to find him, because he felt her awareness through her energy—she did not try to hide her power within the palace walls, as if she wished to flaunt her prowess before him. He ignored her for now, instead focusing on the second presence that crept into the palace, hiding behind her larger spiritual energy. He almost missed it.

Continuing along his route through the palace, he evaluated the second intruder. At first, he thought the second arrival was the Okami, but as he tried to get a better read on the energy, it disappeared, leaving a void in the energy field. Meaning it was a lesser Yokai. *Strange.*

Before he could search out this invader, the witch appeared dressed as a miko, though he doubted she was a real priestess. She materialized from the shadows and kept her face averted from him. She moved on soundless feet from the opposite end of the veranda. He nodded to her as she approached.

"Evening, Captain," she said in a low voice.

"Priestess," he replied.

"The night is dark and something lurks."

He nodded. The second intruder had a foul, dark aura. Until he knew it did not belong to the priestess, he would not move. But he was curious; using his energy probes, he unmasked the creature's clumsy shield. He was not here to protect the humans, but the slimy caressing of his probes raised his defense. It moved sluggishly, its spiritual vibrations so low they would not alert a Yokai with less training in reading the aura of others. *This is a tricky one, it could be dangerous.* If he focused, he could feel its slow progress and read its malcontent as it snuffed and slithered through the palace. It was hunting for something. This did not belong to the witch; it reeked of Akio. *I should have known Akio would discover the witch eventually, or perhaps it's Rin he seeks.* Either way, he would need to be on the alert.

"Is that why you've come? To warn me?"

She chuckled. "I came to meet our Kitsune and check on her progress. This disturbance followed me in. I believe your master sent it for her."

"Ah. Then should I take care of this?"

"Yes." She tilted her head as if listening to a voice only she could hear. She turned back to him and he saw the dark shadows that cast her face in relief like a garish mask. "I want her safe until the time is right. We cannot sacrifice her to Akio's whims."

"Just your own?" he asked. He wanted to leave the Kitsune out of this, lest he bring down the Dragon's wrath upon himself. But what choice did he have? The witch was his last hope to save Tsukiko.

"Yes, just my own. Go, the creature is out for blood."

He bowed to her once more and ran in the direction of the creature. But he could not rush, or the humans would see and suspect. It was headed for Rin's chamber, just as the witch said. Damn Akio. He was too impatient by half. Naoki turned a corner at a stroll. He nodded at the guards on duty, who stood at attention as he passed by. He knew once he was gone they would slouch and continue gossiping. The real Sadao's memories had helped his transition. They had not even blinked an eye when he arrived and assumed the role of captain. They were too blind to see the truth. Despite their superstitions, they were blind to the real monsters among them.

A scream rent the night's stillness—the Yokai had struck. He ran now as the household stirred and the humans were shaken awake. It was over in an instant; he felt the Yokai exulting in the kill. It hummed with pleasure, sending a sick spasm through Naoki. He withdrew his probes and cut off his connection before he took in the dark poison from the Yokai's aura. At times his ability was a blessing and a curse. He had a better understanding of other Yokai's intentions, but he also took on their thoughts and energy, clouding his own. He followed the sound of the creature's murmurs and found it gloating over its kill, a dark form hunched over a woman's body. He could not see the face, but he feared he was too late.

The Yokai looked up as he approached, long pointed teeth dripping with blood. Its doglike snout was matted with dark fur, and it had large beady black eyes. The flesh fell off the carcass, revealing femurs and hip bones that jutted out like white maggots. One of Akio's favorite errand boys.

Drawing his blade, he waited for it to abandon its kill. Then growling, it lifted its bloody snout and bared bloody teeth. But it was too slow to be even a challenge, his sword cut through the decayed flesh as if it were paper, and the separated pieces fell to the ground with a wet flop. He stared down at the dismembered monster bleeding black blood onto the ground. He looked to the woman, fearing what he would find. The kimono was stained with blood, and her throat ripped out, but her face remained intact. It wasn't Rin. He knew this woman; it was Rin's maid lying on the ground, beside her a pile of silk. Rin's dirty kimono. The creature had mistaken her for Rin. She was too young for such a fate, not even seventeen. *This is a pity; only Akio would send a creature that was this sloppy.*

Just then a woman came around the corner. Upon seeing the bloody mess, the girl cried out, a wailing devastated sound. She fell to her knees, screaming, her face strained, and tears rolling down her cheeks. If anyone in the household was left asleep, they slept no longer. She did not see the creature dead beside her. Even when they were dead, Yokai were invisible to most humans. He would need to dispose of the body before Hikaru woke, however; he would surely have questions Naoki was not ready to answer.

A SCREAM WOKE HIM FROM A DEEP SLEEP. HIKARU SAT STRAIGHT UP IN bed. Once he was awake, he realized it was more of a long echoing wail than a scream. It seemed to roll through the palace, building in intensity.

"What was that?" Kichirou shouted outside Hikaru's door.

Hikaru grabbed his sword off the stand by the door. He never used it and he toppled over the stand as he clumsily snatched for it. It was almost laughable to grab the sword, but if they were under attack, he did not want to be without some sort of protection. He threw open the sliding door and it hit the end of the track with a thunk. The flimsy wood and paper shuddered beneath the force of the collision. He ran out into the hall, where all manner of cousins and extended family tumbled out into the night, lightly dressed in their sleeping robes. His uncle's sparse white hair stood up on end in every direction. Hikaru doubted he looked much better. His brothers stood to one side, conversing. Hikaru went over to them as the other family members chattered nervously amongst themselves.

"That sounded like a woman," Hotaru said to Kichirou; then noticing Hikaru, he sneered. "What do you plan to do with that?" He jutted his chin towards the sword Hikaru held limply in his hand.

One of their cousins burst out into the hall, preventing Hikaru from answering. His cousin brandished his sword as he shouted, "Are we under attack?"

"Put your sword away," Hotaru said. "We're not being attacked. There was just a woman screaming. Perhaps it was some nightmare."

"I doubt it," said Kichirou. "I am starting to think there is some evil spirit haunting this place." He shivered.

Hikaru bit his lip. Kichirou did not say it, but he knew he was thinking about Rin. The fear of her had only spread. There had been no word from the Nishimoris, and worse yet, the messengers had never returned. Three had gone out now, never to be heard of again. He wanted to believe Rin had pure intentions, but she had propositioned him twice now. The servants feared her and now the Nishimoris could not be reached to corroborate her tale. *All the evidence is stacked against her, but I cannot believe she means us harm.* Perhaps it was because he wanted to believe the fox woman was real, and she was Rin. Or maybe he was thinking too much with his nether regions.

"I'm going to investigate," Hikaru replied, not taking care to disguise his anger.

"Careful, brother, there's monsters out there!" Hotaru called after him.

He stormed away from his brothers and cousin. Hotaru was the fuel to this fire of superstition, he just knew it. There was no way to prove it, but this reeked of Hotaru. He would use Rin to shame Hikaru and better his own position. Perhaps he hoped this would be the final straw that would change their father's mind about who would be made heir. The screaming had ceased, but he need only follow the stream of soldiers and servants to find the source.

He found a group gathered in the outer ring of the palace in one of the gardens. He pushed his way through to the front. His heart pounded in his chest. When he broke through the crowd, he saw an old woman sobbing on the ground. She was bent forward, pounding the earth with her fist. A guard had hold of one of her hands, trying and failing to get her on her feet.

"What happened here?" Hikaru said.

The soldiers glanced in his direction but did not answer. The servants did not even flinch. They were all transfixed on one spot. Sprawled on the ground, limbs at odd angles, lay a woman. He stared for a few moments, trying to comprehend what was wrong with her, and then he saw the gashes across her throat, hidden in the shadows, and the dark stain on the ground was her blood. Blood stained her kimono as well.

Bile rose up in the back of his throat. He turned to a nearby bush and retched. When the spasms stopped, he stood upright. The servants did not look at him; in fact, everyone nearby made a point to avoid eye contact with him. *I am a disgrace. How can I hope to rule one day when the sight of blood turns my stomach?*

He took a deep breath and looked once more at the corpse. He knew this woman. It was Rin's maid, Yuri. *This has to be a terrible coincidence.* He could not look at her blank staring eyes any longer. He looked across the crowd for the captain. He found him with three of his men. He gave a few quick commands and the men went into the crowd, shooing them away.

"Captain Sadao, what happened here? Who did this?" Hikaru asked. His voice shook. No matter how he tried to remain in control, he was terrified. *There are enemies among us.* He hated himself for it, but his mind jumped to Rin first. She was the only outsider in the palace. He had heard stories all his life about Yokai that tricked humans and caused mischief inside a household. If Yokai were real, he doubted they troubled themselves with humans. Besides, this went beyond some simple mischief, this was murder. He stared at the captain, willing him to implicate anyone other than Rin. He could not imagine her doing such a thing.

"My lord, we are questioning the servants. But it appears her throat was torn out by some beast."

"An animal did this? How is that possible?" he asked. He felt as if his world had been turned upside down as of late. Nothing made sense anymore. Murder within the castle walls? Because despite the captain's assessment, Hikaru knew in his gut this was murder. A wild animal could not reach this far into the palace without help.

Captain Sadao's expression was difficult to gauge. He looked at Hikaru as if he saw past him. He had seen Hikaru vomit at the sight of blood and thought little of him for it, he suspected. Hikaru stood a little straighter in an attempt to look more imposing and worthy of respect, though he feared he was failing at it miserably.

"My lord, perhaps someone let the animal into the palace."

Hikaru scowled. He had been thinking the same thing. And he sensed the answer was hidden behind the captain's shuttered expression. "And who would be able to let a wild animal into the palace without anyone noticing? Or without being attacked themselves."

Captain Sadao's expression did not change, but he said in a slow deliberate manner, "There have been rumors of Lady Nishimori being seen with a wolf. Perhaps..."

"That is not possible," Hikaru said and slashed his hand in the air. "She is a lady and a friend of this court. For you to say that is an insult to me and to my family."

The captain bowed. "I do not mean to offend, my lord."

But you doubt still. The captain was difficult to read, but Hikaru sensed he knew something about Rin that he was not telling Hikaru. The question was on the tip of Hikaru's tongue. *Who is she really?* But he lacked the courage to ask because once the truth was revealed, he could not go back. This sweet torture, taunting himself with the idea of Rin, consumed him and he dared not ruin the fantasy world he had crafted for himself. Captain Sadao looked to Hikaru as if waiting on an order or a response.

"We'll find this culprit. And if anyone spreads these rumors about Lady Nishimori, I will have them flogged. Is that understood?"

The captain gave him a curt nod. Hikaru turned to storm away, but as he did he saw Rin standing on the veranda that overlooked the garden. *Did she hear us arguing?* He hoped not, he would hate for her to get the wrong impression about his clan. He hurried up the stairs to her.

"My lady Nishimori, you should turn away. There has been a terrible incident this night."

She looked past him to the courtyard beyond. She had not changed into her nightclothes and her hair was still styled. He looked at her, trying to imagine her as a powerful witch. He could not see her calling down a curse or unleashing a bloodthirsty beast on an innocent.

He thought once more of that strange woman he had met in the woods. Rin did seem to resemble her, but with each passing day he grew more uncertain. Had that woman been real at all? He wanted to shake himself. There was no such thing as Yokai or witches.

The guards lifted the body up to take it away. Rin's gaze was transfixed on Yuri. There was no fear in her expression, however, just a sadness, one that spoke of loss and deep sorrow. It seemed impossible, but those eyes seemed to have seen ages beyond imagining, and death was just one painful truth among many.

"Rin." He touched her gently on the elbow.

She flinched. She looked at him with terror in her eyes.

"I did not mean to frighten you. It is not right for a lady to see such things."

She gave him a defiant stare. That vulnerable girl disappeared behind a mask.

He shook his head. "I do not mean to insinuate you are delicate. In fact, I am certain you could handle this better than me. There has been some gossip and I would protect you from it. Would you indulge me?"

She tore her eyes away from the garden beyond and he led her away. She walked beside him, and though he wanted to reach out and comfort her, he kept his distance. He did not need to tempt fate any further. He should not even be spending this much time with her. He should have summoned a servant to do such a menial task. *Why do I continue to torture myself this way?*

When they reached her chamber, he thought he saw something moving within. *Could the beast have come here as well?*

He held up his hand to stop her from entering. "Do not move. I saw a shadow beyond the doorway. Wait here," he whispered.

The color drained from her face and her eyes darted to the

room. She reached out as if to stop him. But he held her hand between his. Just the touch of her warm skin against his was enough to bolster his confidence.

"Do not worry, I will be fine."

He slid open the door just enough to let him pass through. Inside the chamber was dark; there was her futon, made up and untouched. She had not slept. He crept into the room and unsheathed his sword. The sleeping platform was pegged in by a reed screen that hung from the ceiling. He walked past the sleeping area to her sitting room. From the corner of his eye, he saw a shadow slip past the open doors leading into the garden. He took a deep breath and approached the garden with his sword raised. Then someone grabbed his hand.

He spun around, his sword at the ready. Rin grinned at him. He lowered his sword.

"Rin, you should not be in here. I saw something in the garden. It may be that beast that killed poor Yuri."

She shook her head. She took him by the hand and led him out onto the veranda. The shadow he had thought was a monster lurking in the dark turned out to be the bare branches of the tree, cast along the floor by the moonlight. He exhaled.

"I may have overreacted," he admitted. He laughed to dissipate the awkward tension.

She smiled and brushed her hair behind her ear. It was an inno-cent gesture, but one that caught his eye and he could not help but wonder if it was done on purpose. She must know his eyes were drawn to every move she made. He wanted to be that hand that could carelessly touch her face. The space between them seem suddenly charged. They were alone in her room, with an empty futon. He swallowed hard. *How can I be thinking about this when there is a woman who has just lost her life?* The worst part was he knew if he made any attempt, she would accept, and that thought sat like a stone in his stomach.

Rin moved closer, her lips parted in an enticing way.

He stepped back. "I should go."

He rushed out of the room before he could change his mind. He hurried back to his room, ignoring his brothers' jibes and the questions from his relatives. He slammed his door behind him and slid down the wall. He rested his head on his palms and a shaking laugh escaped his lips. *Either I am a fool, or I have too much honor. I do not know any longer.*

ELEVEN

Rin slid out of the silk layers of her kimono. She had sent away the new maid, who tried to undress her. The feel of unfamiliar hands made her skin crawl. She kept thinking about poor Yuri, killed by a Yokai, she was certain. And as much as she wanted to pretend she did not care about the humans, she felt guilty for the girl's death. And now the servants watched her as if she were about to grow a third eye and sharp pointed teeth. *I cannot stand this.* Footsteps thumped on the ground and she spun around, clutching the silken fabric to her chest to conceal her naked body.

Shin looked her up and down slowly, starting with her feet and heading up. She scowled and pulled a hairpin from her hair. It had a sharp point. She spun it towards him, and it flipped over and over before grazing his ear as he dodged it. It embedded in the wall behind him.

"Don't stop on my account," he said with a barking laugh.

Rin snatched up her sleeping gown and went behind the privacy screen to finish dressing. *I am going to get you for this, Shin, just you wait.*

When she emerged from the other side of the screen, she found Shin lounging on her futon, twirling a scroll in his hand. She crossed her arms over her chest and made a gesture with her hand, indicating he should explain his presence. *I had hoped he would not come back. I suppose it was too much to hope for.*

"I've been intercepting messengers," he said, showing her the scroll. "Lord Kaedemori is not very trusting. But no need to worry, when a third came through in a week, I knew he would not be sated until he had an answer. I used all my forgery skills to send a letter explaining your presence. It should appease them until we can find a way to break this curse."

Rin rolled her eyes. He could be so arrogant. She plucked the scroll from Shin's hand and skimmed it over. He was not mistaken. It seemed Lord Kaedemori was more suspicious of her than she initially thought. *I will need to move quickly, before he gets it in his head to do something more drastic than writing a letter.* She took the document over to a brazier and held it to the flames. The fire caught and curled up the paper before she dropped it inside, destroying the evidence.

"Before you ask, no, I have not found out anything about breaking your curse, but do not fear, I will find the answer soon enough." He sat on her futon and grinned at her. She gave him a halfhearted smile. She knew he was trying to stay positive for her. But without knowing anything about the spell, it would be difficult for him to find any way of helping her. She hoped he would go on a wild-goose chase while she worked on ending the treaty. She had not accounted for how damnably persistent Shin could be.

He continued, "I tried going to Akio for help, but he would not even let me through the forest. What did you do to anger him?"

She shrugged her shoulders and plopped down next to Shin. *Go back to the Dragon's palace. You'll be safe there.* She couldn't say that, of course, and Shin was too stubborn to realize when he was in the way. Hikaru had almost seen him tonight. She sighed and flopped back on her futon. Shin hogged up most of the space, making it difficult to get comfortable. She elbowed him and kicked until they were lying side by side. Their hands brushed against one another and he pulled back. She rolled over to face him. She raised a brow in question. *There's something you're not telling me.*

"I could get used to the quiet," he said. "You were always blathering on before."

She slapped him playfully on the arm.

He laughed and the vibrations rolled over Rin. His laughter subsided and they stared up at the ceiling for a few moments. It was nice, almost as if things were back to normal.

"The Dragon returned to the palace. That's the reason it took me so long to return."

Rin sat up and stared at Shin with wide eyes. *Please say you did not tell him I was turned into a human. I could not face the humiliation.*

"I covered for you; he doesn't know anything about this," he said, responding to her unspoken question. He would not look at her.

He's holding back. She tugged on his ear.

He pretended it hurt, yowling in mock pain. Rin gave him another playful swat. *Grow up, you big baby.*

He chuckled and then sighed before saying, "He's not the same. He's been moping around the palace. He won't eat or sleep. Something's happened." He looked at Rin from the corner of his eye. "Do you know anything about it?"

Her stomach constricted. *It would be vain to think the Dragon is pining for me.* Rin closed her eyes. *When I get back to the way I was, I'll have to face him. But everything is different now. I cannot go back to where I was, not with the court's judgmental looks and their whispers.* She wasn't sure which was a worse fate: living out a brief human existence, or an eternity trapped with gossiping Yokai intent on ruining her reputation more than she had already.

She covered her eyes with her arm. Shin drummed his fingers along it, and she lowered it and peeked up at him.

"You're being overdramatic again. Why not go to him?"

Rin tried to laugh, but no sound came out. She rolled over and punched the futon in frustration. The witch had a powerful curse. She never knew how much she would miss her ability to speak until it was gone. Or how demoralizing it would be to not be able to utter a single sound. Shin grabbed her wrist to stop her from punching. She panted as he gently lowered her fist.

"I'll find a way to break your curse, I promise, and then you can go back to the Dragon."

She touched his face, stroking his cheek, and smiled. *You've always been there for me. What would I do without a friend like you?*

He turned away from her touch. "Go to bed, Rin. I'll watch over you while you sleep."

She shook her head and tugged him down on the futon beside her. She draped his arm around her waist and snuggled up close. *Just like when we were kids. He always used to sneak into my bed whenever it thundered. I miss those days. They were much simpler.*

He coughed. "Rin, we're not little kids anymore. What if I took advantage of you?"

She twisted around to press her finger to his lips, and shook her head. *You would never dare. We're friends and I love you like a brother.* She knew he could not read her thoughts, but she thought the message was clear.

He huffed. "You're right, you're the one woman I could never take advantage of. You're too stubborn."

She ignored him and listened to his breathing. The steady in and out made her drowsy and her eyelids sagged. For just a little while she wanted to forget about the curse, forget about Hikaru and his damn honor.

Shin wriggled behind her. She peeked an eye open. There was something on his mind. She could not ask him directly, so she had to settle for him being ready to tell her. After a few moments of silence, he said, "I smelled blood. A human died here tonight and they were killed by a Yokai. You're not safe here."

I know and that's what scares me. Because I can't leave, the witch's spell won't let me.

THE RESTLESS ENERGY IN THE PALACE KEPT HOTARU AWAKE. THROUGH the thin walls he heard the muttered conversations between his relatives, who were terrified there was a murderer in their midst. Whispers had exploded in the palace moments after the scream. Second and thirdhand accounts were being tossed about, without substance or proof. But Hotaru had a sinking feeling they were right. *It has to be that woman, the one pretending to be Lady Nishimori. We've never had this happen before; it cannot be mere coincidence.* Waiting for more information gave him cause to fidget. He folded and unfolded his arms for the tenth time in the past few minutes. Then he saw the shadow outside his door. He stood, too eager to pretend he hadn't been anticipating bad news.

"Come in," Hotaru said.

Rokuro bowed from the waist as he entered. Hotaru clutched his hands at his sides with difficulty. The lieutenant knelt low at Hotaru's feet and he waved his hand to dispatch with ceremony.

"Tell me, Rokuro, are the rumors true?" Hotaru asked.

"Yes, my lord, Lady Nishimori's maid was killed—they say by a wild animal."

Hotaru heard the doubt, the accusation. The rumors about Lady Nishimori were rampant, and now with blood on the ground, the clan would be even more terrified than before.

He swallowed hard and folded his arms over his chest to hide their shaking. He felt like he was living in a nightmare. How could Hikaru do this to them? By bringing that woman, no, that monster, into the clan, Hikaru had endangered them all. He never would have let this happen. He had seen what she was from the start—inhuman, dangerous. If he was in charge, he would have expelled her from the palace. Why his father had allowed her to stay, he could not understand. It was probably a fatherly indulgence to his heir, but this favoritism could ruin them all. Nothing had been the same since Hikaru brought that woman into the castle. His brother was obviously under her spell. How else could he be so blind to her otherness? *This must be her revenge. Sayuri's taint still clouds the palace and left its mark on Father. Hikaru cannot rule; no child of hers would be fit to lead the clan.*

"Have they found the creature that did this?" Hotaru asked as a formality. He knew the beast was resting comfortably in her chambers, waiting for her next victim.

"No, my lord." He clamped his lips shut; there was more to it he would not say. Hotaru saw the truth written in his expression. He liked Rokuro, he was a good lieutenant, and the men respected him. Hotaru also knew he was loyal to him alone, a valuable trait in a man.

"But you have doubts?"

Rokuro nodded slowly, eyes focused on the ground. Hotaru could see how it pained him to speak against his superiors.

"Do not hold anything back," Hotaru said, coaxing him into expanding on his previous statement.

"My men have reported seeing a wolf going in and out of Lady Nishimori's chambers late at night. We've investigated time and again, but each time we find nothing, not even a footprint. We believe she may have something to do with the girl's death."

This confirmed his own suspicions, but he did not want to appear overeager to accuse her. "What would she have against her maid?"

The warrior looked around the room as if he expected the walls to have ears. And he supposed in some ways the walls did. Spies abounded; Hotaru was not the first second son to aspire to greater things. He focused instead on the warrior in front of him.

"You can speak freely here."

"Well, it is no secret Lady Nishimori is strange. We believe Yuri may have learned her true nature and lost her life for it. At least that's what the rumor is about the palace."

Interesting. I will need to tread carefully. If she is a witch or Yokai, she may realize I am onto her and retaliate. I must proceed with caution. "Thank you for bringing me this news."

Rokuro let himself out with a promise to bring Hotaru news of any new developments. Hotaru waited a few moments before leaving on his own errand. He had to tell his father. Lord Kaedemori could only pretend to be blind to Hikaru's faults for so long. Now their people were dying and it was time Lord Kaedemori admitted that his oldest son was bewitched and unfit to rule.

He went to his father's bedchamber, omitting the formal meeting room. A servant was exiting as Hotaru arrived. When the servant saw him, he dipped a hasty bow, hardly disguising his confusion and curiosity.

"I need to speak with my father," Hotaru said.

"His lordship is resting." The servant glanced nervously to the chamber door behind him. Lord Kaedemori was awake, there was no way he would have slept through the ruckus. Knowing his father, he probably had spoken with his captains about reinforcing their protections, and sent out a hunting party to capture the beast that killed Yuri.

"It cannot wait. I must speak with him straight away."

The servant, trained not to argue, bowed again and followed his order, disappearing behind the sliding door. After a few moments he returned and showed Hotaru in. His father sat at the far end of the room, dressed in a white robe, and his hair cascaded across his face, softening some of the strong angles of his normally frowning expression. It was rare to see his father in such an informal setting. Though his father appeared composed, he sensed a disgruntled undercurrent radiating off him.

He bowed to his father, then rose up and said, "Father, I apologize for the late hour, but there are urgent matters that could not wait until daylight."

"If this is about the girl, I've already received a full report from Captain Sadao."

"No, Father, it is not about that unfortunate soul."

His father scrutinized him with a dark gaze, then said, "What is it, then?"

"That woman, the one who claims to be Nishimori, I believe she may be the one who killed Yuri."

His father clenched his hands on his thighs but otherwise made no other indication Hotaru's words affected him. "You saw this yourself?" he asked.

"No, but the men have seen a wolf sneaking into her chamber at night. She is a strange woman, unlike any noble lady I have met. She does not bow, and she often goes without sandals and shuns assistance from her maids. I approached her—"

"You must stay away from her." His father's interruption startled him. His father, who lived and breathed ceremony, would never be so rude.

He smoothed over his shock with a nod in his father's direction, then continued, "I think my brother is under the spell of that woman. We have to do something before everything we've worked for comes to ruin."

His father steepled his fingers and did not look at Hotaru, but a vein jumped along his jaw as if he was biting down on his words. What did his father want to say that he hesitated to speak? True, his father had never sought Hotaru's counsel, but his father had never seemed more vulnerable or more afraid than he did in that moment. *We are certainly in danger if even my father fears Lady Nishimori.*

"Father?"

"I will see to this. Now go back to your room and speak of this matter to no one. Do you understand?"

He stared at his father for a moment. This had not gone as he'd planned. All hopes of being the savior of the clan and exposing the Yokai were blotted out like spilled ink on parchment. He choked down his disappointment and nodded. He rose and left the chamber without another word, clenching his hands into fists.

TWELVE

The sliding door creaked in the track and then clicked into place. Hikaru's father's inner sanctum yawned before him. He took a deep breath. *I am sure he just wants a report about the servant's death.* His father sat at the far end of the room on the raised dais. So many of his memories of his father were inside this room, it was almost impossible to think of him anywhere else. *One day I will sit in his place; will I too look down on my own son with such disdain?* Hikaru knelt down in front of his father, his hands pressed against the floor. He could feel his pulse thrumming in his fingertips. When his father did not speak, he feared the worst. *Is he angry about how much time I've been spending with Rin?* His neck ached from leaning forward and his legs trembled from kneeling. The only sound in the room was the ragged sounds of Hikaru's breath.

"You have brought evil into this house," his father said.

Though his father had not given him permission to do so, Hikaru raised his head and met his father's gaze. "Father, what are you talking about?"

"Do not pretend you do not know." His words were like a whip crack.

Hikaru flinched and lowered his gaze. His heart hammered in his chest. He knew his father did not approve of Rin, but to have him make such a blunt accusation was unlike him. The rumors about Rin had been swirling about the palace for days, but he never imagined his father, a man of reason, would fall prey to the falsehoods. *Does he think Rin caused that servant's death?* The urge to defend Rin nearly overwhelmed him, and he had to keep his head down to hide his feelings from his father.

His father spoke, unaware of the internal struggle raging inside Hikaru. "Kitsune can bring great fortune, this I know is true, but they also bring calamity."

He thought back to the woman who had saved him in the forest. *He cannot mean Rin.* There was a wild look in his father's eyes. His clothes were disheveled and his hair, normally slicked back in a topknot, was falling into his face. Something was not right. He chose his next words carefully. "Surely you do not think there is a Kitsune in the palace. They're not real."

"You have been beguiled by her, my son." His father's words were delivered calmly but sharp as a knife. His father glared down at him with black eyes full of accusation. Lord Kaedemori knew Rin was more than she seemed. He had known it from the moment he met her. Only Hikaru refused to acknowledge what was right in front of him.

Hikaru swallowed past a lump in his throat. He could not believe that Kitsune were real. Perhaps his father was under an unusual amount of stress. "I do not know what you mean."

"Rin!" his father thundered. He stood up abruptly and the table rocked on its legs, nearly overturned by his father's sudden movement. He loomed over Hikaru, and he saw the bags that hung under his father's eyes and the gaunt hollow of his cheeks. How long had it been since he had slept? "She has bewitched you!"

"Lady Nishimori and I have spent some time together, I admit it is true. But there is nothing unseemly happening. I would never risk our alliance with the Fujikawas."

His father pressed his lips together hard enough that they nearly disappeared among the lines surrounding his mouth. Lord Kaedemori inhaled and exhaled; a vein in his cheek jumped. He did not speak though he seemed poised on the edge of another outburst. They stood locked in a battle, Hikaru on the verge of confessing all of his concerns to his father. He ached to share his feelings to ease the burden that his secret feelings for Rin had weighed upon his shoulders. He had a wife and a duty to the clan; that, above all else, was paramount. To speak his selfish thoughts would not be proper; his father would be ashamed of Hikaru's weakness.

"Lady Nishimori is our kinsman's daughter. We have a duty to make her feel welcome. I have thought only to see to her comfort. Nothing more." Hikaru met his father's eye, but his hands shook as he bunched them in the fabric along his thighs. With one word from his father, Rin would be cast from the palace. That's what Lord Kaedemori wanted. Hikaru saw the desire to do so in his father's eyes. He had to protect her; at least he knew she would be safe back with her clan.

"The Nishimoris and the Kaedemoris are two branches of the same family. Yet I see nothing of Lord Nishimori in Rin. What I do see is a Kitsune who has come for revenge." Lord Kaedemori's voice rose as he spoke. He paced back and forth, his hands clenched in the small of his back. Hikaru watched his progress. Agitation rolled off his father like a wave.

"The Nishimoris are known to be eccentric. I know Rin does not act like most ladies—"

"Because she is not human!" Lord Kaedemori slammed his hand onto the table. The table shook and an ink block went tumbling onto the ground along with a brush, and parchments were scattered. Hikaru scooted forward to pick them up, but a look from his father halted him and he sat back again.

His father sank back down into his seat. Like a sack of grain with a hole in it, he seemed to be deflating. He stared at the tabletop, as if the whirling patterns in the wood would answer all of his questions. He had always been the epitome of calm and collectedness. He had never raised his voice to Hikaru before. With dark circles under his wild eyes and skin that was near translucent, Hikaru saw how fragile his father was. *He will not be around forever. Could my time be coming soon?* The heavy mantle of his duty weighed down upon Hikaru, suffocating him with the reality of his responsibility. *Am I ready for this?* He tried imagining his position reversed, sitting in his father's spot. *The men do not respect me, and until I produce an heir, my position will be in danger from Hotaru.* Hikaru dragged his fingers across the rough tatami mats. The silence between his father and him was a thick miasma creating doubt in Hikaru, both in his father's ability to rule and Hikaru's as well.

"What would you have me do, Father?" Hikaru asked. He had never felt more lost.

His father looked up. His eyes were wide, the pupils just pinpoints in the center of his dark irises. "This is your mother's revenge. This is my punishment." He bowed his head, resting it in his palms. His father's eyes appeared wet, but Hikaru could have been mistaken. He waited for his father to continue. He looked upon his father with new eyes. He had always seemed infallible, strong and wise. Now he only saw a broken man. Lord Kaedemori never spoke of his first wife, though Hikaru had made the mistake of asking about her once when he was very young. It was the only other time in his life he had seen his father lose control. Lord Kaedemori had struck Hikaru and told him never to speak of her again. And so from a young age he learned to never speak of the woman who had given birth to him. All he knew of her was from whispers from clansmen and taunts from Hotaru, which were probably cruel inventions meant to hurt Hikaru.

Fearing his father's wrath, he decided to sneak out while Lord Kaedemori was preoccupied. His father was absorbed in the past and did not notice as Hikaru slipped out. *If Father is losing his mind, he will not want to step down, not willingly, but we cannot have a madman running the clan.* He clenched his hands at his sides. *Am I ready for this?* The thought kept circling around in his head. *I expected many more years before I would take up this mantle. If I were a different man, I would flee and become a priest, living a life of thoughtful tranquility.*

He opened his eyes, and the visions of a life that could never be faded, but what appeared before him was even lovelier. Rin walked along the opposite gallery, wearing a white kimono with orange leaves and red flowers. She looked like the sun goddess come to earth, brightening up an otherwise gray fall day. She frowned, and he imagined she was thinking about something that troubled her. Despite his own problems, he wanted to ease her burdens. He wanted to make her smile again. He also knew he should slip away without greeting her. When she had tried to kiss him the night before, he had been too terrified to face her. Even now, his own desire for her sparked like an ember, and every moment spent in her presence fanned the flames.

Rin turned and saw him, and her eyes locked on him, as if they were bound together by a single red thread. He swallowed and watched transfixed as she hurried over to him. She did not take small dainty steps as so many court ladies did. She picked up the edge of her robes and ran to him, her bare feet slapping on the wood floor.

She reached him and smiled, a bright flash of teeth against her pale face. A long dark lock of hair had fallen forward and brushed against her cheek. He wanted to push it back just to have an excuse to touch her face. But that would be inappropriate. Every moment they spent alone was a scandal waiting to happen. The clan's treaty with the Fujikawas was tenuous at best. She tilted her head and very gently touched his cheek. Even when he tried to push her away, she was always reaching for him, trying to offer him comfort he did not deserve. He had a wife and a duty to his family to uphold. But even so, he relished the feel of her soft hand against his cheek. He grabbed her wrist and pulled her hand away.

"Do you worry for me, my lady? I do not want to trouble you. I have had a trying morning is all. But I am already beginning to recover."

She smiled as if she knew what troubled him and understood. She seemed to have an uncanny ability to read his thoughts. *Could she be a Kitsune?* In this light he was almost certain she was the same woman. If that woman had been real and not a figment of his imagination. *If only I could hear her voice, I could be sure.* He wanted to shake himself; perhaps his father's ravings were catching.

She pointed at him, then pressed her fingers to her temple. *You can tell me what's on your mind,* that is how he interpreted her mime.

He grinned. *I'm being silly. Rin is not a Kitsune. There is no such thing.* "It is nothing a lady would find of interest, just matters of estate."

She gave him a coy smile in return. *Let me decide that,* she seemed to be saying.

He sighed and said, "I do not know how you can coerce me without words. It is as if you have some magic way about you."

She shrugged her shoulders, but the smile did not leave her face.

"I fear my father is unwell. I went to speak with him about the murder and he raved about Kitsunes." Hikaru shook his head.

Rin touched her chest. *He thinks it's me?*

Hikaru looked away from her. "He is under a lot of pressure is all."

She touched Hikaru lightly on the shoulder. And it amazed him how such an innocent brush could speak so much. He desired her; that much was plain. But if it had been a simple matter of lust, he would have been able to squash the feelings. It went deeper than that, he wanted all of her. He wanted to know her thoughts, to learn all her secrets. He wanted her as a wife. As the thought manifested itself, it could not be undone. It formed, taking shape as a jagged shard inside his heart. The only thing that could cure him would be to take her into his arms and press his lips to hers. She could never be his, so instead he tactfully stepped out of her reach, but turned to face her.

"My mother, I am told, exhibited similar symptoms before her death. I have heard it told that my father had to lock her up at the end. I was too young to remember it. But they say she was possessed by a Kitsune. That cannot be true, though, can it?"

He never intended to reveal this much about his past. He had spent his entire life running from it, and without warning it had come out unbidden. There was something about Rin that put him at ease, and he felt he could reveal even his deepest secrets to her. A strange emotion flickered across her expression. Perhaps it was alarm or maybe fear, but it was so quickly gone he could not be certain. She drew close to him. He was acutely aware of the distance between them, or lack thereof, and the scent of jasmine that clung to her skin. Without thinking, he tucked the hair he had noticed before behind her ear. When he moved to pull his hand away, she grabbed his hand and kissed the palm. He stood like that for a moment, her lips against his skin. He savored it before he gently pulled away.

"Excuse me, my lady, I should be going." *This is dangerous. Perhaps I am bewitched.*

Thirteen

Rin approached the shrine and the hairs on the back of her neck stood on end. She'd sought this place looking for solace. As a human, her connection with the mystic world of the Yokai had been severed. And as such, she felt the ache of its loss like a hole that had been carved out of her chest. It was growing larger every day, threatening to consume her. As she drew closer to the shrine, the feeling of unease settled in her gut like a stone. The witch had taken Rin's ability to sense her own kind when she turned her into a human, but this place had a hollow dead feeling to it that even as a human she could sense. She could see why the humans thought it was haunted.

Covered verandas boxed it in on all sides. An overgrown maple tree shaded the space, casting long eerie shadows over the ground. The ground consisted of packed earth. Nothing grew apart from the tree. *This is not right. If a Kami resided here, every-*

thing would be in bloom. The sunbaked earth warmed the soles of her feet as she crept closer. *What have they done to cast out even the gods?*

Rin looked over her shoulder, her body tense. The four pillars at each corner of the courtyard had markings carved into the wood. She did not know much of the written human word, but all Yokai knew what these words meant. They were binding spells. *Someone kept a Yokai here.*

When Hikaru had told her the story about his mother, it had disquieted her, and she thought back to Hotaru's tour. Humans often tried to explain away what they could not comprehend. A Kitsune could not possess a human body, but a Kitsune could take on the form of a human. She felt compelled to learn more about his mother; who was she? Her quest led her here, and now, standing in this desolate place, she almost wished she had not come at all. It would have been better to let this ghost lie.

Perhaps she had been hoping to find a reason in all this madness. Why was the witch trying to stop their treaty? Why was there so much hate in their family? Why could she not get Hikaru out of her head? The gooseflesh rose along her arms. Rin crossed them over her chest, but nothing seemed to abate the unearthly chill. She had never thought about the humans keeping Yokai until the witch trapped her. *Am I not the first to fall victim to the witch?*

She examined the spells, and beneath them were long score marks made by nails. Her hand hovered over them. *Who were you? Why did they do this to you?* Tears pushed at the back of her lids. She turned her head away and went to the shrine instead.

She knelt down before it. The shrine was small, around the same height as Rin and twice as wide. The roof had been red once until the paint had started to bubble and peel. The figure inside, a fox with golden eyes and red paint for fur, stared forward, both imperial and majestic. *They worship the Kitsune, yet Lord Kaedemori fears them. Why is that?* Her hands rested against her thighs, but they twitched to reach out and touch the idol. *What if I am not worthy in this form?* The paint on the feet of the idol had been worn away, exposing the graying wood beneath. *Someone prayed here. They begged for their life.* She closed her eyes and she could almost imagine her. A beautiful lady, long hair trailing in the dust. She raised her hands up in supplication, waiting for release that would not come. Rin opened her eyes. She too longed for the freedom to return to who she was. She reached out to touch the idol.

"I would not touch that, or you will anger the Kami."

Rin jerked her head backwards. Lord Kaedemori stood along the gallery. He looked down on Rin as one might a rabid dog—with both fear and contempt.

She bowed, pressing her head to the ground. *I should have known he would come to me. He has not trusted me from the moment we met.* Her heart hammered in her chest. She had never felt this sort of fear when she had her powers.

He did not speak. His mouth looked immobile, as if she had imagined him speaking at all. His eyes skimmed over her and then past her to the various wards scattered across the court-yard. There were prayer cards wedged into window frames; sutras hung from the eves. The entire space had a thin sheen of dust. She would think no one came here, but an offering bowl had been filled recently with the same food the witch had used to trick her with. She now knew the food was called fried tofu.

"I have seen you wandering the halls of the palace like a ghost. Why are you here?" he said.

I would ask you the same. Why do you fear my kind so? Her encounter with Hikaru that afternoon had left her wondering. Rin turned away from him and pretended to pray at the shrine. She pressed her hands together and lowered her head.

Lord Kaedemori padded over to stand beside her. He said nothing, but the threat of it hung in the air. The tension between them was taut as a cord. She squeezed her eyes shut and dared not look at him. *When did I begin to fear humans?*

"I loved her," the lord said.

Rin looked at him from the corner of her eye. As much as she feared him, he was also a source of curiosity. No one in this household seemed to have any spiritual power but for Hikaru, and he seemed unaware of his ability. Even in her human state, she could see that Hikaru was different than the others and his father knew it. He feared his son as he feared Rin. Lord Kaede-mori knew enough to recognize her as a Kitsune even when she was trapped in a human body. Which could only mean he had met her kind before. He knew about her world but could not see it, not really, and that, she thought, was the root of the problem.

He spoke as if addressing the shrine itself and Rin was invisible. She wanted to look upon his face and try to read the emotion there, but she did not know how he would react. "Your kind can be cruel, with your tricks. I thought to keep her, but she could not be held."

You captured a Kitsune? How is that possible? Rin kept her expression neutral though her mind raced. This place was more than a family temple, it had been a prison for one of her own. Her throat clenched and she balled her hands into fists. *What happened to the Kitsune? Did she escape, or did she meet some worse fate?*

"My son is wed; you cannot take him. I paid my price. You can take nothing more from me. We are even. Remember that."

Her kind were known to play tricks on humans; she was as guilty as any of her kin. Her sisters had told her of their exploits with men. They often disguised themselves as human women and lured men into their beds. Sometimes they did it for gold, silk, jewelry or maybe just to ease their boredom. If the man was kind or handsome, her sister might bless his house with good fortune, but if he was cruel or tried to take more than was willingly given, she might steal and humiliate them. What Lord Kaedemori alluded to was worse than she could imagine. He had imprisoned a Kitsune and kept her away from the forest and from her family. Surrounded by these holy items for too long, she would have become weaker and weaker; it would have killed her. The rage bubbled inside Rin and eclipsed her fear of Lord Kaedemori. She jumped up and cut the lord off as he tried to leave. She pointed at the shrine. *What happened to her?*

Lord Kaedemori looked past Rin and into the courtyard. He might as well have been thousands of miles away. She was not sure if he had understood her. The sutras pasted to the eves waved at her, mocking her. They had no power over her in this form, but she was trapped nonetheless by the witch's spell. The wind rippled the branches of the tree and a few maple leaves fell down onto the ground, like bright drops of blood.

"She died. I killed her," he replied.

Rin covered her mouth with her hand though no sound would come out. His expression was mild, but she saw the pain that sharpened his gaze and carved lines into his mouth as if he could hold back the tide of his grief. *Why!* she wanted to scream. If you loved her, why kill her in such a slow and agonizing way?

"You think you are very clever to have deceived my son, but I will not let him suffer as I have." Then just as quickly as it was revealed, the emotion was snapped shut behind his eyes and the cool and distant lord replaced him.

She smirked at him. Whatever madness had driven him to kill the Kitsune did not matter now. She would revel in the ruin of his treaty. *You think you can stop me? I will have vengeance for my kinswoman.*

He scowled at her, his eyes burned like twin flames. He hated her, but his anger only fueled her resolve. "You will not leave this place. You should never have come here," he said.

He turned to walk away. Rin ran after him and grabbed his sleeve. His eyes bulged out of his skull and he shook his arm to rid himself of her. She clawed at his face in a blind rage. He swung his hand backwards and caught her cheek with his hand. The force of it knocked her backwards and she fell onto her backside. She touched her cheek and found a streak of blood from where her lip had split. *If I had my powers, I would tear him to shreds.* Her emotions were in a jumble. She had never felt this anger before; it churned in her gut fiercer than anything she had felt as a Kitsune. *This is what it means to be human, this rage, this complete lack of control.* She would scream, tear, bite anything to ease this boiling inside her.

He stood on the steps, his hands balled into fists. He trembled. His eyes narrowed into dark flint sharp enough to cut. Rin stared back at him with a defiant tilt to her head. She had already climbed back onto her feet. She was not so easily defeated. He could knock her down all he liked, she would always get back up.

"You will regret this," he said, letting his words hang in the air.

She raised a brow, mocking him.

"Save your ire, your time runs short. The priestess comes at dawn to exorcise you."

FOURTEEN

"You look like you could use a drink."

Hikaru looked up from his translations and his vision swam. He rubbed his tired eyes with the back of his hand. "Kichirou, do you have any idea what time it is?"

His brother shrugged. He carried a jug of sake and a devious look in his eye, which could only mean trouble.

"What are you doing here?" Hikaru asked.

Kichirou sat down cross-legged across from Hikaru. He rested the jug on his knee. "Like I said, I thought you could use a drink." He produced two cups and poured the clear liquid into them, dribbling some onto his hands.

"The last time we drank together, I was in bed for a day with a splitting headache," Hikaru said, looking dubiously at the jug.

Kichirou handed Hikaru a glass and laughed. "I remember that." He tossed back his own drink and then poured a second.

Hikaru stared into the cup. The liquid rippled, crashing against the sides. He looked at his own distorted image in the dim light cast by the braziers. His face was sunken and hollow from lack of sleep. He had not rested much since he returned from the Fujikawa clan house. *I have not slept the night through since Rin arrived.* She was a fever he could not sweat out, no matter how he threw himself into his responsibilities. She constantly hovered at the edges of his mind, taunting him.

"Marriage doesn't seem to suit you, brother. Perhaps because you're not utilizing all the benefits." Kichirou waggled his eyebrows.

We are not having that conversation. Hikaru gulped down the sake. The pleasant burn seeped down his throat, warming his gut. It did not numb his anxieties as he hoped it would, however. It would take much more liquor to bury these feelings.

Hikaru held out his glass to be refilled and said, "I'm sure there's better drinking companions than me."

Kichirou nodded his head as he poured his fourth glass. "They're all busy—something about that mute woman."

"What!" Hikaru jumped up and leaned forward onto the table between them. He slapped his hand on the lacquered surface. "What happened to Rin?"

His brother tossed back another glass and his eyes shifted to Hikaru. *That's why he came. Hotaru must have sent him to taunt me. The two of them have always been thick as thieves.*

Kichirou swirled the jug back and forth and did not answer right away. He looked as if he was contemplating another drink. "They say she's the one who killed the servant."

"That's not possible." It would have been better to hide his concern; this was what they were waiting for. If Hotaru was looking for Hikaru's weakness, he had found it in Rin.

Kichirou set the glass down and leaned back. He laced his fingers behind his neck. He looked at Hikaru through slit eyelids. "Lieutenant Rokuro has a witness, I hear."

Hikaru clenched his hands into fists to stop himself from reaching across the table and shaking information out of his brother. "Who?" he asked through clenched teeth.

"I didn't ask."

Hikaru sat back and pinched his brow. *If this is some prank of Hotaru's...* He took a deep breath. He couldn't help Rin if he lost control. But there was no time to sit around and wonder at his brothers' motives. He had to find out for himself. He jumped to his feet, but his head swam. Perhaps it was the combination of the alcohol and his lack of sleep. He held out a hand to steady himself. When the world stopped spinning, he straightened his robes—which needed no adjusting. His brother watched him, a smile playing at the corner of his lips. He did not blame

Kichirou for playing messenger in their brother's schemes. Kichirou was a pawn, one easily won over with women and drink.

"Excuse me, I'm going to speak with father." Hikaru bowed to his brother. He would rather dispatch with the niceties given his mood, but habits died hard. He seemed incapable of being rude even when he wanted to be.

When Hikaru reached the door, Kichirou said, "It won't do you any good."

He paused at the door. He wanted to strike him, to make him pay for their brother's scheming, but that would be not only inappropriate but fruitless. Hotaru used Kichirou to shield himself from Hikaru's anger. If Hotaru had been there, he would not have held back—niceties be damned. With his back turned to his brother, Hikaru said, "We shall see."

Hikaru marched to his father's chambers. Despite the late hour, the palace bustled with activity, all of it centered around his father's audience hall. Two warriors stood guard at the door, backs straight and eyes trained in front of them. The door to his father's chamber slid open and Captain Sadao stepped out. He was dressed in half armor, wearing a breastplate over his robe and overcoat. The captain bowed when Hikaru approached him.

"I need to speak with my father," Hikaru said.

The captain looked him up and down. "Lord Kaedemori is not seeing anyone."

"He will speak with me." Hikaru squared his shoulders and jutted out his chin in an attempt to look more formidable.

The captain's expression was made of granite, unmovable. If he thought anything of Hikaru's attempt at posturing, Hikaru could not tell. The captain stared at Hikaru, his gaze dark and hooded. The moonlight made his eyes look like dark pits. He held his hands at ease at his sides, but his jaw was clenched tight. Hikaru's anger boiled just beneath the surface and manifested in the tapping of his foot and the reflexive opening and closing of his hand. The man to the right of the captain peered at his companion from the corner of his eye. When he saw Hikaru looking at him, he snapped to attention. Hikaru's brows pulled together. This was not going as he expected.

"Consider your position. If you disobey me now, it will cost you later," Hikaru said.

The captain bowed. "My apologies, my lord, but I have my orders."

Hikaru clenched his hands into fists and turned to walk the other way. His first impulse was to go look for Rin, but he knew if his father had men at his chambers, then Rin would be just as heavily guarded. *I should have acted sooner. I saw the signs, but I decided to ignore them.*

"My lord!"

Hikaru stopped and waited for a young warrior to catch up to him. He did not recognize the man. He was tall and lean with long brown hair and a mobile mouth that was pulled back in a smile.

"That is no way to greet your superior," Hikaru snapped back. He had no patience and the admonishment came out without thought. He regretted it as soon as the words escaped his lips. He would never win men to his side by acting superior.

The warrior did not seem to mind. His smile did not fade as he said, "Forgive me, I heard Rin—that is the lady, is imprisoned, is it true?"

Hikaru frowned at the man. He had never heard anyone call Rin by name. Who was this young warrior? Jealousy raised its ugly head. "What is your name?"

"Shin," the young warrior replied. His smile grew wider, displaying straight white teeth. For a moment Hikaru thought he spotted elongated canines. Hikaru squinted to get a better look, but the warrior closed his mouth—the smile wiped from his face. He looked at Hikaru a little closer with a curious tilt of his eyebrow. They were of an age, and unlike most of his warriors, his hair was long and shaggy. And it may have been a trick of the light, but it appeared he had pointed ears poking out from beneath his hair. *I must be imagining things.*

Something about this man unsettled Hikaru. He wanted to be rid of him. "Do not speak so informally about Lady Nishimori."

"My mistake." He waved away Hikaru's scolding with an impatient gesture. "Is it true, then? Can you get her out?"

Hikaru looked the man up and down a bit closer. Upon closer

inspection, his clothes were not the standard warrior's colors and he wore no armor

"You are no warrior. Who are you?"

He laughed. "She did not tell me you were so clever. That is rare in a human. No matter, I will rescue her myself."

"Wait—" The stranger turned to walk away and Hikaru grabbed his sleeve, but as he did, the material deteriorated and crumbled to dust in Hikaru's hand.

When Hikaru looked up from the smeared ashes in his palm, the man was gone. Hikaru was paralyzed. He had to have imagined it. There was no possible way a man could disappear in the blink of an eye. He spun in a circle to be certain the stranger was not waiting behind him with a knife. Hikaru was alone; only the shadows cast by the pillars of the covered walkway accompanied him. *I'm imagining things is all.* But the doubt lingered at the back of his mind, like a sore that would not heal. The ashes were still on his hand, no matter how he looked at it. He rubbed his clean hand across his face. *I have to do something.* He walked because he did not know what else to do. Everyone was asleep. The night insects played their lonely music to the moon. He kept on walking, his feet guiding him while his mind spun in circles. He knew what he had to do, but once he made the decision, there would be no turning back.

He stopped in front of the rice paper door. The thin barrier felt more like a mountain to be climbed and he was no athlete. He took a deep breath and knocked.

A grumbled reply came from within. Hikaru waited, his hands folded in front of him. He rolled his thumbs over one another. He could not stand still. His mind kept wandering back to Rin. *I should have been there to protect her.* He listened as heavy footsteps approached. The door slid open a crack. A round face peered at him from within.

"This cannot be good if you are coming to me at this hour." The door slid open the rest of the way and his uncle, Arata, regarded him with hands folded over his gut.

"Uncle, forgive my late arrival, but this cannot wait."

His uncle grunted and stepped aside to let Hikaru in. He followed his uncle's wobbling gait as he thudded on the ground in front of a table with a game of Shogi laid out. The wooden board and white tile pieces looked like men lined up on a battlefield, awaiting the commander's order before charging forward to certain death.

"What is the problem, then?" Arata asked.

Hikaru wrung his hands together and stared at the board for a moment longer.

"You did not wake me just to play, did you?"

Hikaru shook his head. His throat was too dry. Perhaps he should call for a servant to bring him something to drink.

"I do not have unlimited patience," his uncle said.

"I've realized recently that the men do not respect me, and if I am to rule the clan, I will need to earn that," Hikaru said. There was more he wanted to say, but even resolved to his task, it left a sour taste in his mouth and he could not speak the words aloud. He met his uncle's gaze. Arata's eyes grew large, and his mouth fell open. His uncle read the underlying meaning in his words.

"Your father—"

"He is alive," Hikaru rushed to say. "But I can see the weight of his responsibility and its burden upon him, and I do not know how much longer he can rule effectively." He hesitated to say any more. He never would have spoken out against his father this way, but the words burned the back of his throat, demanding release. "He's imprisoned Lady Nishimori; he believes she is a Kitsune."

His uncle's eyes grew wide for a moment before he wiped the expression away. Arata stroked his chin and avoided Hikaru's gaze. They shared the same thoughts; Hikaru had been thinking about his mother ever since his father had started raving about Kitsunes. He had always thought the rumors were just that. He could not believe his father would torture and imprison his mother like that. But now history was repeating itself and he had himself to blame for it. Hikaru ran his finger along the edge of the board. *Am I ready to control other men's lives? They do not respect me. How can I possibly lead the clan?*

"Is it possible this Lady Nishimori is a Kitsune?"

Hikaru's breath caught in his chest. The immediate denial dangled from his lips. A week ago he would not have even considered the notion, now... "Do not be ridiculous," he said, but not with nearly the conviction needed.

His uncle sighed. "There are many things in this world that cannot be explained."

Hikaru shook his head hard enough to rattle his brain inside his skull. "There is no such thing." He wasn't sure who he was trying to convince, his uncle or himself.

"You need to gather men to your side by strengthening the bonds with your father's allies." His uncle twirled his long beard, pulling on the hair and the skin along his chin with it. "The men are looking for someone they can respect. Someone who can lead."

The unintentional jab hit him like a blow to the stomach. "Do you think the men will follow me?"

Arata dropped his hand onto his lap. "That I cannot say; only time will tell."

A lump formed in his throat. It was as he feared. "I shall win them over, I have to."

"You'll need to do more than that. You will need their utter devotion if you do not want your brother to attempt to take your place."

The fear of that had always been at the back of his mind, haunting him. "I did not wish for any of this. Sometimes I wish he were the heir and not me."

His uncle nodded and stared at the Shogi board. He took a piece and flipped it over, revealing the red promotion character on the other side. He turned the piece between his fingers for a few moments. Hikaru watched his actions, transfixed.

"You'll need to bring your wife here," Arata said.

Hikaru sighed. Fate was a fickle thing; no matter how he wanted to change it, he could not. He had delayed bringing his wife to the clan house. But his excuses had all run dry. *It's for the best if it keeps Rin safe. I need more influence to protect her.*

"And we cannot do anything until it can be proved that this woman is *not* a Kitsune."

"You cannot—"

"If you want my support, you will do as I say. This woman came to us without explanation and acts strangely. If the priestess declares her pure, then you will cast off all suspicion."

Hikaru's hands dug into the fabric of his robe hard enough to tear. They all thought he was bewitched. *And what will I do if I find out she is a Kitsune and she has been playing with me this entire time?* He did not have an answer for that question. But he left four parallel snags in the silk running up his thigh. "As you say. Gather our supporters and I will write to have my wife sent to us at once." Hikaru stood.

"If she is who she says, then it is past time she went back to her clan. She has no place here."

Hikaru nodded. His next question was on the tip of his tongue; despite his attempts to swallow his own doubt, he asked, "And if she is not?"

"Let's hope her intentions are good."

FIFTEEN

Rin paced the length of the courtyard. Her bare feet had acquired a thin sheen of dust. *He won't come tonight. He'll stay away and I'll find a way to send him a message in the morning.* Two guards stood at the door, one facing the hallway that led to the shrine, the other facing her. The one watching her regarded her with a blank expression as lifeless as a mask. She met his gaze and held it. He frowned but did not look away. She would not be the first to surrender. She refused to let them think her weak. For the space of a breath they were locked in time. Then he lowered his eyes.

"What have you done now?"

Damn him. Rin turned slowly. Shin leaned against the shrine. He smirked at her in his charming way. She wanted nothing more than to fall into his arms at that moment. But she wrapped her arms around her waist instead. *You should not have come. The priestess cannot harm me in this form, but she can hurt you.*

He glanced around the courtyard, his eyes skimming over the sutras and binding charms. He even touched one with the tip of a clawed finger. "Binding spells." He looked to Rin. "What is the meaning of this?"

She shrugged and went to sit down on the steps of one of the adjacent covered walkways. Every pathway had been boarded up. The warrior watched her from the corner of his eye, but if he saw Shin, he gave no indication. Most humans could not see her kind—Hikaru was one of the few exceptions.

"Rin, what happened?" Shin knelt down in front of her, taking her hands in his.

She yanked her hands away. *Leave, Shin, and don't come back.*

"Is this the young lord's doing? I should never have let you stay." Shin growled. His canines elongated as he clenched his fists.

Rin shook her head. *He can't stay here. What if the binding charms trap him here?* She yanked at Shin's elbow and led him to the door, where she pointed out. The warrior tensed as she approached. He reached for his sword but did not draw it. His fellow guard glanced over his shoulder at her. She ignored them. She was more worried about getting Shin out of there.

"Stay back. I won't tell you again," the guard that faced outward snarled.

Shin bared his teeth at the men, but they did not see. They looked through him and at Rin.

"You're crazy if you think I'm going to leave you here alone," Shin said.

She huffed and stomped back over to the shrine. She knelt in front of it. Sitting near it gave her a measure of serenity—something she needed desperately right about now.

"I'm not leaving, Rin." Shin sat down on the ground beside her, his back to the shrine.

You stubborn idiot.

"You're probably cursing me, calling me a stubborn fool," he said with his usual levity, but his expression was severe.

Idiot, but close enough. He had an uncanny ability to read her thoughts. She pointed at the sutras and scowled at him. *You're not safe here.*

His eyes flickered to the sutra. He snatched one that was posted above the shrine and ripped it to pieces. "These are just paper. Without spiritual energy they cannot harm us."

She bowed her head. The shredded fragments were scattered on the ground and one of them bumped against her toe, which peeked out from beneath the dusty hem of her outer robe. *I should have known that. If I was myself, I would have sensed that there was no power here.*

"I will not summon the Dragon, if you wish it, but even my patience has its limits. This has gotten out of hand."

She did not want to involve Shin and she definitely did not want the Dragon to come to her rescue. She had fancied herself in love with him at one point. The Dragon was handsome, daring and powerful. He ruled the entirety of the largest island in Akatsuki. Coming from a minor household, she never thought she would catch his eye. Her family were servants to the Dragon, at times messengers, at other times they tended to his guests, and as for Rin, she tended to his personal needs. When they became lovers, she thought she was in a happy dream. But it became quickly apparent all that she had idealized was nothing but girlish fantasy. The Dragon was powerful, but he was still just a man. She had enjoyed their time together, but when it came to an end, she did not grieve it.

It was not until the rumors started and the stares that she realized how being with the Dragon had ruined her reputation and that of her family. She was nothing but another of the Dragon's conquests. Desperate to win some honor back, she had gone to bring the Dragon's most disobedient vassal to heel. As usual, she rushed in without a plan and Akio had outsmarted her. If Shin went to the Dragon now and asked him to fix her, she would never recover from the windfall of scandal. The Dragon's plaything turned human by a mere priestess. They would probably think she had done it to win the Dragon back. *I have some dignity. I got myself into this and I can get myself out of it.* Shin had no reason to keep trying to fix all of her mistakes. She shrugged again. *Not your problem.*

"I know you don't think it's my problem, but damn it, Rin, it is. We've been friends for centuries. What would you expect me to do? Leave you here to rot as a human? What would you do in my place?"

She looked away from him and at the Kitsune statue. The empty painted eyes stared at her, unfeeling and uncaring. The Kami who guarded this family had fled long ago. Now all that remained was a hollow shell. *If Lord Kaedemori has his way, I will not live long as a human.* She sighed. *But Shin's right, I would do the same.*

"You know I am right."

She nodded. She hated to admit it to him, but she couldn't lie to him either. She needed his help as much as she resisted it. Her pride just kept getting in the way.

He grabbed her by the shoulders and pulled her against his chest in an unexpected embrace. It shocked her at first, not that he had hugged her. They were no strangers to physical affection. There was something different about him lately. He held on too long and too tight. He was afraid, she realized. He clung to her as if when he let her go, she would slip away for good. That thought terrified her. She grabbed a handful of the silk on the back of his kimono. She inhaled his musky scent, but it brought none of its usual familiar comfort. She could not smell the layers of the scent; his emotions and his unique signature were hidden from her. He might as well have been a stranger to her.

She pulled away and put distance between them. She did not need another reminder of everything that had been stripped from her. Shin was her last link, and losing any sort of connection with him made her heart sick. From the corner of her eye, she could see the warriors conversing with one another. They must have seen them and wondered what she was doing. From their prospective, she would have looked like she was doing pantomime. She turned her back to them and focused on Shin. She besought him with her eyes. His gaze traced over her features. *He can see it, can't he? He knows he has to let me take care of this myself. He must know I would never forgive myself if I lost him because of my own error.*

"Who's there!" the guard facing the corridor shouted.

Rin's head popped up and Shin snarled. His face half transformed into a mix between man and wolf, his snout elongated and his hands tipped with long claws. Rin held up her hand to still him.

"I've come to speak with Lady Nishimori," Hikaru said.

Rin's heart leapt. *He came.* She had hoped he would stay away even as much as she wanted to see him. Then reality crashed down, shattering like a dropped vase. Shin was inching towards the guards. Though she could not see Hikaru yet, she knew he would be able to see Shin, though the guards could not. And with Shin's temper, it could only end badly.

"Lord Kaedemori said there is to be no visitors," the outer guard said.

"I speak as my father, and heir of the clan of Kaedemori. You will let me pass." There was a hard edge to Hikaru's tone that she had never heard before. A ripple of premonition ran down her spine.

The guards shared a look. The guard who had been watching Rin turned his back to them to whisper in the other guard's ear. She pulled on Shin's arm, trying and failing to drag him away. He shrugged her off and marched up the steps to the guards.

"We are leaving, Rin," Shin said.

She ran after him and reached out to grab his arm. Just then Hikaru looked up. He saw Shin approaching and opened his mouth to warn the guard, but it was too late. Shin slashed a clawed hand across the man's back and tore through the silk like paper. The man spun, fumbling for his weapon, but not quick enough. Shin lunged and landed on his chest and clamped down on his throat. The second warrior had time to get his sword. He swatted the air as he spun in slow circles, looking for Shin. Rin beat on Shin's back, trying to get him to stop. *You cannot kill them, Shin!* She opened her mouth to scream at him, but nothing came out other than a strangled choking sound.

She wrapped her arms around Shin's throat and squeezed as she clung to his back by twisting her legs around his torso. Shin shook and snapped at her; he clawed at her arm, scoring it. Bright red blood bloomed on her forearm. The severity of the pain startled her and she seized her hand back. She toppled backwards and hit her head on the hard-packed earth. The pain sliced through her as blood seeped out of her wounds. They were shallow and nothing serious, but her every nerve seemed focused on the sensation. In the chaos around her, Rin's mind focused on the pain. *So this is what pain feels like.*

The second warrior dropped his weapon and fled. As he ran he shouted, "Yurei! There is a ghost in the temple!"

With the warrior fled, Shin turned to Rin. He leaned over her, staring at the blood and inflamed skin on her arm, his eyes somewhere halfway between the brown of a man and the yellow of a wolf.

"Get away from her!" Hikaru shouted.

Shin growled. Shin's head now resembled that of a wolf. Red gore matted the fur around his muzzle as he pulled back his lips and bared his teeth. Hikaru stood with his feet planted, facing Shin. He had no weapon. Rin was not sure if she was impressed or worried. She grabbed onto Shin's hand, pleading silently with him to spare Hikaru. *Not him, he is an innocent.* He looked down at her with now golden yellow eyes. *Please, Shin, leave before things get worse.*

He leaned forward and brushed his muzzle against her face. She smelled the coppery scent of blood on his mouth, and the soft hairs against her cheek smeared blood on her face. She hugged him tight but then shoved him away. He fell to his knees as he transformed into a wolf. He ran past Hikaru and towards the exit. Hikaru watched him go in mute shock. *Goodbye,* she said.

Hikaru looked down at her. She remained kneeling on the ground. She never wanted him to see her like this, imprisoned and covered in blood. His hands visibly shook.

"What are you?" he asked.

She met his gaze, pretending to be unafraid of the judgment he laid on her. *I came here to end their truce and start a war. I never thought I would come to care for him.*

"That thing, it killed one of my men."

She nodded.

"I thought—" He ran his hands through his hair. "Does it even matter what I thought anymore? A man is dead."

She did not remove her eyes from him. If she did, she would crumble under defeat. If she did, she would admit that the witch had won and that there was no hope left for her.

Hikaru shook his head, his eyes focused on the blood on Rin's face, and then he turned and fled. She would not chase after him. She had not sunk quite so low. *Perhaps there is time to repair the damage that has been done.*

Rin stood over the corpse of the man Shin had killed. He seemed so young and small now. His narrow thin face was pale. The blood from his wounds had soaked the front of his robes and the armor was stained with it. The pool beneath him reached outward and brushed against her toes. She leaned forward and closed his eyes. *I am sorry.*

"You have done better than I would have expected."

Rin's entire body went rigid.

The witch sauntered over. She stepped over the body of the fallen warrior and tracked bloody footprints into the courtyard. She went over to the shrine. She tilted her head and regarded it before caressing the face of the idol.

Then she said with her back turned to Rin, "I was summoned by Lord Kaedemori to exercise a Yokai."

Rin balled her hands into fists. *What is she doing?* She wanted to lash out at her, but she feared the old woman's powers and her own weakness in human form. Rin touched the raised edge of the scratch Shin had given her. As a Yokai it would have been healed by now, but the flesh burned and the tingling would not go away.

The witch laughed. "Do not worry, the game is not over yet. It has only just begun. Tomorrow when I come to proclaim you innocent, you must pretend you were possessed."

Her words felt like knives in her gut. She wanted nothing more to do with the witch's plots. *Why are you doing this?*

"Do not worry, once my plan is complete, I will set you free." She grabbed Rin by the chin.

Rin could feel the crackle of her spiritual energy like pins and needles along her flesh. Somewhere buried beneath this human exterior was Rin's own energy fighting to break free. *I will defeat you. One way or another.* Rin narrowed her eyes as the witch smiled.

"Do not think to disobey me, though, or your wolf will pay the price."

Rin deflated. It was as she feared. If she did not do as the witch said, Shin would be in danger. *I'm sorry, Hikaru, but I have to do this.*

SIXTEEN

"My lord, the priestess has arrived."

Hikaru jumped and swiped a black mark across the inventory he had been working on. He set down his brush and took a deep breath. He did not want to face the priestess. *How much longer can I deny what is before my eyes? I saw that creature kill a man—and Rin, she embraced it.* The image of her bloodstained face staring at him, both serene and withdrawn, had kept him awake all night. *The clan comes first— above all, even her.* His stomach was in knots and his eyes ached from lack of sleep.

He couldn't show his fatigue. A leader should be strong or at least appear so. To do that meant putting aside his personal concerns and focusing on what was best for the clan. "Ah, yes. Can you show her to my audience chamber?" he asked.

The servant bowed low to the ground, his forehead nearly

pressed against the floor, before he exited to do Hikaru's bidding.

Hikaru stood up and paced the length of the room while he waited for the priestess. He tugged at a loose thread on the hem of his sleeve, worrying at it, unraveling it and exposing the raw silk. He let it be and faced away from the door. He ran his hands through his hair and hovered over the parallel scars on the top of his head. They were from an injury he had sustained when he was too young to even recall. From time to time, the spots itched—usually when he was under duress. He ran his fingers along the smooth skin, it soothed him for some mad reason. He closed his eyes.

The door clacked against the track as the servant let the priestess into his audience room. He took a deep breath. He could see the silhouette of the woman through the transparent rice-paper doors. The servant rolled the door open. An old woman sat with her head bowed; her long white braid fell over her shoulder. She wore the red and white of a miko, but even if she hadn't been, he would have known what she was just from looking at her. He felt an aura about her, a shimmering veil that surrounded her. It wasn't often that he saw these sorts of things, and most often he disregarded them, but after everything he had seen as of late, it was harder to forget. As he approached, she lifted her head. Her dark eyes pierced him through as if she could read his thoughts. *That is preposterous,* he thought. *No human can see that.*

"Thank you for coming," Hikaru said as he sat down across from her.

"The pleasure is mine, my lord." She folded her wrinkled hands onto the tabletop. Not once did her dark gaze leave his face. There was a hint of a smile that brushed the corner of her lips. "How may I be of service?"

Staring into her ageless eyes, he could believe that all the strange things that had happened to him as of late were real. There was an unearthly quality to this woman, as if there were centuries' worth of knowledge hidden behind her placid gaze. He sat with his back straight and his fists planted on his thighs. No matter how he rehearsed what he wanted to say in his mind, he could not force the words out. Because once spoken it would mean admitting Rin was something other than human.

"I believe there is a strange woman in your household. She does not act as a lady should, am I correct?" the old priestess asked without prompting.

"Yes—my father must have mentioned it when he summoned you."

"He did. I am surprised it is not Lord Kaedemori who greeted me," she replied.

"My father is indisposed. As heir, I have taken over his duties for the time being." It had taken a lot of cajoling to get his father to hand over control of this matter. He knew Lord Kaede-mori still thought him possessed or bewitched, but he needed to prove to his father that he could take responsibility.

"Is that so?" The old woman smiled. It stretched out her wrinkles and enveloped her eyes until they nearly disappeared beneath the extra flesh.

Hikaru cleared his throat. "You will want time to purify yourself and prepare, I am sure."

"She is beautiful."

"Pardon?" The back of his neck burned and his throat constricted.

"This young woman, she is beautiful. You found her by the side of the road, is that right?"

Hikaru cleared his throat. "My father told you much."

She chuckled softly. "No, he did not. I have just dealt with her kind before."

"Perhaps—" he started to say, but the priestess cut him off before he could utter a denial.

"You are in love with her, I can see it."

Hikaru stood up without thinking. He realized too late his reaction spoke more than words ever could have. He glanced down at the priestess and considered a carefully worded warning, but he could not make the words pass his lips. "I will leave you to your prayers."

She watched him go, her dark eyes focused on him. The flesh along his arms prickled as he hurried out of the room and back into his own inner private sanctum. He slid down to the ground, his heart pounding. *I cannot love her. It is an infatuation, nothing more. Besides, she's some sort of monster.* The servant returned and escorted the priestess out. Hikaru leaned forward and cradled his head in his hands.

He jerked upright when a knock came from the door that separated his private chambers from his audience room.

He stood up and brushed himself off. "Speak."

The door slid open enough to reveal the servant kneeling just beyond the threshold, head bent forward.

"My lord, your uncle is here to see you."

Hikaru glanced past the servant to his uncle, who sat where the priestess had been moments before. Hikaru's limbs felt as if they were hung with stones. He looked over his shoulder to his futon; the bedding looked very enticing. *I should send him away.* Hikaru sighed before nodding at the servant, who pulled back the door the rest of the way so he could join his uncle.

"You may be clan elder sooner than we expected," his uncle said before Hikaru could settle in.

"What do you mean?" His uncle's words were like a cold bucket of water dropped over him.

"Lord Kaedemori killed his serving man this morning. He slashed his throat."

Hikaru grasped at his own throat. "No!" What sudden madness had taken hold of his father? Was this Rin's doing? Was it some Kitsune spell?

"He has lost all control. You must make your move; you have to take control before your brother does."

Hikaru pinched his brow. Everything was moving too fast. He'd thought he had time, years before this day would arrive. *There is no turning back now; the wheels are in motion.* His uncle looked at him, expecting an answer. He realized the moment he had gone to him for advice, he had been setting the stage for this moment. "I will not take control completely until I know for sure my father cannot be cured. For now, gather the men who are loyal to you, and let it be known I will be acting on my father's behalf."

"And if the men revolt and claim it treason?"

Hikaru suppressed a shudder. Now more than ever was the time to be strong.

"Then do what you must, but make it bloodless if you can. I do not want to be seen as a tyrant."

His uncle nodded. "I will see it done. And what shall you do?"

It was a challenge and Hikaru knew it. He also knew the proper answer would be to speak with those noblemen in the clan who could make his rise to elder easier—but his mind kept going back to Rin.

"I will be taking care of a few things. We will meet again, later."

He stood up before his uncle could pin him with any more questions. He hurried out the door and down the hall. He could not hide from it anymore. He had to see Rin. He wanted to speak with her even if she could not tell him with her own mouth. He wanted to know for certain if she was a Kitsune. Was she a monster, or was this a misunderstanding? Had she been the woman who saved him from the boar?

The temple where she was held captive had been a place of fear for him from a young age. He had memories of his mother there. He had been young when she died, but her gaunt face stretched tight over angular bones still haunted him. That was his only memory of her—a ghost lingering about the temple. The servants claimed she was possessed; others swore she had been a Kitsune his father had lured into the palace then trapped there. His father denied it all with his silence, never speaking of the matter, so Hikaru had learned to pretend the strange things he saw were not real. He had been successful in blocking them out until he had met that fox woman in the forest. All his life he had made an art of doubting, but he was starting to run out of excuses.

Four guards stood at the end of the hall as he approached. They all drew their swords in unison.

"You cannot pass," the nearest warrior said.

"Move aside," Hikaru said with a sweep of his arm.

The warrior did not move. He stared at Hikaru with a grim determined expression. He would cut Hikaru down if he had the chance.

"We have come to see the lady," the priestess said from behind him.

Hikaru looked at the old woman who stood at his elbow, then back to the guard.

"She is here to exorcise the evil spirits from the house and Lady Nishimori," Hikaru said.

The man frowned at them. His brows pulled together, creating a V over his eyes. After a moment of careful scrutiny, he bowed and then stepped aside. One by one the warriors backed up and bowed to Hikaru. *I must learn to command men, as I will be lord here.*

Hikaru gestured with his hand for the old woman to go first. She hurried down the hall into the courtyard beyond. Now that he was close to her, he felt the guilt of his actions from the night before like a stone upon his chest. He had seen Rin with that monster and had fled. *I should have tried to understand. What if she was in danger? I am a coward.* He intended to avoid her gaze, but his eyes were drawn to her. She knelt before the shrine in the courtyard, her back to him, her head bowed in prayer. He wanted to comfort her, to try to explain. He looked down at his feet; there were bloodstains on the wooden floor. He looked away. The warrior's death was an all-too-painful reminder of just how different Rin was.

The priestess approached Rin directly. She moved about with a self-assured air—she did not seem to fear her. Rin turned and her eyes went straight to Hikaru. Instead of anger or sadness, there was only a blank reservation in her gaze, which hurt like a punch to the gut.

He could not meet her gaze, so he watched them from the

corner of his eye. Rin's eyes slid from him and glided over to the witch, where they stayed transfixed. The priestess grabbed Rin by the chin and turned her face from side to side. She dropped her hand and then reached into a bag. She pulled out a handful of salt and sprinkled it around the courtyard, singing as she did so.

Rin's eyes were glued to the woman. She looked torn between fear and hatred.

"She is possessed by a spirit who has not found rest," the priestess said.

She reached into the folds of her robes and removed a long narrow piece of white paper with black characters painted onto it; it was an ofuda. She chanted over the paper and it seem to flutter and come alive in her hand. She placed the ofuda on Rin's forehead. Rin's eyes crossed as she looked at the paper, but she did not move. Hikaru held his breath, hoping beyond hope that there was nothing wrong with Rin. And then the priestess sang. It was a melancholy song, the words blending together to create a string of incomprehensible syllables. Then Rin threw her head back, her mouth open, and pouring forth from her mouth, a black miasma. It created a cloud over her head and coalesced into a humanoid shape.

Hikaru held his breath, watching as a woman with long black hair and dark eyes stared at him. She seemed familiar to him though he could not say how.

"Speak your name, spirit!" the priestess commanded.

"I am Sayuri," said the apparition.

"Mother?" Hikaru shouted without thinking.

The apparition turned and looked at Hikaru. "My son," she said in a hollow ringing voice full of sadness. "What has he done to you?" Silver tears slid down her face.

"Why have you taken hold of this woman's body?" the priestess asked the spirit of Sayuri. The priestess threw her arms out as she spoke.

"For revenge." The apparition flickered and looked back to Hikaru with translucent eyes. He wanted to reach out and touch her. Could this really be his mother, who had been taken from him at such a tender age? "My husband murdered me. He trapped me here because he feared my true nature." She motioned to the courtyard with a sweep of her hand.

"And what is that?"

Sayuri answered the priestess but did not take her gaze from Hikaru. It felt as if they were the only two there. "I am a Kitsune. My husband, Yoshirou, found me in the forest and fell in love with me. He married me, not knowing what I was. When he discovered my true nature, after our son was born, he grew angry and locked me here to rot."

"Was your son different than a normal child?" the priestess asked, her voice rising and falling like a chant.

"Yes. He was born with fox ears and a tail."

Hikaru stumbled backwards and fell onto his rear. His hand

went to his head and felt the parallel scars. *This must be a trick. It cannot be true!*

"Well, revenge is yours," the priestess shouted. "As we speak, your son is to take control of the clan."

Hikaru whipped his head towards the priestess. How could she know? He had only just given the order himself.

The spirit reached out to Hikaru with a hand made of black vapor. "Is this true, my son?"

Hikaru's throat had clamped shut. *I cannot be a Kitsune. I am a human!* He wanted to shout at her, deny that this was real. But the doubts he had secretly harbored his entire life had been exposed. The whispers he had pretended not to hear were revealed.

"It is true," he choked out, his voice a thin impostor.

"Then I can find peace again."

She pressed her hands to her chest and tilted her head back and skyward. She glowed with a bright white light, and with one last sad look at Hikaru, she disappeared, dissipating like mist in the morning. Hikaru's hands trembled as he clutched the hems of his sleeves, balling them into his fists.

The priestess looked down at Rin, who had fallen over to the side, her arm stretched out, pointing to the shrine behind her. *I should go to Rin, but I cannot make my body obey my commands.* Footsteps approached him from behind.

"Is it done, my lord?" one of the guards asked.

When he opened his mouth to speak, bile threatened to spill out instead. He swallowed hard and then said, "Yes, the spirit is gone."

"Your father—he murdered your noble mother," said another guard.

"Yes, it is true. Lord Kaedemori brought this evil upon this house, which plagued this woman," the priestess said. She pointed at Rin, who lay unconscious on the ground. "The Kami who rules this house holds the Kitsune sacred. To kill one goes against the god's will. Lord Kaedemori has defiled this place with his actions. Go to your fellows and tell them what you have seen here."

They bowed to her and ran to do her bidding. Hikaru could not even open his mouth to stop them. He crawled over to Rin and stared down at her sleeping face. He traced his fingers across her cheeks. *What have I done by bringing you here?*

WHISPERS TRAVELED FAST IN THE PALACE. HOTARU'S SPIES HAD BEEN IN a flutter since his father had been locked away, by Hikaru, no less. What game was his brother playing? He could not be thinking of seizing control, could he? The lords were scrambling, looking for a leader in this time of chaos. Now was Hotaru's chance to prove he was worthy to be the next elder. And finally he could get it, with the right backing. So here he was, outside his uncle's doorway. His father's sole surviving sibling was in some ways equal to their father in influence in the clan. Hotaru took a breath. This next step meant there was no turning back, no pretending he was happy with his place as second son. But seeing the palace fall apart brick by brick, through uncertainty, magic and danger, he felt as if he was being torn apart little by little along with it. *I cannot let my brother destroy us.*

He slid open the door an inch. His hands shook. He dared not have a servant announce him; the fewer people that knew about this rendezvous, the better—he had not even sent his uncle a message to let him know he was coming. Rumors would fly and he needed the advantage of surprise if he hoped to take control of the clan from his brother.

"If you're coming in, do it," his uncle called from within.

Hotaru slid the door open the rest of the way and slipped inside, closing the door behind him. His uncle looked up from his Shogi board. He did not seem surprised to see him, which meant Hikaru had been here, as the whispers said.

"Nephew." He looked away from Hotaru and back to his board.

Hotaru sat down across from his uncle, on the opponent's side of the board. His uncle, one of the greatest generals and right hand of his father; Hotaru was in awe. How long had he dreamed of being in this position, asking for his uncle's advice, but never daring because of the order of his birth? He felt elated and maybe a bit reckless for doing this. But he could no longer watch idly as his brother obsessed over a Kitsune, oblivious to the problems that were plaguing the clan. His father had imprisoned the Kitsune, but he knew that would not last. Hikaru always found ways to get what he wanted. The neighboring clans were looking for any weakness, any flaw, and he was handing it to them on a silver platter. His affair with the Kitsune could only end in scandal, and now he was trying to seize control before his time. Did he want to destroy them all? Or was this the Kitsune's plan? Hotaru refused to stand aside any longer.

"Uncle, I think you know why I am here."

He nodded but did not look up. "You want to usurp your brother's position as future elder."

Hotaru bit his tongue, silencing a childish excuse. It sounded so blunt coming from his uncle's mouth. But his uncle was not a man to mince words. It was something Hotaru admired about him. But as Hotaru was a second son, so was his uncle, and he knew even aspiring for his brother's place went against every law and tradition.

"Usurp is an ugly word. I merely mean to protect our clan and heritage."

"Will you steal his wife and kill him? Because if you do not have the backing of the Fujikawas, you have nothing."

He took the rebuff with a stony expression. He had expected some resistance; his uncle was a man of honor. And what man would plot a coup? But he also knew his uncle was open to hearing his side when he did not silence him immediately. "I know that. And I am prepared to marry Lady Fujikawa if that is what it takes. But I will not kill my brother. I thought to offer him exile."

His uncle shook his head. "And wait for him to raise an army to come and usurp you?"

"What man would follow him, when his own men despise him?"

His uncle glared at Hotaru, measuring him, waiting for him to back down. Like the pieces on the Shogi board, his uncle used his words to manipulate, cornering his opponent to get the desired result. In essence, this was a test. How far was Hotaru willing to go to win what he sought? He thought he had the resolve, he was willing to sacrifice it all for the good of the clan, but killing his brother, that was where he drew the line. He might find him unfit to rule and selfish to a fault, but he was still his own blood.

"How can I support what is treason? Do you doubt your father's wisdom?" His uncle's tone was more scolding than accusatory.

"I do not doubt my father, but you know what Hikaru is, what my father tried to hide when he locked his first wife away in that shrine. He's not *human*."

His uncle tugged at his beard and did not respond. Hikaru's unnaturalness, the ears and tail he had been born with, were mostly rumor. But he had heard from his personal servant that there was a long scar along his tailbone where a tail should have been. He would have continued to deny it if Hotaru had not sought out the woman who helped give birth to Hikaru and learned the truth. Hikaru as an infant had an extra pair of ears on top of his head, red and furry like a fox's, along with a long tipped foxtail. Lady Sayuri had paid her handsomely for her silence and saved her from his father's wrath. But when Lord Kaedemori found out, he locked his wife away and had a priestess remove the ears and tail, hiding the entire scandal. Until Hotaru's own curiosity had gotten the better of him. He had doubted his brother's right to rule ever since. How could a Yokai rule them? It was not natural.

"That is not something you should speak of. He is still your brother."

"And he's always hated me."

"Now, now."

"He does! Do not try to lie to me and pretend there is any affection between us." *It is because we share our father's blood that I have not killed Hikaru for the abomination he is.*

His uncle sighed. "What do you want from me? To support your claim?"

"You know this is what is right. Please, from a second son to another, you must understand how I feel."

"As a second son, I know how dangerous these thoughts can be. I served my brother and gave him the best advice I could. I never dreamed of more."

"And what about when he married a Kitsune? Did you believe him then?"

His uncle tugged harder on his beard.

"Hikaru is not fit to rule. Parentage aside, the men do not trust him. They are rallying to my side, but it is only treason if I lose."

He let the words hang there. His uncle would not meet his gaze but twisted his beard around his fingers.

Then quietly, almost at a whisper, Hotaru said, "I need your help. I need the lords' assistance. I know Hikaru has come to you with the same request against our father. Tell me it is not so and I will leave now and we will never speak of it again."

His uncle unwound his beard from around his fingers and then folded his hands inside his long sleeves. He was a master of strategy and a hero beyond renown. If they failed and Hikaru won, they would both die. All the men who had sworn themselves to Hotaru would die. *But if I do not try, the entire clan will be wiped from the history books.* "You're right, he came here asking me to support him in forcing your father to retire. He thinks he is mad because he imprisoned Lady Nishimori and called her a Kitsune."

"You were around when my father married Sayuri; do you think my father is mad?"

"I think your father is haunted by his choices."

"Let me ask you plainly, is this woman a Kitsune?"

He nodded and then looked away. Hotaru's chest constricted;

193

he felt as if he had won a small battle. But the war remained to be won.

"Regardless, Hikaru will set aside Lady Fujikawa and try to marry Lady Nishimori. And we will lose our hard-won treaty. I have seen the way he looks at her; he is besotted. Just in the short time she has been among us he has neglected almost all his duties. Even if he did not set aside his wife, can you not see how this will affect our clan?"

His uncle stared at the board. Hotaru folded his own hands into his long sleeves. He wanted to appear the picture of calm. Looking down at the board, he saw his uncle had been in the middle of a game. He made a move, taking his uncle's ōshō and winning the game. His uncle smiled down at the board.

"Perhaps it is time we saw a change."

Hotaru grinned. Finally everything was going as planned.

SEVENTEEN

Rin woke back in her original chamber with a faint headache and a foul taste in her mouth. She rolled over and touched her temple. *The last thing I remember was the witch coming into the shrine dressed as a priestess.* She sat up and looked around the room. The chamber she had been staying in for the past few weeks looked all but the same. She ran her hands through her dark hair. Her hands shook. *What will I do about Shin?* She knelt on the futon and crawled over to grab a robe that had been hung over a screen in the corner of the room. She slid it on. It felt good to dress herself again. *I suspect the servants are too terrified of me to even try to come attend me. That suits me fine.*

She went barefoot out into the adjoining garden. She inhaled deeply the decaying scent of leaves on the ground and the dirty water of the pond. *I thought I would never leave that place.*

She raised her hands palm up and let the wind twine in her fingers. She inhaled and exhaled, trying futilely to access her fox fire. It remained locked away, as good as extinguished by the witch's vile spell. She opened her eyes and stretched her mouth open into a scream, but no sound came out. All she managed to do was strain her throat from trying. She flung her arm in an arch and her hand collided with the tree. The pain was bright against her skin. She looked at her blotched red skin with disdain. The pinpricks traveled along her flesh, reminding her of her mortality. The scab on her arm broke open and bled anew. *Now all I have is a sore hand for my troubles.*

"Lady Nishimori?" Hikaru called from beyond the veranda.

She did not turn around. She would rather have a moment's peace. She was beginning to wonder if the witch would ever turn her back. *She uses me as her puppet. I doubt I was ever meant to break this spell.*

He stepped into the garden, his sandals clacking on the cobblestones as he approached her. She held her breath. She knew she should be putting on a smiling face for him, doing her best to seduce him and break the spell, but she just didn't have the heart for it. When he had looked at her with fear and damnation the night Shin killed the guard, something inside her snapped. She had not realized how much she had come to care for him until his affection was taken from her.

"I'm sorry to bother you. I wanted to see how you were feeling." His address was formal and full of uncertainty. He knew he had hurt her and he was sorry for it. *It would be better if he went on fearing me. What future could we possibly have together?*

She waved her hand in a dismissive gesture.

He exhaled. She imagined he was wringing his hands together, searching for the words to say. He was probably staring at the ground in that charming insecure way of his. She glanced over her shoulder at him, just a peek. But instead of avoiding her gaze as he had done so many times before, he watched her. His expression was difficult to define. It was hungry, and she felt her own feelings reflected there. She wanted him more than she should. It was not just an infatuation; this was stronger than anything she ever felt before.

"I wanted to apologize for how I acted before. I should have tried to understand, but instead I ran away." He frowned but did not look away. "It was shameful. I did not even give you a chance to explain." He pleaded with his eyes. He wanted her to tell him that she was human, that she had nothing to do with Shin's actions. But the truth was if she had not brought Shin into this household, that warrior would be alive. It was her fault.

I should let him go now, his brother can work to my purpose, and I won't run the risk of breaking any hearts. She raised an eyebrow as she crossed her arms over her chest, playing at being upset with him.

"I have always prided myself on being a man of reason, but for some reason with you, that all goes out the window. You drive me mad."

Her eyebrows shot up almost to her hairline. She bit her lip to keep from smiling. She couldn't even properly pretend to be mad at him.

He ran his hand through his hair, stopped at the top of his head and jerked his hand away as if burned. "I don't mean it that way. But you must see what a fool I am for you?"

She nodded and that was the problem. She had never had a man treat her as if the sun and moon rose and set to the rhythm of her heart.

"I have had my entire life planned out. My days are ruled by routine and schedule. Everything in its place, my entire destiny mapped out before me, and then you came along..." He laughed and shook his head.

She moved closer and for once he did not step away or try to avoid her, he was focused on her only.

"Recently, I went into the forest on my way back from a political meeting with a nearby clan. I saw a woman in the forest, or something akin to a woman. She had coppery hair and..."

She smiled. She remembered him. Saving him in the forest had been an impulsive thing; she never imagined it would bring her here.

He stared at her for a moment. "That was you, wasn't it?"

She nodded again.

He tilted his head back and laughed. "I must be losing my mind."

She touched him on the shoulder; he did not tense this time.

"Why are you here? Why can you not speak?"

Even if she could explain, she would not. These sorts of spells always had repercussions if they were revealed. So she leaned forward and planted a kiss on his lips. Curse be damned, and consequences be damned, she wanted him, and for once she would take what she wanted. He grasped the back of her neck and suddenly her entire body was aflame. She wrapped her arms around him, pulling him closer, needing him more than she thought possible. Then without explanation, he pulled away.

She scowled at him and crossed her arms over her chest. *Not again! Can you not forget your damn honor for one moment?*

He ran his hands across his scalp. "You have to understand, I am very much infatuated with you, but I cannot take advantage of you. I have a wife. She is on her way to the palace, in fact. Your honor would be ruined if even a rumor of any of this got out. You could never make a good marriage—" He caught himself and laughed again. "Do your kind care about these sorts of things?"

She smiled and shook her head. Humans were so melodramatic in their affairs. What difference did it make if you had a casual partner or two? Love and lust were two different things. He kept her at a distance, and when she tried to fill the gap, he moved his head away.

She huffed and turned away from him. She was fed up with his excuses and his unfailing duty to his father and the household. But when she turned away from him, he grabbed her shoulder and spun her around.

"Do not mistake me, I care for you more than I should."

She shook him off. *Words will not break my spell.* She was not one to weep, but she realized tears were falling down her cheeks despite that. Rin touched the stream of tears. *Why am I crying?*

Hikaru's eyes had grown large. "Please do not cry. I came here to make amends."

She shook her head, but before she could walk away from him, he pressed his lips to hers again.

He pulled away and paced a few feet from her. "I should not have done that. Why can I not get you out of my head? Is this some spell?"

She walked over to him, grabbed his shoulder and twirled him to face her. She kissed him hard and fierce. He was stiff at first and then little by little he relaxed, and he grabbed onto the back of her kimono and they were nothing more than two parts of one heartbeat. His hands tangled in her hair and she traced the clenched muscles along his back. She kissed the side of his mouth and down his neck while he whispered her name over and over like a prayer.

She was burning; all the frustration and the rejected advances had culminated into this moment. His hand slid up her side and brushed against her waist and then cupped her breast beneath the layers of fabric. She gasped. It was all the sound she could make. There was no turning back now. She pulled him by the hand and led him into her chamber.

He looked at her with a hooded gaze and she kissed away any protests before he could form them. He undressed her first, fumbling with the multitude of layers of her kimono, and when she was down to nothing but her undergarments, he stared at her, eyes wide and mouth slightly agape. She was not inexperienced, but standing before him, she felt vulnerable and exposed. *This has to be some side effect of being human.* She tried to cover her naked body, but he held onto her wrists to stop her.

"You are the most beautiful thing I ever laid eyes on," he said.

She blushed. She had never been one to do that before. Then she slid off his kimono, kissing the exposed flesh on his chest and downward. He groaned as she released the last of his clothes and then they lay on the futon together, nothing between them but the fire that threatened to consume them both.

"Are you sure? Once we do this, there is no going back."

She smiled up at him before pulling him down for another kiss. *That's what I am hoping.*

YOSHIROU'S IMPRISONMENT HAD LEFT HIM PLENTY OF TIME TO WORK, not that much had been done. Every so often he would get up under the pretense of stretching his legs only to pace the room like a caged animal. Of all his children, he never expected this from Hikaru. Hotaru was the one he had watched and feared would rise against him. *Why, Sayuri, is your son doing this to me? Is this also my punishment for my sins?* The guard, one of his own men turned against him, watched him warily. Yoshirou had not neglected to see the way the young man's hands hovered near his sword or how his eyes skimmed over the lord, his muscles tensed, ready to pounce. Keeping his cool was getting harder all the time. He had woken on the first night of his imprisonment with his futon torn to shreds and feathers scattered across the room with no recollection of how it had happened.

"My lord?" The warrior backed up an inch as he glared at him. The coward.

"Yes?" Yoshirou said, filling his tone with all the icy remoteness of a detached ruler. Because even if his son betrayed him and locked him away, he was still the elder until he drew his last breath.

"The priestess is here to see you."

He made a sharp gesture with his hand, indicating she should enter. The guard scurried backwards, eager to be out of his presence.

She entered, head bowed, but he knew her in an instant. When Hikaru had made his move and imprisoned him, he had felt her hand moving the pieces. Not Sayuri's son, who loved to learn more than to fight, and who trembled beneath his stare. Hikaru did not have the forethought to do such a thing, but this was the witch's type of game. He had seen it before, but had never been on the receiving end. He clenched his hands tight on the edge of his table, hard enough to splinter the wood. The guard slid out the door, and as he did, she raised her head, a wicked smile on her face. He broke a nail and blood welled along the bed, but he did not move to wipe it away.

She sat down in front of him and spent a few moments arranging the folds of her sleeves and straightening the billowing folds of her her haori, then folded her hands on the table in front of her and glanced up at him. He clenched his jaw. He must not let his temper get the better of him, the witch wanted something, and losing his cool now would play into her hands. He folded his hands in front of him. The blood from his broken nail rolled down his finger and onto the tabletop. He ignored the throbbing pain, he was numb to it by now, as he was absorbed by the witch and her knowing smiles. Let her play her games as long as the Kitsune was gone.

"It is done, then, you've exorcised the Kitsune as promised?"

The witch smiled, a slow creeping smile that made his stomach drop. "She was no Kitsune, my lord, just a woman possessed by the spirit of Sayuri."

Hearing her name again after so many years felt like a knife to his gut. Old wounds reopened to bleed anew. He thought he had buried her and the guilt over her death long ago, but since the Kitsune's arrival, he had become obsessed. He could not sleep, he refused to eat, and all the while he was wondering about her, waiting for the revenge he knew was coming.

"You're lying."

"Why would I lie?"

He slammed his hand on the table. She had to be a Kitsune! Why else would she taunt him, never speaking, but she moved as Sayuri did, every gesture an echo of his lost love. She even resembled Sayuri, dark eyes, round face and her smile. If he closed his eyes, he could still see Sayuri laughing in the garden, feeding the koi, carrying his child. He opened his eyes. The witch looked on him with an expression of pity. She thought he was mad, but she had been the one to warn him. She had been the one who told him how dangerous Kitsune were. He opened his eyes to the truth that Sayuri would destroy him had she gotten the chance. So he tried to exorcise the Yokai energy from her, to make her human, truly, but it had killed her instead. He ran his hands through his hair. Sayuri's gaunt face haunted his nightmares. Towards the end she had been nothing but skin stretched over bones, begging, pleading for her life.

"Sayuri..." he moaned.

It had to be her. Lady Nishimori had to be Sayuri's kin come for revenge. He looked up and he saw her standing there behind the witch's shoulder. She looked sad, so sad. He reached out for her, but when he tried to grasp her outstretched hand, she disappeared into the mist. Had it been an illusion or a vision? He could not be certain.

He turned back to the witch. "You told me a Kitsune was in the area, that they were coming for me."

"They are. Their kind and Sayuri will never be satisfied until you are dead."

His hands trembled. *Sayuri, why will you not forgive me? I loved you, I still love you.* I was a fool to do what I did.

"What can I do? How can I stop this?"

She shrugged. "Your death is what she wants. Blood pays for blood."

"And the girl, she is bewitching my son. I can see it, I am not blind."

"Then deal with her. I have done all I can, it is up to you now."

She rose to leave, but he did not watch her go. His eyes were drawn to the guard standing outside the door and the sword at his hip. Sayuri had returned and she pointed one pale ghostly hand at the weapon. He knew what he had to do.

EIGHTEEN

Waking up next to Rin had to have been one of the most blissful moments of his life. He felt her warm body formed against his and thought it would be better to never wake. Because when he woke, his life and responsibilities would come crashing down. *Just a few more moments to pretend.* He nuzzled her neck and she squirmed a bit but did not wake. *I should leave, the servants will be coming soon to get her dressed, and they would be shocked to see me here.* Yet he could not help but stay a few moments longer.

After a while, Rin's stirring went from restless sleep to waking. She rolled over and came nose to nose with him. He smiled at her and she leaned forward to kiss him. What started as an innocent brushing of lips quickly escalated, but he could not let it go further. It was just the one night. That was what he told himself. He ended the kiss and she smiled at him innocently. She drew her fingers across his face. It pierced him more than he thought it would. This was only a brief respite. When he left this room, it would mean goodbye.

She seemed to be coming to the same conclusion. She sat up and looked at him for a moment.

"You did not transform into a fox as my father would have thought." Hikaru chuckled. He thought of what his mother's specter said and his final words. *I was born with fox ears and a tail too. What does that mean, what am I?* He pushed away these troubling thoughts. He did not want to cloud these precious moments with Rin.

She frowned. Her neat brows pulled together over her eyes.

"Did I offend? It was not my intention."

She shook her head. But he sensed there was more she was not telling him. Like why she appeared as a woman when she had been a fox when they first met. Why could she not speak? They both had their secrets, he supposed; let her keep hers and he would keep his. *Either way, she must leave this place for her own protection.* He dressed in a hurry and left her in contemplation on the futon. He stood for a moment watching her. She sat on her knees, naked and unashamed. Her thoughts appeared to be turned inward. Once again he wished he could read her thoughts to better understand what she was thinking, or better yet how he could help her.

"I cannot stay. I am sorry to leave you."

She did not respond. He touched her lightly on the shoulder and she startled and stared up at him. Seeing the tops of her naked breasts and her come-hither smile made him want to climb back in bed with her. But he had delayed this moment long enough, his uncle and the others would be waiting for him. It had been an indulgence just to spend the night with her.

He sighed and went down the hall. The day was young, but he suspected this matter would weigh on his mind for much of it. He snuck into his room just before Yori came to dress him and fortunately he was none the wiser. As Yori dressed him, another servant entered with a scroll. Hikaru took it and cracked the seal. He skimmed over the correspondence and then his stomach contracted.

He crumpled the note in his hand. *So soon, I thought I would have more time.*

Sensing Hikaru needed time alone, Yori departed with a bow and left his master with his thoughts. Hikaru smoothed out the paper and read the message once more just to be certain he had not misread it. But it was there in plain words. She was on her way; his wife was coming to the palace. She would arrive in a matter of days. *I cannot have her here without this matter with my father settled.* He tossed the paper aside. *She cannot know about Rin. If they think I am having an affair with another clansmen's daughter, it may get back to her father and impact the treaty. What will Rin do if I turn her out, will she return to the forest?* He cradled his head in his hands. *What is wrong with me? There are more important things at stake than a Kitsune. Damn it. I've fallen in love with her.*

The palace did not rest and he had duties to attend to and important nobles to flatter and bribe. He went about in a fog. Time seemed to be slipping through his fingers. He planned to set aside Rin and start over with his wife. When he was elder, he would need an heir to secure his succession and weaken Hotaru's claim. He spoke with the noblemen in the clan, who nodded and smiled but made no promises. He hung around the practice yard and tried his hand at swordplay only to fail miserably. His only consolation was that his brother had not been there to see him humiliate himself.

Tired and dejected, he walked through the halls on his way to yet another meeting with his uncle. Yori scurried after him, carrying a teetering pile of documents he intended to review with his uncle. Then he spotted Rin from afar. She stood in a shaft of sunlight, the rays picking out the red highlights in her hair. For a moment he glimpsed the fire that had been diminished since she came to the palace. He remembered the powerful woman who had saved him in the forest and his chest constricted. She was waiting for him, he knew it from the mischievous smile. Though he had promised himself that he would put her aside, he could not follow through. He felt compelled to go to her. Despite his better judgment, he sent Yori away with an excuse for his uncle and went to her.

She had dressed, looking radiant in red, orange and gold. When she saw him coming towards her, she winked and disappeared around a corner. He chased after. A sliding door had been left open and he followed her into the empty room. When he crossed the threshold, she launched herself at him, her hands twining around his neck as she kissed him.

It was unexpected but welcome. The logical part of him shouted to stop, they would be caught for certain, but the part of him that craved Rin silenced it. He walked her backwards and pressed her against the wall. His hands pinned her on both sides as he explored her mouth with his tongue. This was what life was meant for, the soft taste of her mouth and the feeling of her body against him. He hated the layers of fabric that separated them. He wanted to ravage every inch of her body. The space between them was too much. He wanted to close the gap and feel that euphoric sensation of oneness when he was inside her.

"What is the meaning of this?" said a voice like icicles down his back.

Hikaru stumbled backwards and spun in place, panting for breath, his kimono half torn open by Rin's needy hands. His father stood in the doorway in all his austere authority. Rin leaned against the wall, staring at his father as she panted. Given the circumstances, she held her cool, leveling his father with an indifferent gaze. Hikaru, on the other hand, could hardly still his pounding heart. His uncle's men should have had his father under guard. How had he escaped?

"Father, you should be in your room, resting." It was a thin excuse and he knew it.

His father glared at him with a stare cold enough to freeze his blood in his veins. "You thought you could force me to retire?"

He looked at Rin and his eyes narrowed. In his hand was a blade dripping with blood. Lord Kaedemori gripped the blade tighter.

Hikaru placed himself between Rin and his father. Blood ran down the blade and dripped onto the tatami floors. Drip. Drip. Drip. Where had the sword come from and whose blood was on it? Hikaru's heart hammered in his chest. He looked to his father and then to the door beyond him.

"Father, you are not well. Please give me the blade and we can talk." He held out his hand, pleading with his father to see reason.

"Enough!" his father shouted and swung the sword about like a madman. "I must kill the Kitsune to save our family."

Hikaru eased towards his father, hand raised as if he were trying to soothe a savage beast. His father lowered the blade but did not loosen his grip. Hikaru knew he had no chance of overpowering his father. He had to win him over with reason. If there was any of his father left to reason with.

"You cannot kill her; our patron Kami holds Kitsune sacred. You will curse us."

"That's not true!" His father slashed with the sword. There was no artifice to it. He might as well have been a child swinging a stick.

Hikaru held his ground and inched closer to his father, his hands palm up in front of him. "Father, listen to me. Rin is no danger to you!"

"Don't you see?" his father wailed. "She is Sayuri come to punish me!"

Hikaru shook his head. "No, my mother's spirit is gone, exorcised by the witch. You have nothing to fear."

"I have everything to fear. I cut off your ears, I cut off your tail. She will haunt me for what I have done." His father fell to his knees, sword clutched loosely in his hand.

Hikaru inched closer, squatting down to reach his father's eye level. Slowly, he held out his hand. Lord Kaedemori stared at the ground. Tears poured from his eyes and down his cheeks. Hikaru put one knee on the ground. His father did not move. He feared to even breathe. He scooted a little closer, hand outstretched to take the sword. If he could just take it from him, they could talk together as they had never done before. His father was hurt by the sins of his past, maybe this was their chance to make amends. When Hikaru hovered over the blade, fingers prepared to close around it, his father jerked backwards. The top of his skull collided with Hikaru's chin. Flashes of white light burst behind his eyes and he fumbled backwards. Lord Kaedemori slashed at Hikaru. Hikaru threw out his hands to shield himself and the blade sliced through his palm. The pain was sharp and unexpected. He wrenched his arm back, and fueled by fear, he took his free hand and made a swipe to take the blade from his father once more. He failed to reach him and his father scuttled backwards.

"What do you think you're doing?" his father said.

Hikaru clutched his bleeding hand to his chest. "Father, let's be reasonable."

"No. You have been bewitched, that is plain for me to see." He pointed to Rin with a shaking hand covered in blood. Hikaru blocked his father's view of Rin. "There is no other choice." Lord Kaedemori raised up the sword and turned the point on himself.

He watched it in slow motion. His mind seemed to focus on the tip of the blade as his mouth fumbled to convince his father to stop. "There is no magic at work here!" he shouted. He took a step towards his father, but he swung the blade at him once more. "Father, listen, I brought in a priestess; she exorcised a spirit from Rin. She is well." He would say any lie it took to stop his father.

"Do you really believe that?" his father snarled as he positioned the blade against his gut. It pierced the first layer of fabric and a single drop of blood bloomed along his skin.

He crept towards his father, but each step seemed weighed to the ground. He could not move fast enough. "I know what I am now. I know what you did. Step down, retire with dignity. There is no need for violence," he pleaded. His voice cracked as he fought back the tears. *I never wanted this; I never wanted any of it.*

His father stared at him for a moment. His mouth was a single line. "You're wrong. Peace only comes with death." He plunged the blade into his abdomen. He grunted as it sank into his flesh. His mouth opened in a gasp and he fell over like a felled tree.

Hikaru ran to his side as the blade entered his father; whatever force had held him back snapped. It was too late. He stood helpless as blood spread from the wound in his father's stomach. It ran down the exposed part of the blade and dripped onto the tatami mats.

Hikaru's hands shook as he stared down at his father's prone body slowly bleeding to death on the ground. "Why, Father?"

His father peeked at him through cracked eyelids. Blood frothed on his lips as he said, "This is the honorable thing to do. I loved her, but I did not trust her." He took a wet rattling breath. "Do not lose sight of what is most important."

Hikaru knelt down beside his father. He had never dared reach out and touch him before, but he brought him close and laid his father's head in his lap. His hands hovered over the wound, helpless to do anything to stem the flow. He turned to Rin. "Call for a healer."

Rin came and knelt down beside Hikaru. She rested her hand on his shoulder and shook her head. His father closed his eyes, his breath gurgling in his throat. Hot tears burned the back of Hikaru's lids, but he dared not let them fall. He was a leader and he would not show weakness.

"Damn you, go. He's dying." He clenched onto his father's shoulders. He had always seemed so large and imposing, but now he could feel the bones of his shoulders beneath his clothes. He was an old man beneath all the trappings of authority.

He gave one more gasping breath and then died. Hikaru was numb. He could not feel his father's dead body in his arms or the blood that ran sticky and thick down his arms. Rin wrapped her arm around his shoulder, but even that went ignored. *I am the elder now.*

NINETEEN

After his father's death, Rin did not leave Hikaru's side. She had seen the despair in his eyes and knew he blamed himself. She coaxed him to her chamber, where she tried to take away his sadness with her body. Their coupling was tender. When he looked into her eyes as he entered her, the deep sadness she saw there stirred something in her chest. She had never intended it, but she had grown to care for him deeply. They fell asleep in a tumble on her futon, limbs wound together. She rested her head on his chest and let oblivion take her.

It was late that night that she woke with a start. The hairs on the back of her neck prickled and the air practically sparked with spiritual energy. She knew there was only one explanation. Rin gently unwound herself from Hikaru's embrace and, after sliding into her night robe, went out into the garden. The witch stood beneath the maple tree. The leaves had all but fallen, and only a determined few remained to cling stubbornly to the branches.

"You have been busy, I see," the witch said.

Rin crossed one arm over her stomach and waved her free hand, indicating the witch should get on with whatever she came to say. *Kill me or free me, it is the suspense that is the worst. The not knowing is driving me insane.*

"Things are progressing nicely, but it appears the Fujikawas have remained devoted despite news of Lord Kaedemori's death." Her mouth twisted into a grim smile. She was enjoying the Kaedemoris' misfortune. *And it is my fault. She brought me here to place a wedge in the family and awaken old prejudices.*

Rin took a step towards the witch. *Enough of your gloating, old woman, what do you want from me?*

She turned to face Rin. She wore the priestess garb again though Rin was certain she was not a real priestess. "I have come to tell you that time runs short, you have only a few days left. And as such, I have come to give you instructions."

Rin held her breath. She had watched the moon change and known her time was coming, but she could not bear to betray Hikaru, not after everything she had been through. It had been convenient to forget, but the witch was right, she was running out of time. *How can I break the spell and spare his feelings?*

"You are to kill Lady Fujikawa. She arrives in two days' time. Once she is dead, the spell will be broken."

She balled her hands into fists. *And if I don't, I will become a fox, is that it?* From the corner of her eye she glanced about for something to throw at the old witch. She could not fathom the old woman's motives, but she was tired of being used as a pawn in her game. And she was also tired of fearing for her life. She had never been this vulnerable as a Kitsune. She could not imagine how humans lived their lives feeling this weak.

"You do not approve of my plan?" the witch taunted.

Who would willingly take a life, you madwoman?

The witch laughed as she stalked closer to Rin while she stood frozen in place. Every inch of her body was alert, preparing for the witch to administer some punishment. A burning fire that set her skin ablaze or a spell that would turn her into a bug to be squashed underfoot. The witch tried to walk over to the chamber where Hikaru slept blissfully unaware. Rin stepped in her way. It was the only thing she would do to interfere with the witch. *Hikaru is in innocent in this.*

The witch smiled and revealed her graying gums. "If you do not kill Lady Fujikawa, then you must kill the new lord Kaedemori."

Rin gritted her teeth to hold back a curse that could not pass her lips even if she wanted to. She clenched her hands hard enough to break the skin. Had she a tail in that moment, it would have been whipping back and forth.

The witch patted Rin on the head. "That's a good girl. Now go back to your lord, enjoy him while you are able." She placed a dagger into Rin's hands. The metal was warm to the touch; the hilt was plain and made of white bone.

When Rin looked up from the blade, the witch was gone. She'd left Rin standing beneath the waning moon. She tilted her head back and looked to the stars. The hand holding the dagger fell limp at her side. The stars held no answers. Before she could return to Hikaru, she heard a low whine. She spun around, and Shin, in wolf form, sat at the foot of the stairs. She sighed and sat down on the steps. She set the dagger down next to her. She stroked Shin's head and wished for the hundredth time she could send him away. *I can just be glad he and the witch did not cross paths. This time.*

Shin nuzzled against her hand and then pulled his lips back in a growl. He shifted into his human form. He appeared before her with arms crossed over his chest.

"You reek of human!"

She looked away with a haughty tilt of her head. *Of course I do, I am a human right now.*

He grabbed her shoulders and she looked up at him. "Have you taken that human to your bed?" His tone was scornful, accusatory, and laced with something else.

She could not meet his gaze and she looked down at the dagger instead. She'd never taken a human to bed before. She could understand Shin's shock. But she had never expected this damnation, not from him. She knew many Kitsune who had taken human lovers. In fact, it was a common practice among Yokai. She had just never had any desire to take one herself. She picked up the dagger and twirled the hilt of the dagger in her hand, to avoid looking Shin in the eye. Shin shook her and it jerked her from her thoughts. Shin had only ever been gentle with her.

She pulled free of his grip. *What has gotten into you? Since when does who I share my bed with affect you? I know there are more than a few young maidens who were seduced by you.*

"What were you thinking?"

She pointed at Shin in a sharp gesture, then to herself and threw her hands up. *My business is my own.*

He raked his hands through his hair. "I know I've bedded my share of human women. But that was different. Those women, they knew that it was just for fun. None of them expected more. That *human*, I have seen the looks he gives you. He's in love with you."

Her stomach fluttered at Shin's words. She had been trying to convince herself that this was a temporary infatuation, but with each passing day he had dug deeper into her heart. Roots had started to spread and there was no dislodging him, it seemed. She could not explain it to Shin. *I think I love him.*

She pointed a finger at him and then grasped her throat with both hands. *I cannot speak. How can I explain so you'll understand?*

"I understand you well enough," he huffed.

She patted his shoulder. *You understand me better than most, but I do not think you would understand this. You've never taken a woman seriously, ever.* He slid his shoulder out from beneath her hand.

"When you can speak again... when all this is over, I think there are some things we need to talk about." He turned away from her.

Under normal circumstances, she would have let it go, but something in his tone made her wonder. He had been acting strangely for a while. Ever since her brief tryst with the Dragon. She frowned as she circled around him, trying to catch his eye. She tilted her head and looked up at him. He stared past her at the ground. A muscle twitched along his jaw, as if he were biting down on his words. Shin had never held anything back from her before. *The only reason he would hold back is to spare my feelings.* There had been too many secrets lately. She placed a hand on his forearm, which was folded in front of his chest. This time he did not move away, but she felt his muscles tense beneath his skin. He was strung tight as a bowstring.

Tell me what's wrong.

"I'm not going to say until you can give me a real answer," he said, seemingly reading her thoughts.

She decided to let it lie, there was no point in arguing.

"I heard what the witch said. You should go take care of him while he's sleeping, it will be easier on you. Just press the blade against his throat and pull; it will be over in an instant."

She stared at him, eyes wide. *He cannot mean that.* She shook her head. Just the idea of Hikaru's blood flowing onto her hands twisted her stomach into knots. *I am questioning my ability to kill a stranger. These damn human emotions are starting to cloud my mind. Before I would not have hesitated for even a moment.*

Shin grabbed Rin's chin and forced her to look at him. "I will not let you sacrifice yourself for him. Kill this Lady Fujikawa or kill him, it does not matter to me. Just see it done."

Rin's eyes grew wide. *When did you change? You were never this cold before.*

They stared at each other in silent contemplation.

"I should take you to the Dragon. No matter what you want. I should drag you out of here kicking and screaming."

She crossed her hands over her chest. *I did not ask you to get involved.*

"Don't look at me that way. You have to see that your stubbornness will be the death of you."

She narrowed her eyes as she glared at him, hoping the power of her evil eye would be enough to end this argument.

"I know what happened. The entire palace knows. What does it matter if he set you aside? He's set aside hundreds of other women."

Rin rolled her eyes. *Do you really think I am so vain as to care about being set aside? This is about honor. One night of weakness and then I became another conquest. I lost the little respect I had. I lost his respect. I have to prove myself, but if I go back now, like this, my reputation will never be repaired.*

"On second thought, your pride be damned, we're going." He grabbed her wrist and yanked her down the steps. She resisted, though it was like trying to move a boulder with a piece of thread. In the struggle she knocked the dagger off the stairs and it went down the steps with a clatter.

"Don't be a fool, Rin, just come with me."

She did not know what else to do. If they left, it wasn't just her that would pay the price, the witch would make him pay as well. She jerked her hand backwards and slapped him hard across the face. Shin startled and dropped her hand. He pressed his fingers against his cheek.

"You slapped me..."

She reached for him to apologize; she had not meant to hurt him. But he backed away from her.

He stared at her for a moment. Something shifted between them. At last Shin spoke and his voice was low and gravelly. "Never mind, you are a fool. I'll leave you to your choice and I hope you are happy with it. I will not stay here and watch you throw your life away."

He shifted into a wolf before she could try to reach out for him. He looked at her with golden eyes before he loped out of the garden, leaving her behind. *He's really mad this time. I've never seen him act this way.* The realization settled on her like a stone on her chest. Shin, her one friend, the one person she knew would support her and love her regardless of her faults, had turned his back on her.

Twenty

The procession moved through the gates at a crawl. The column, headed by warriors, carried banners depicting the clan's insignia, a light blue field with a river bisecting it. The warriors in matching blue armor, their identical dark blue masks topped with spiral horns, flanked the procession. Their mouths were thin lines like the stroke of a brush against fresh parchment. Next to the warriors were a few noblemen on horseback, and in the center of the retinue, two muscular men pulled a cart. The cart pullers' upper bodies, corded with muscles, pulled with little effort. They stared forward as the procession made its slow march into the inner layers of the palace.

Hikaru had watched for what seemed thirty minutes as they passed through each ring of the palace before they reached this point, the innermost ring of the palace and the home of the clan leader's family. Hikaru fought the urged to fidget; this was his wife who was arriving, after all. *Shouldn't I be pleased?* Were most husbands this miserable when their wife came to his clan home? True, they had not spoken but a handful of words at their wedding feast. And their wedding night had been dark and obligatory. She had said not a word the entire time. He had been so uncomfortable afterwards that he had slipped out after consummation. He had not seen her since. Come the next morning, he could not face her and decided to return to his own clan house. *What if she is with child?* This thought was accompanied by guilt. He had spent every night since his father's death with Rin.

After what felt like an eternity, the procession came to a final grinding halt. The warriors that boxed in the cart and the noblemen fanned out, their footsteps stamping on the stone of the courtyard. The cart pullers were the only ones left moving as they eased the cart forward. The wheels creaked and bells dangling from the four corners of the cart jangled. The cart was a simple construct of beams, gilded wood on the front and back, and then two crimson curtains on the sides. They had stopped the cart so that one side faced Hikaru and his brothers, who flanked him.

An unseen hand pulled back the curtains. They were meant to protect the ladies within from being seen by their inferiors, but as the curtain slowly rolled back, it felt like another part of the theatrics surrounding their arrival. When the curtains were opened, they revealed five women sitting within. The four in front had long ebony hair and wore bright-colored kimonos. A servant with a step stool rushed forward and placed it on the ground in front of the ladies. The lady's maids stepped down first, covering their faces with their fans and keeping their eyes lowered.

Then his wife stepped down. She wore a kimono with so many layers and colors it was a surprise she could stand beneath the weight of all that fabric, let alone walk. Her face was painted white and her ebony hair fell in a curtain down her back. She glanced up at Hikaru from behind her fan. Their eyes met, but there was no connection. He may as well have been locking eyes with the wall. Her expression, what he could see of it, was flat and without animation. *It is as I feared, she is dull and stiff.* A part of him had hoped he would feel that spark; it would have made it easier to set aside Rin. He still struggled with sending her away. He knew he should, his uncle urged him to do so, but he could not. He loved her and he did not want to be parted from her even if she was a Kitsune.

Hikaru stepped forward, his arms spread apart in greeting. "Lady Fujikawa, welcome to our home—" He fumbled over the next words. Someone in the crowd coughed and cleared his throat. "I am happy to have you join me here."

His father would have had a better speech prepared, but given that Hikaru was new to his position, he thought he might be forgiven this once. His proclamation was followed by the restless shifting of bodies. The servants had been kneeling down on the ground since the procession had arrived. Hikaru imagined they felt even more uncomfortable than him. At least he had the luxury of standing.

The lady nodded from behind her fan and said in a soft but direct voice, "It is my pleasure to join your clan, my lord husband."

Any other man would be happy to marry someone so beautiful and gentle, not to mention rich... But he could not help but think about Rin. She was mixed into the crowd, near his younger brothers and the other noblemen of his house. He had spotted her as soon as they had come to wait for his wife to arrive. His eyes were always drawn to her, no matter where they were.

When all the formalities were seen to, Hikaru showed his wife to her rooms. They walked side by side, not saying a word. Her ladies followed after them, silent as ghosts. He felt the need to make some small talk.

"I hope your journey was pleasant," he said.

"It was, thank you." There was nothing else to be said. He bowed when he left her at her room, and went to look for Rin.

Hotaru had planned a banquet to celebrate the arrival of Hikaru's wife. And now that the staff had been dismissed, they were preparing for the feast. There was much to prepare for another round of ceremony.

As Hikaru waded through the crowds, he spotted Rin standing still in the center. She stared at the carriage, her expression distant. She knew his wife was returning, he could not very well hide it from her. But though the truth had lain between them, he had not breathed a word about it. He was married and his wife was here. He would be expected to spend time with her and produce an heir. Despite his better sense telling him to do otherwise, he weaved through the crowd towards her. A selfish part of him wanted to indulge in these moments while he could.

She turned without seeing him and headed down the hallway, trailing after a crowd of servants headed back to their daily tasks. Despite the press of bodies, she stood out. The servants and even the other nobles kept their distance from her. But it was different now, they bowed their heads with reverence. Despite his orders to silence Rin's true nature, it had spread through the palace like wildfire. Now instead of fearing her, the servants revered her like a Kami among them. When she walked in a crowd, it was like the wind blowing through the trees, everyone parted before her. But once she passed through, the gaps closed up and Hikaru lost sight of her.

As bodies closed the distance between them, she slipped away from him and perhaps his last chance for a moment alone with her. He shouted out her name. Heads swiveled in his direction, but he did not care. She stopped when he called out to her and turned around with an eyebrow raised in question. She nodded her head sideways, daring him to follow her.

He hurried over to her. When he reached her, he wanted to hold her, to kiss her and remind himself of what love felt like. *It is not meant to be a business transaction. Being with her is what it should be.* "I should have forewarned you, my duties will keep me rather preoccupied now that my wife is here. I will have to leave you alone more often than I like..." He trailed off, not sure what else to say. People flowed around them, watching with curiosity. He put them from his mind and focused on Rin. "I just wanted to say..." That if the circumstances were different, I would have made you my wife. I find you beautiful and enchanting. He dared not say any of those things; instead he said, "If you would like, I am sure I can arrange some distractions for you, just until you choose to leave. You are not a prisoner here. You may go whenever you wish." The very idea sat in his stomach like a burning stone. He did not want to think about a time when he would not have the luxury of catching a glimpse of her from afar. Or those quick passionate embraces in an empty room.

She frowned before forcing a smile. She nodded and walked away. There was a swish of her hips that he knew was meant to entice him. He looked over his shoulder. There were matters to be seen to, Lady Fujikawa had brought men with her and they would need to be entertained, but Rin was an addiction he could not give up. She glanced over her shoulder at him with a faint smile. When she caught him looking back at her, she winked at him before disappearing around a corner. He knew he should head back to his chamber to change for the banquet, but he could not resist her call. He went after her.

The crowds had dispersed and the halls were predominantly empty once again. He found Rin in the garden. She sat on a bench beneath a maple tree. She smiled when he arrived and tucked a loose hair behind her ear. He stood there for a moment, drinking her in. *I want to remember this moment because one day she will be gone, and all I will have left is my memories of her.*

He sat down beside her and put some distance between them. If his wife's family saw him with Rin, then it would cause a scandal. He ached to reach out and brush his hand against her skin or to run his fingers through her hair. But he knew even an innocent touch would lead to much more.

A servant appeared at the mouth of the garden. She was a young woman. She looked both ways before approaching them. In her hand was clutched a small bowl. She thrust it towards Rin, who took it with a smile.

"I ask for your blessing, Kami-sama," the young servant said.

Rin rested a hand on the girl's head. The young girl trembled for a moment and tears gathered along her lashes. She backed away and then scurried out of the courtyard.

Hikaru laughed. "Where once they feared you, now they worship you. What did she give you?"

Rin grinned as she showed him the bowl full of fried tofu. Her favorite, he knew. He laughed as she picked out a plump piece with her fingers and popped it into her mouth.

He reached into the bowl, but before he could grab a piece, she snatched it away. He chuckled and put up his hands. "I'll let you keep it, then."

She finished her treat and set aside the bowl. She leaned back on the bench, exposing her neck to the sun's rays, and kicked her bare feet back and forth.

I wish it could always be this way. He pulled on a thread along his sleeve. *And why can't it be?* The thought took hold and it could not be dislodged. He spoke his mind before he lost his nerve. "My father chose my bride for me, and though I am sure she will be a good wife, I cannot help but wonder, would it be better to live a life of my own choosing? What sort of man would I be if my life had not been dictated by our society's rules? Who would I choose if it were my decision?" He had never spoken these sorts of thoughts aloud before, but he knew he could speak freely with Rin.

Rin watched him as he spoke. She had gone very still. Her lips, parted slightly, looked soft and inviting. He touched her cheek with the back of his hand. Her skin was warm to the touch.

"I would make you my consort, the wife of my heart."

She dropped her gaze and looked away. It was unusual for her.

"I have offended you?" he asked.

She opened her mouth as if she would say something, but no sound came out. Before he could probe further, a servant appeared. Hikaru stood up and put additional distance between himself and Rin. Her answer would have to wait. Judging by the servant's expression, he had seen and he did not approve. There were still a few who distrusted Rin. The servant pursed his lips as if he had tasted something sour. Rin remained seated. He could feel her gaze on the back of his head. He itched to turn around and kiss her just to spite the servant. He was the lord here now.

"My lord." The servant cleared his throat. His eyes flickered to Rin.

"Yes?" Hikaru snapped. He felt tight as a bowstring.

"Lord Hotaru has requested an audience with you."

"Very well, I will be there in a moment," he said in what he hoped was a commanding tone.

"He said it was urgent, my lord." The servant swallowed past a lump in his throat; it was difficult for him to speak to Hikaru in such a way. Rumors of his parentage were whispered through the palace. They called him Hanyou—a half Yokai. Born of a human and a Yokai. He did not know what to believe.

The parallel scars on the top of Hikaru's scalp itched. If being a Hanyou helped earn his people's respect, then perhaps that was a good thing. *That's not it, this servant fears us.*

Hikaru turned to Rin. "I am sorry; I must do as duty commands. I will come for my answer later." He leaned down and pressed a kiss to her brow.

Hikaru followed the servant to his audience chamber, where he found not only Hotaru waiting but his uncle as well. Hotaru stood at the far end of the room, on the platform that just a week ago had been where his father sat when he received guests. He stared down at Hikaru.

"There you are, brother," Hotaru said.

Hikaru glanced between his brother and his uncle. Why were they together? His uncle would not meet Hikaru's gaze.

"What is this about?" Hikaru said.

"I think you know why I am here," Hotaru said as he took a seat in the same place their father had always sat.

"I do not. Enlighten me."

"You're an unfit ruler. A mongrel who has neglected his duties, placing them on uncle and me in favor of chasing after your Kitsune."

"I am the heir."

"That means nothing to me. You are not *human*."

"Hikaru, be reasonable," his uncle interjected, pleading with him. "Some men are made to be leaders and others—"

"You too, Uncle? I thought you were on my side."

Hotaru jeered down at him; the look on his face was reminiscent of their father. "See, you cannot even keep our family's support."

"I know you've wanted this from the beginning. How long have you been plotting this?"

Hotaru shook his head. "I do not want to do this, believe me. I would rather you were capable of leading on your own. But since you give me no choice." He flicked his hand.

Hikaru turned around to find two of his own men closing in on him. He spun around to face his brother. "You cannot do this. I am the elder."

"Correction, you were the elder."

TWENTY-ONE

S o *this is it,* Kazue thought as her gaze skimmed over her new chambers. The Kaedemori clan was not so different than the Fujikawas'. The room even reminded her of the one from home, a painted screen in the corner with a forest motif, a futon with a reed curtain, a sitting room just beyond, and a private garden all to herself. Along with her own lady's maids she had brought with her, she may as well be back at her father's palace. But it wasn't the same. The air felt different; her skin prickled with dark energy. This palace held secrets, and even when she should have been resting, she could not. She paced her chamber, fussing with this and that and sending her maids on useless errands.

She felt something like a spark of lightning. She turned in place but saw nothing out of the ordinary. Her maids bustled about the room, hurrying to unpack her things and prepare for the night's festivities. *I am imagining things. It's probably because I'm nervous about starting over here.*

After a month apart, she would be reunited with her husband. Would he expect to share her bed? Her father had been disappointed when the young lord left shortly after her wedding night, and more upset with Kazue that she was not pregnant. She rested her hand against her empty womb. Their child would rule over the combined clans of Fujikawa and Kaedemori, making them the largest and most powerful clan in the islands of Akatsuki. Without an heir, her father depended on Kazue to preserve his line. *If only I had more time to get to know him before he ran away.* He seemed kind, but seeing him again, she felt no attraction, no love. *Perhaps it can grow.* She had told herself the same lie over and over since the marriage was announced and she had given up on Kaito returning.

Kazue wandered over to the painted screen and ran her fingers along the hills in the picture. When she learned what Kaito was, she knew it would never last long. They were from different worlds and she had a responsibility to her clan, to protect her family. And yet, in her selfish heart she had hoped she could keep the Dragon. Perhaps she had been a fool to think he would want her the way she wanted him. She gave him her everything, her heart, her soul, her virginity. The day she married Lord Kaedemori she had prayed that Kaito would come and take her away to his palace beneath the sea, but that was a foolish dream. He was gone and he was not coming back.

"My lady, the banquet will be starting soon. Shall we change?" Aoi looked at her with large doe eyes. As servants went, she was faithful, but a bit naive. That was why she brought her, she did not want any of the scheming girls who tried to manipulate her to gain favor with her father.

"Give me a few more minutes." She smiled at Aoi, knowing she would not deny her request. "The journey has left me tired. Why don't you and the girls go into the garden?"

Aoi bowed. "Yes, my lady."

They all departed, and when they were gone, Kazue went over to her trunk and pulled back the lid. She glanced both ways before digging to the bottom. Buried beneath layers of silk was her most prized possession. She removed a bundle and unwrapped the fabric around it. Inside, a mirror inset with pearls reflected the light coming from her brazier. It was the only gift the Dragon had given her. Her last link to him, she wished it was enchanted or gazing into would reveal his face; instead there was nothing but her own disappointed gaze staring back at her. Brushing her fingertip along the pearls, she counted them, wondering what he was doing now. She sighed.

Then she felt it again, the spark. Light footsteps fell on the tatami mats. She shoved the mirror beneath the folds of her kimono and turned to look over her shoulder at the intruder.

"Aoi, I told you to wait in the garden." She knew it was not Aoi, but after keeping her powers a secret from childhood, she dared not reveal them now.

An old woman stepped into the light coming from the braziers. "My lady, it is I."

She could have wept from relief. If anyone could explain this ominous aura, it would be the priestess. She did not even waste time wondering how the old woman had found her way into the palace. She seemed unconfined by walls or society; how she envied her.

"Teacher, I am so glad you're here." Kazue jumped up to greet her.

She embraced the old woman, clinging to the one thing that was hers in this strange place. "Why did you not tell me you were coming here?"

"I did not know I would be in this region for certain, child. But I am glad I came here. There is danger around."

"I feel it too. What do you think it is?"

"I do not know for certain, but I came to warn you, be careful."

She nodded her head. She had prepared herself for this; she was ready to face whatever monsters lurked in the night. "I will, teacher."

"And there's more, the Dragon is missing; none can find him. If he comes here for you, you must refuse him. Do you understand?"

Kazue recoiled. She pressed her hand to her chest. The Dragon come for her? That was laughable. He cared nothing for her. What they'd had was nothing but a short liaison, a tryst. He held no love for her. But the question escaped her lips before she could stop it.

"Why?"

Her teacher grabbed her by the shoulders. Kazue looked into her wrinkled face, the lines that framed her mouth from years of laughter, eyes full of ancient wisdom. She had risked much to teach Kazue about her spiritual powers. If her father had found out—she did not want to think about the repercussions.

"I have seen a vision of the future, and if you were to go with him, it could mean destruction."

She looked away from her mentor, afraid she would see the longing in her eyes. Despite her warning, she still wanted him to come for her. "It does not matter either way, he would not come here. I am married now."

"That does not matter to a Dragon."

"I understand, teacher."

Her teacher pressed a kiss to Kazue's brow. "Be safe, child. I will return soon."

The mysterious woman left in her usual way, like a puff of smoke, though Kazue still harbored doubt in her heart. She had not told her teacher, but she too had a vision, and it showed a child. And though her vision was not certain, she knew it belonged to the Dragon.

I wish Shin were here and that I could speak with him. Rin stood up. She had lingered in the garden, thinking about Hikaru's proposal. She had not thought about the future or even the potential of a future with Hikaru. He was married and a human—well, a half human. She was not completely immune to the gossip. She could not imagine why he had not told her himself. It hurt her that even now he was keeping secrets from her. Not that it mattered, even with Kitsune blood in his veins, his life span would end, and thinking about that just constricted her chest. *I cannot even consider a future until I break this spell.*

She started walking before she could change her mind. Her bare fleet slapped on the wooden walkways. The servants, who were busy with their tasks, still stopped to bow or try to press offerings of flowers and food into her hand. She shook them off and ran down the hall. She darted down the first empty passageway she could find and leaned against a wall. *I almost miss when they hated me.* After taking a moment to collect her thoughts, she continued, this time down the deserted halls that led back to her bedchamber. Much of the activity was centered around the main hall, the centermost building where the family entertained.

When she reached her door, she looked both ways before sliding it open. She went straight to her futon, and kneeling down, she reached under it and pulled out the dagger from underneath. She clamped her hand down on it and just held it for a moment. Testing the weight against her palm, she resigned herself to her task. *It's her or me.* She swallowed past a lump in her throat. *I have no choice.*

After poking her head out to check for any casual witnesses, she headed out. She hid the dagger in her sleeve just before a servant appeared at the opposite end of the walkway. The young woman bowed so deep to Rin her head nearly touched the ground. Rin smiled and scooted past her, her arm pinned behind her back. Rin went in the opposite direction of where she had originally intended to avoid suspicion, then doubled back once she was certain the servant was gone. Guards were stationed along the cross section that led to the inner ring; she came across blue-masked warriors. They watched her slip past without expression. They were not Kaedemori guards, but Lady Fujikawa's. *Damn, they will not know I am a Kitsune. I doubt they will let me pass.*

Hidden in the shadows, she sized up the guards and reevaluated her plans. A garden nearby had a trellis, which she could climb. She recalled her last adventure on the palace roofs. *I can do it again, and this time no one will be chasing me.* She removed the dagger from her sleeve and placed it in her sash. She could not risk it sliding out. Her palms were slick with sweat, so she wiped them on her thighs before taking a deep breath. The guards faced the garden. She would need to distract them to get by. While searching for inspiration, there came shouting from behind the guards. The men turned in unison, pulling their swords from their sheaths as one. Rin seized her opportunity and ran over to the trellis, praising her good fortune.

As she climbed, her hands trembled. The climb seemed to take an eternity. *They'll turn around any minute and I'll be done for.* In reality it was but a matter of moments. She reached the roof, where she collapsed, taking large gulping breaths. She rolled over and looked down at the guards, but they had disappeared. *No matter. At least I was not seen.*

She ran along the rooftops. Every few feet she peeked her head over the edge. She found mostly empty rooms. Then she came to a large barren garden. The plants were all dead, the tree at the center was nothing but empty branches. Four young noble ladies sat talking in low voices. They were Lady Fujikawa's maids. Rin squatted on the roof. She wished she had taken off her robes; all the exertion was making her sweat. She swiped the sweat off her brow with the back of her hand.

"Ladies, where are you?" Lady Fujikawa called from within her chamber.

"In the garden, my lady," said the lady in the center of the three others.

Lady Fujikawa glided into the garden. Her long ebony hair fell over her shoulders like rivers of silk. She wore her layers of robes with ease. Rin watched her with a distant pang of jealousy. This was Hikaru's wife. Did he love her? she could not help but wonder. Human relationships baffled her despite spending nearly a month in their presence. *Tonight is the last night.* She looked up at the moon. It glowed above, mocking her. It seemed cruel to murder an innocent human. She could have laughed. Being among the humans had changed her.

Lady Fujikawa joined her ladies and sat on the bench.

"Shall I read to you, my lady?" asked a woman to her right.

"No, thank you," was the lady's despondent reply.

"Does something trouble you?" asked the third woman.

Do they take turns speaking to her? Rin readjusted her legs, which had begun to burn from squatting. She could not just plop down in the garden and kill the lady. She would have to catch her alone. And there were likely guards about. *I did not think this through very well.* She removed the dagger from her sash and rolled it in her hands as she concocted a plan.

"Nothing is the matter. Leave me," snapped Lady Fujikawa.

The ladies rose together and scattered like fall leaves. Lady Fujikawa stood up and walked to the far side of the garden. Her head was lowered as if she were deep in thought. Now was her chance; Rin prepared to leap down. But before she could, another voice called out to Lady Fujikawa.

"My lady?"

Lady Fujikawa turned in place and furrowed her brow as one of her blue-masked guards approached her.

"I asked to be left alone," she said, her lips pressed flat together.

"Pardon my intrusion, my lady, but you have not been yourself since we left the palace."

"It is not your concern." She turned to walk away, and now the warrior faced Rin's direction and Lady Fujikawa's back was turned to Rin. The warrior was so intent on Lady Fujikawa he did not notice Rin watching from above.

"My lady, I have sworn my life to you. Your happiness is of the greatest concern to me."

She laughed and said, "Those are empty words. What is real devotion? I would say it is nothing but a romantic notion."

He smirked. His smile seemed familiar. *It cannot be.*

"A man has broken your heart; I can see it on your face."

She raised her hand to slap him, but he grabbed her wrist before she could do so. With his free hand he removed the mask. Lady Fujikawa gasped and slowly lowered her hand. The Dragon let the mask fall to the ground with a bang.

"Kazue, did you think you could run?"

Rin could not see her face, but from the way she balled her hands into fists, she knew the Dragon had stirred her ire. "You left me—without warning... without saying goodbye."

He chuckled. "I told you I would break your heart."

She scoffed. "You are a terrible liar."

He moved closer to her and Rin edged closer. *Is this where he has been? My master?* She knew she should have felt something more, a twinge, anything that indicated there had been real feeling between them, but there was nothing. The Dragon, the greatest ruler in Akatsuki, was in love with a human. Though she could see it in his eyes, she could not believe it. Rin watched in a trance as he moved Lady Fujikawa's hand away from her mouth and kissed her. She backed away, leaving them to their private moment. She could not kill her, not with the Dragon protecting her. But when she tried to walk away, her foot slipped and she went sliding off the roof. She clawed at the roof tiles, knocking loose a few in the process. Then she went toppling over the edge and landed in a bush, which broke her fall.

Everything hurt. Her body was covered in hundreds of small pains, all shouting at her. She rubbed her aching limbs and looked up to see an angry Dragon glaring at her. She opened her mouth to explain, but no words came out.

"What are you doing here?" he snarled.

She waved her hands, showing that they were empty. Then from over his shoulder she saw Lady Fujikawa pick up her dagger, which had fallen on the ground alongside the broken roof tiles.

"Kaito, look at this."

Kaito? Rin had never called the Dragon anything other than the Dragon. Had the human given him a name? She could have slapped herself; there were more important things to worry about than pet names. Like the ice that glossed over his eyes that she knew did not bode well for her.

"Are you here to kill Kazue?" He shook Rin hard enough to rattle her brain inside her skull.

It's me, do you not recognize me? She looked him in the eye, willing him to see her, but the witch's spell had blinded him. She should have known the witch was devious—her last hope had been snatched away. If her master could not save her, then...

"Speak, damn you!" he snarled.

His hands on her shoulders were like ice. The cold burn of his touch crept into her flesh, freezing her from the inside. She opened her mouth to cry out, but no words would come out. The witch's spell had muted even her ability to express pain.

Kazue grabbed the Dragon by the shoulder. "Stop, Kaito. I do not want to see any more bloodshed."

He ground his jaw, a habit Rin was all too familiar with. He wanted to kill her; he would have had Kazue not stopped him.

"You escape with your life, but if I see you again, you are dead." He stepped backwards and took Kazue by the arm. They hurried out of the garden through an adjacent walkway, not bothering to go through her chamber.

Rin sat in the bush, numb. Her master, who she had served for centuries, had not recognized her, and on top of that, she had failed to kill Kazue. *Which means I cannot break the spell without killing Hikaru.*

SHE STARED DOWN AT SHIN THROUGH LONG LASHES FRAMING WARM brown eyes. A wicked smile pulled at the corner of her cherry red lips. Her dark hair fell in a tangle, framing her pale face.

"It has been too long since you visited," Aimi purred as she languidly traced his pectoral muscles with the tip of her finger.

Shin folded his arms behind his neck, stretched his legs out on the futon, and closed his eyes. The tension he had sought to relieve still wound him tight, and no amount of pretending would ease this churning feeling in his gut. He should never have left Rin behind. He should have dragged her out kicking and screaming, curse be damned. *And where is the Dragon? The bastard should be fixing this mess.*

"You cannot ignore me, Shin." Aimi pouted.

"I can do as I please, woman," he snapped, but it was half-hearted.

Aimi knew him well enough to not be offended, not really. But she enjoyed pretending she was. She scoffed. "Perhaps I shouldn't tell you about Akio, then."

He sat up, leaned on his elbow and fixed her with a hard gaze. Aimi had her uses outside the bedroom as well as in. It was why he had sought her out in the first place. As a spy she was top notch. Akio never suspected that she was feeding Shin, and by extension the Dragon, information about all his movements and every plot. But this time it was personal. Shin had heard the whispers, and he was certain the forest guardian had something to do with Rin's curse.

"Don't play games, Aimi. We both know why I'm here."

She jutted out her bottom lip and crossed her arms over her chest. "You're cruel, Shin."

He sighed and she flashed him a smile.

"You're no fun lately." She tossed her hair over her shoulder before standing up to cross the room. She sauntered, naked, over to a screen, where her robe had been hastily tossed in their hurry to make it to the futon. She dressed slowly, exposing her flesh in small glimpses and with sly glances over her shoulder. Though he had seen every inch of her body, had taken her in more ways than he could count, it never satisfied him. Aimi was beautiful, clever, dangerous, but never enough for him because she was not Rin. He was never sated, no matter how he tried to drown his feelings in the indulgence of the flesh, fighting, or drinking; everything left him wanting and empty. *I have to tell Rin how I feel before I go mad.*

When she finished dressing, she knelt in front of him as she pinned her hair into place on top of her head. He waited for her, because he felt like he should spend time with her at least. He never wanted a woman to feel like he was using her. It wasn't Aimi's fault he was too afraid to tell Rin how he felt. A part of him feared Rin's rejection and losing what they had together.

When she finished, she placed her hands in her lap and said, "I've made inquiries, as you requested. It seems Akio is looking for someone."

"Is it Rin?"

She shook her head. "No. He's angry with her, but he's made no real effort to capture her. When she stormed in here, he was livid, but he's not fool enough to start a war with the Dragon over nothing. If she comes into his forest, however..." She shrugged.

He sighed. "Damn her." Rin's impulsive nature always got her into trouble. It was one of those traits he simultaneously loved and hated.

"I heard she really made a fool of him. Right after he sent a few of his pets to hunt for her. But came to his senses not long after."

Yes. And she was nearly killed by one. But something killed it first, and that's what's been bothering me. There's a powerful Yokai in that palace. But they've masked themselves, so I do not know who it is.

"Did you find out who Akio is after?"

"Do you doubt my abilities?" She arched a perfectly sculpted brow.

He forced a smile. "I never doubt you, my pet."

She smiled, seemingly satisfied. "Well, it seems Akio has found a Kitsune-Hanyou. If the rumors are true, he's the son of some human lord. He sent Naoki to fetch him."

Ah. It all makes sense now. I knew there was something different about the human, though I could not say what at the time. And Naoki is haunting the palace. Of course, who else could cloak themselves so completely?

"What does Akio want with a Hanyou?" he asked.

She shrugged. "Well, they say Kitsune-Hanyous have special powers, don't they? I had a friend who swore the liver of a Kitsune-Hanyou could break any spell."

And that's why Akio wants him. I have to get Rin out of there. If Naoki discovers her, he'll be sure to take her back to Akio.

He got up to leave. Aimi didn't stop him. She never did. She knew what this was. It was one of the other reasons he kept coming back; she never expected more.

"You'll be back again soon, I suspect," she said as he slid on his robe.

"Hopefully not," he replied with his back turned. He did not see the ghost of the smile on her lips as he exited without a backwards glance.

TWENTY-TWO

Hikaru paced the length of the chamber. Every so often, he went to the door and rattled it with the fruitless hope that it would open. Even if it did, there were guards outside, waiting to cut him down if he tried to escape. He ran his hands through his hair, pressing his fingers against the scars on his scalp. *I am half Kitsune.* His new reality had yet to sink in. He dropped his hands to his sides. He should have known Hotaru would try something like this. He had always resented Hikaru's place in the household, and Hikaru had been too blind to stop him. *And that's the problem. I knew he was ambitious. I knew he had no love for me and I still did nothing to stop him. If I were a better leader, I would have been able to prevent this. This is my fault.* He ceased his pacing. He could see the silhouettes of the guards outside his door. Hikaru never wanted to be a leader; that responsibility had been thrust upon him. *Perhaps it will be better if I never become elder. If Hotaru lets me live, that is.*

The guards talked together in low tones, their voices like a distant hum, the background to Hikaru's tormented thoughts. Then he heard a familiar voice mixed in with the other two. Curious, he crept closer to listen to their conversation.

"Lord Hotaru has asked to see the prisoner," Captain Sadao said.

"Can't imagine what good it will do. He's destined for the after-life," replied one of the warriors.

"You will show respect; this is our lord's brother."

The men bowed; Hikaru could see their shadows through the door.

The guards moved aside. Hikaru backed away, looking across the barren room for some sort of weapon. He would not go without a fight. Rin needed him. He needed to protect her. If his brother had moved against him, then he might try to capture everyone that was close to him.

The door slid open and Hikaru, defenseless, squared his feet and prepared to rush the door. But the captain came into the room and shut the door after him. Every muscle in Hikaru's body tensed. As a matter of posturing, Hikaru raised an eyebrow, hopefully to taunt the captain into action. Not that the captain seemed anything other than composed.

"Follow me," the captain said.

Hikaru stared at him for a moment, trying to assess if he could fight him and win. The answer was a resounding no. If the captain could best his brother, then Hikaru might as well be a fly. He decided to switch tactics. "What does my brother want from me? He's already taken control of the clan. Does he expect me to accept an honorable death by my own hand?" he said, with a self-depreciating tilt of his mouth.

The captain said nothing. He slid the door open and commanded the guards to leave. Then he gestured for Hikaru to step out first. Hikaru did so with some hesitance. Glancing down the hallway, he formulated the beginnings of a plan. He might not be able to outfight the captain, but he could surely outsmart him.

He headed towards the elder's chambers, but when he did, the captain stabbed a finger in his back. "Not that way."

"The elder's chambers are that way." Hikaru pointed in the opposite direction the captain had bullied him into. *Is he onto me?*

"They are."

Hikaru went down the hall, his heart hammering in his chest. The servants that passed them would not raise their heads. He felt as if he were on a death march. He bided his time until his chance came at last. A servant carrying a platter of food came from the opposite direction. Hikaru hurried his pace before the captain noticed. He grabbed the servant by the shoulder, spun her around and grabbed the platter from her. He tossed the platter and bowl of soup at Captain Sadao. Hot broth splashed his face as Hikaru used the momentary distraction to run.

He could not hope to outrun the captain, so he turned a corner, disappearing from sight. Thundering footsteps pursued him. He slammed open the nearest door; inside, a group of ladies chatted together. They looked up as one, eyes wide and curious. He ran through them, scattering them like a flock of birds. They shrieked and shouted curses at him as he slipped out into the garden beyond. The captain, hot on his heels, burst through the door. The ladies shouted instructions at the captain, inadvertently detaining him with their outrage.

The garden beyond was ringed by verandas and more rooms on each side. He turned a sharp right and went into a nearby room. Jumping over an empty futon, he got himself tangled in a hanging reed curtain, slowing his progress.

"Stop, you fool!" the captain shouted from the garden beyond.

Hikaru knocked over a changing screen as he left the room, creating an obstacle for the captain. He did not stop; he kept running, his mind working faster than he thought possible. Then he turned a corner and ended in another garden. He cursed his ancestors for their love of decorative plants. There were a few low bushes and a decorative pond to the right. A single pathway ran alongside it, the only escape route. Jogging up the opposite end of the path, three more guards rushed towards him. They had heard the disturbance and now they raised their blades at him.

Hikaru skidded to a stop, panting and clutching his chest. He was no athlete by any stretch of the imagination. Footsteps fell in behind him; the captain had caught up.

"Hikaru, come to me. I can help you escape."

Hikaru looked to the captain and then to the men who closed in from the opposite side. It was most likely a trap. No matter which side he chose, it meant his demise. He inhaled, then dived into the pond beside him. It was not much deeper than his shoulders. The soldiers shouted as they ran around the pond and the plants that blocked their way. He swam the short distance across the pond and then dragged his dripping body out and onto the opposite veranda. He ran through another room and burst through the other side, but the wet clothes weighed him down and made his progress slower than before. They would catch him for sure. But he had to save Rin. Nothing else mattered unless he knew she was safe.

A hand came down hard on his shoulder and he tumbled to the ground. He twisted up with his arm to punch the captain. He connected with his jaw; it felt like punching a stone. The captain pinned him to the ground, his mouth set in a grim line.

"Stop fighting me, you fool. I am trying to save you."

Hikaru panted, staring up at the captain. "You are my brother's man, you never respected me. Why would I believe you?"

"Because I am not from this household. I am not even human."

His face shifted and his eyes were a bright purple, like twilight, and there was a marking on his forehead like a tattoo or a symbol of swirling lines, which he did not know the meaning of.

"What are you?" Hikaru bit out. "How could I not see you this way before?"

"Because I am stronger than you. Will you come quietly?"

Hikaru nodded as he choked down the paltry explanation. Did it matter what he thought? No matter how far he ran, he could not escape. If the captain was not human, and he had no more reason to doubt, then there was no choice.

The captain eased off him. He grabbed his sword, which had fallen on the ground, and returned it to his sheath.

"Wait here." He slipped away, leaving Hikaru alone with his shifting reality.

Now would be the perfect time to run. But he could not make his legs obey him. So Hikaru waited for the captain to return, ears straining as he listened for the other guards. *Can I trust him? What does he have planned for me? Why save me?*

The captain returned. And he motioned for Hikaru to follow him.

"Why are you rescuing me?" he asked.

"I'm following orders."

"Whose orders?"

He did not answer.

Hikaru dug in his heels. "I'm not going anywhere with you until you tell me who ordered you to save me."

The captain looked over his shoulder. At first he thought he would not answer; then he said, "The forest guardian ordered me to save you."

His mouth fell open. This had to be a joke. But then he had thought Kitsunes were a thing of fantasy until recently as well. It wasn't that much of a stretch to believe the forest guardian wanted him. *But why?* He held his questions to himself. They slipped out into the hall, where Hikaru saw three bodies on the ground, the soldiers that had been chasing him before. He looked away. He couldn't take the guilt if the captain had killed them for his sake.

After a few moments, Hikaru spoke up. "I have to find Rin."

"There's no time."

Hikaru shook his head, but the captain's back was to him. He turned down an adjacent hall towards Rin's chamber. The captain chased after him and grabbed his arm.

Hikaru shook him loose. "I will not leave without her."

He met the captain's gaze. At first his expression was firm and it seemed unchanging; then with a heavy breath, he nodded. "But make it quick."

Hikaru ran ahead. He threw open Rin's chamber door, but found it empty, her bed unslept in. *Could she have gone to the banquet?* Fear tightened his throat. *I have to find her.* He ran out in the hall.

"She is not here," the captain said. He glanced at the sky, as if he could tell time by the stars.

"My brother may have her. If he does, he will kill her."

"If he knows what she is, then he would have brought her back to the shrine."

Hikaru headed that way.

The captain's heavy footsteps followed after him. "You cannot go there. Your brother's men will be about."

"Have you ever loved someone?"

The captain did not respond. It was a ludicrous question, and inappropriate. After a few beats, he said, "I do love someone. I will find her. Stay here."

He pushed Hikaru into an empty room and then leapt into the dark. From the doorway Hikaru saw him running along the rooftops like a bird through the clouds.

NAOKI RAN ACROSS THE ROOFTOPS AS MEN SHOUTED DOWN BELOW. Hotaru had made his move and now the palace was in chaos. Warriors raced along corridors, calling out to one another, while clan members screamed and shouted. Many would die tonight. But that was not Naoki's concern. He stretched out his senses, searching for the Kitsune in the palace; as he did, he brushed against something that surprised him. The Dragon, one of the rulers of Akatsuki, was in the palace. How he had gotten past his net was a mystery. As he brushed against his power, he sensed the Dragon's awareness. He retracted before the Dragon could get a clear read on him. He was lucky he'd cloaked his probes; to the casual observer he would appear as a lower Yokai. As he withdrew, he caught a spark of the Kitsune; they were together. *Now this could pose a problem.*

If it came down to it, he would not be a match for the Dragon. Though he was curious to meet him, he was also bound to Akio. If the Dragon knew what the guardian had planned, it could mean war among the Yokai. And he had to prevent that at all costs. Alongside the Dragon's energy was a strong spiritual presence, though it was raw like an uncut jewel. He had sensed it when she arrived; there was more to Lady Fujikawa than met the eye. They withdrew from the Kitsune, and the Dragon and Lady Fujikawa were headed in his direction, running along the rooftops. He shielded his energy and dropped into an empty courtyard below.

Pressing his back against the wall, he waited for them to pass overhead. As they approached, he felt his heart beating in his chest. The Dragon was stronger than him, a first generation Yokai, and as such, if he paused to look, he would notice the void that Naoki's shield created. His hand hovered over his sword. The Dragon stopped overhead; he imagined him scanning the horizon, drawing closer to the edge of the roof and peering over. The Dragon's energy probed against his shields, pressing against it, straining and nearly overpowering him. Naoki held his breath and focused all his energy on maintaining the shield.

"What is it, Kaito?" Lady Fujikawa asked.

"There's someone there." His footsteps drew closer, and the pressure from his energy closed in. He could feel fractures in his shield; another push and it would break and leave him exposed.

"Kaito, let's go before the guards see us."

The Dragon stepped away from the edge and said, his voice pitched away from Naoki, "You're right, I promised no more bloodshed."

Naoki listened as their footsteps receded, and did not risk expanding his own energy to track their progress. When he was sure they were gone, he resumed his search, using the halls and cutting through chambers instead. Using cloaking, he avoided guards and clung to the shadows. Men bearing blue armbands hunted in packs, murmuring to one another about Hikaru. They were looking for him. Naoki should give up this fool's errand and remove Hikaru from the palace. Then he heard shouts of the men.

"We've found the Kitsune!" Rokuro shouted.

The lieutenant held no love for Hikaru, or Rin. If he abandoned her now, her death would be on his conscience.

Cursing himself for his damn honor, Naoki slid in behind the men as they closed in around Rin. She was trapped in a garden, men in a half circle around her with blades drawn. Her eyes darted from one to the other as she backed up slowly. Naoki drew his blade. He would avoid spilling human blood if he could, but he had his orders.

Silent and unseen, he crept up behind the first man. His blade slid into his back before he had time to cry out, blood bubbling up to his lips. "I am sorry," he said as the man dropped to the ground. A second man saw the man drop dead; from their vantage point he would have died from a wound delivered by an invisible hand. He shouted, pointing at his brother in arms. As he lowered his sword to gawk, Naoki swung his blade across his gut. The man clutched at his wound; then a third and fourth turned, spinning in circles, looking for their unseen assailant.

"This is the Kitsune's power. Kill her before she kills us!" Rokuro shouted.

Rin watched him. She alone could see him as he swung and slashed, killing them with ease. As each man fell, he whispered their name. He knew each one, had drunk with them; Sadao's memories flooded him, weighing him down. Though the skin he wore was false, for a time he had shared their lives with them; he would never forget them. Last of all was Rokuro with his back to Naoki.

"You killed my brothers! Just like you killed Jun in the forest. I'll make you pay!" He raised his sword and ran towards her.

Rin looked away as Naoki swung his sword a final time and

separated the man's head from his body. Humans were no match for his skill with the blade. It was not fair to them that they must die. Then he turned to the Kitsune. She faced him with composure, but he saw how her hands shook. He sheathed his blade as he took a step towards her. Then suddenly her eyes fluttered shut and she pitched forward, collapsing into his arms. "What would you have me do with her?" he asked the witch, who had crept up behind him. It was her spell that had put the Kitsune to sleep.

"Bring her to the young lord," the witch said.

He did not want to trust the witch. But even now with the blood of innocents on his hands, he wanted to save his beloved more. He had come this far, he could not turn back now.

"I know you're not going to let her go, why not take her?" he asked.

The witch smiled. "Because she still has a job to do for me. She must kill Hikaru."

SHIN ARRIVED TO A PALACE IN CHAOS. THE HUMANS SHOUTED TO ONE another, their voices melding together into one agitated humming sound, the backdrop to his search for Rin. The Dragon was near, he could feel him and a human with immense spiritual power very close by. The Dragon would know what to do; together they would be able to stop Akio.

He found them running along the rooftops, hand in hand. When the Dragon saw Shin, he held up his hand to stop the woman. She looked at him, curious but unafraid. She was pretty, by human standards. He wondered what she was doing with the Dragon. A part of him had hoped he had come here to save Rin. But perhaps he had been hoping for too much.

"Shin," the Dragon said. There was a threat in his tone and Shin took a step back.

Shin bowed low to the Dragon. "Master, we've been looking for you."

"And you have not found me."

"Master?"

"Do I need to explain? You cannot tell anyone we met here. If my enemies discovered..." His gaze slid to the side where the woman was holding his hand.

The truth hit him like a punch to the gut. He had thought Rin and the Dragon... then the real reason he had disappeared was because of this woman. The Dragon had taken a human lover, more than that, a human with spiritual powers. Then the rumors were true. He never thought he would see the day. If Akio, or any of his other enemies knew, they would use her against him. For someone in the Dragon's position, a human could be his greatest weakness. For a moment his loyalty to the Dragon warred against his desire to save Rin.

In the end, loyalty won out. "I will keep my silence, Master." He bowed his head.

The Dragon smiled and patted Shin on the shoulder as he passed by, whisking his woman off into the night. Shin let him go. If the Dragon lingered any longer in this place, then they would be found out. He would have to save Rin on his own.

He ran along the rooftops in the opposite direction of the Dragon to Rin's room. He landed in the courtyard. The entire place smelled of her, but she was not there. He could tell right away. Nothing was disturbed, but he could not shake the sense that something was out of place. The humans were running around; blood was on the air. *What is going on here?*

He crept out into the hall, and invisible to the humans, he listened to their conversations.

"Report!" said a grizzled warrior in a blue mask.

"Lady Fujikawa is missing, and we cannot find Lord Hikaru," said his underling.

"Do not stop searching until you find them both," the leader snapped. The younger warrior bowed and hurried to do his bidding.

He continued his search, following the scent of Rin. She had climbed over rooftops to the heart of the palace. The scent of human blood was everywhere. Rin's trail ended in a garden; he dropped down into it. Bodies of slain men lay on the ground, their limbs at odd angles. Shin walked through the carnage, searching for Rin, but her scent had been overpowered by the smell of death. She had been here. Perhaps moments before, but she was gone.

"She is no longer here, Shin," said an unfamiliar voice.

The hairs on the back of his neck rose up on end. He turned around to find an old woman grinning at him.

"Who are you? How do you know my name?"

She cackled. "I know much about you. As for me, I lost my name long ago."

He frowned at her. His energy burned just beneath his skin, waiting to be unleashed to transform, should she prove dangerous.

"Did you do this?" he asked, motioning to the dead bodies.

"No, but you know who did."

"Naoki." He said his name like a curse.

"He has your Kitsune."

He swore and motioned to chase after her when her words stopped him. "You cannot hope to defeat him on your own."

He stopped and turned to look at her. He had not felt her spiritual power at first, but now he could, and she was even more powerful than the woman who had been with the Dragon. "And you can?"

She laughed. "I am only a human. But you can, with my help."

He raised an eyebrow, inclined to be skeptical, but he wanted to hear what she had to say.

"I have a charm here. If you use it, you'll be able to control Naoki. Just place it on his forehead and he'll do as you bid."

She held out a small stone with swirling markings on it. He stared at it, afraid to take it from her. Getting this on Naoki would be no easy task. He was a skilled swordsmen, known all through Akatsuki as a great fighter.

"Why should I trust you?"

"Who said anything about trust?"

He hesitated a moment longer before snatching it from her hand. "If this does not work, I will find you, old woman."

She bowed her head. "I am counting on it."

HIKARU WAITED FOR WHAT SEEMED AN ETERNITY. HE WRUNG HIS hands to avoid pulling at the tattered threads at the edge of his sleeve. Then he saw the shadow approaching—two figures. He stepped out from within the room until he realized the two approaching were not Rin and the captain but an unknown man and Lady Fujikawa.

At first he thought he should be alarmed until his wife reached for the unknown man's hand and squeezed. The look she bestowed upon the stranger held all the emotion and warmth Hikaru had never received from her. He held his breath and watched as they disappeared over the edge of the roof. In his heart he had known they were not meant for one another, but he was glad she had found her happiness. His only reservation was the ruined treaty. Before he could consider it further, the captain appeared with Rin in his arms. Her head lolled to one side.

"What happened to her?"

"It is safer to transport her this way," the captain said.

Hikaru eyed the captain but held his tongue. Hikaru took Rin from the captain, despite his protests. She was his responsibility. The weight of Rin's head on his shoulder was reassuring; he could feel her heart beating against his, steady and alive. With the captain leading the way, they slipped into the night through the palace.

"I saw a man with my wife. A friend of yours?" Hikaru asked.

The captain hesitated and then with a nod said, "I know of him."

"Care to explain? That's my wife he has with him."

"Who do you care about more, your wife or her? I can only rescue one woman tonight."

He felt guilty for not fighting for Lady Fujikawa, but there was only one choice for him. "Let's get out of here."

They managed to steal their way into the courtyard, where horses were waiting for them. They were not like any horses he had seen before. They had hair that rippled in the wind as if their very manes were made of living fire. Their coats were pure white. Hikaru reached out a hand to touch their fiery manes. It was warm but did not burn. He gently laid Rin over the back of the first as the captain swung into the saddle of the other. The warm flames tickled his skin as he rested Rin's head against his chest.

The gate to the palace was closed as they cantered through the courtyard. Guards stood guard, weapons drawn. Hikaru looked to the captain for guidance, but he did not break stride as they galloped full speed straight for the men. The guards held their ground, unblinking. Hikaru closed his eyes, prepared for a collision. But before they collided, the horses leapt into the air, sailing over the palace walls. He looked down as the ground came rushing back to them. The guards had not even turned their heads. It was as if they had not seen them at all. The animals landed silently and then they flew through the night, racing over the countryside. The horses' feet did not even seem to touch the ground. They were some distance from the palace when a wolf appeared. It was a massive beast, larger than any of the smaller forest creatures he was accustomed to. It ran alongside them and then abruptly cut in front of them. The captain brought them to a sudden stop and Hikaru nearly fell from his saddle.

The wolf growled at them, its teeth bared.

"Move, Okami," the captain said.

Then from a rumbling throat the wolf replied, "I will not let you take Rin."

TWENTY-THREE

Rin fell, her shoulder slammed into the ground, and her eyes flew open. The air crackled. She scrambled away just in time to avoid the stomping of the horse's hooves. Flaming hooves, these were no average horses. *These animals are from the forest.* She got to her feet and saw the back of a man as he swung a blade at a wolf. *Shin!* She ran forward, intent on stopping the man from attacking Shin, but someone grabbed her around the middle and stopped her.

"Rin, don't, they'll kill you," Hikaru whispered into her ear.

She wrenched her neck backward, tensing in his grip.

What is going on?

Shin and the man circled one another. The hairs on Shin's back were raised and his lips pulled back, revealing rows of pointed teeth. He growled and snapped, goading the man into attacking. *I thought he had left me for good.* She was relieved he had not abandoned her but also furious he had come back. She could see from the way the man struck like a snake, he was no mere mortal. She knew him; it was the guardian's man.

Hikaru pulled her back and she watched in horror as Shin and Akio's dog battled. They met in the middle, blade flying and white fur all ablur. Rin clutched onto Hikaru's arm, unable to tear her eyes away from the fight. The man swung his sword and it bit into Shin's shoulder. Blood poured from the wound in a sickening trail down his foreleg. Rin clenched tighter; she must have been drawing blood from Hikaru's flesh. Shin snapped at the man's arm and caught a length of his sleeve, which he tore free.

Shin spun around, putting himself between the man and Hikaru and Rin.

"Get Rin out of here," Shin snarled at Hikaru.

Rin shook her head. She looked at Hikaru, begging him not to do it with her eyes.

"We cannot stay here," Hikaru agreed.

Whose side was he on? She did not know. She tried to pull away, but he had a firm grip on her arm.

"I don't know what either of them wants, but my first goal is to keep you safe."

Shin lunged for the man again, heedless of how powerless she was in this form. But Hikaru pulled her back before she got very far. The man grunted as Shin's jaws grazed his collar. Hikaru guided her away, holding onto her shoulders as she strained to watch her best friend fight for his life. Hikaru helped her onto the back of the Yokai horse. The animal was accommodating, but it flicked its tail back and forth and its ears pointed back. These creatures had a master, and because they were willing, it meant their escape was their master's will. She felt powerless. If she had her fox fire, she could help Shin instead of abandoning him.

Hikaru kicked the horse in the ribs and then they were flying through the night. She did not know where he was taking her and she did not care. Whoever provided the horses would find them no matter where they went. Her mind with Shin, she clung onto Hikaru's arm as she looked over his shoulder, watching the fight as it grew smaller and smaller in the distance.

They ran over rice paddies and closer to the forest they went. She wondered if the horse was taking them to their master, but then they made a sudden turn onto a country road. Hikaru pulled up short and the horse came to a stop. It pawed the ground with its flaming hooves and snorted clouds of sulfur. Hikaru slid down and then helped Rin join him on the ground. When they were both safely on foot, he slapped the horse on the rear and sent it running. He watched it go for a few moments before turning back to Rin.

"I do not trust that beast or Captain Sadao. So I thought we should send it away."

She nodded if only to placate him. Akio would find her; it was only the question of whether it would be before the witch's spell turned her into a fox or not. She linked hands with Hikaru, looking for comfort. The road was empty but for the moonlight that guided their path. It was not that different than the place where he had found her after the witch's spell had stripped her of her voice.

He squeezed her hand and smiled. "There's somewhere we can go where I think we will be safe."

She smiled at him, though it was halfhearted. Tonight was the last night; there was nowhere he would be safe with her. She still had to choose, him or her. They walked down the country road in silence. Rin's thoughts chased themselves in circles. When she wasn't worried about Shin, she was wondering why the Dragon had not recognized her, or worrying how she would break the spell without killing Hikaru. If she didn't break it, then she would turn into a fox come sunrise.

They skirted the forest; sparsely spaced trees rustled in the breeze. They watched them like dark sentinels. Rin peered into the gloom, cursing her human vision. There would be Yokai in the shadows watching them. As it was, the short hairs on the back of her neck prickled in warning. The witch should be here any moment to taunt or gloat, but she had not come to find her. The forest grew dense all of a sudden and the shadows longer, and she swore she saw eyes watching them from behind trees. The hillside went upwards into the mountains. On the right-hand side of the road, there was a red archway. One the humans used to keep out evil spirits. She stared up at it for a moment. The paint was faded and worn, splintered wood exposed beneath the peeling paint.

"Up here," he said as he tugged her along. She followed him up the multitude of steps. The forest had started to creep in and the undergrowth grew over the steps and obscured them from view. Rin tripped and Hikaru caught her around the waist. She smiled at him in thanks and they continued their climb. At the top of the steps, the shrine was in disrepair. The roofs had holes and the cobblestones were patchworked with grass and roots that had pushed through. There were two buildings total, one temple and one caretaker hut. Hikaru let go of Rin's hand.

"Wait here. I am going to make sure we're alone."

She let him go, but the uneasy feeling had not left her. She could not be certain if it was because they were being watched our just her own anxiety creeping up on her. Hikaru returned a few moments later.

"There's some bedding in the caretaker's cottage. We should rest while we can."

She followed him into the caretaker's hut. A worn futon, with frayed edges and patches on it, was laid in the center of the room. She looked to Hikaru. *How did you know about this place?*

"I've been coming here since I was a boy. It was my escape when the palace became too much to bear," he said as he rubbed the back of his neck.

She touched him gently on the shoulder. *It's nice.* They went into the hut and she sat on the futon. *I cannot keep worrying about Shin. He can handle himself. It's me I should be worried about.*

Hikaru knelt down on the futon beside her. He had his back to her at first.

"This is not how I thought this would happen." He sighed.

She looked down at her hands. This was not her idea of a happily ever after either. For one of them this would be the end.

"You never answered my question, but I guess I should rephrase the question. My wife, it seems, has run off with another man."

Rin smiled. *Indeed she has.*

He turned around and took Rin's hands in his. "Rin, will you be my wife?"

His question stole the breath from her lungs. She had no proper answer because there was no future for them. So she kissed him instead. Time was so precious, there was no use wasting time explaining. They shed their robes, his sopping wet, and fumbled under the slightly musty sheets. When they were finished, Hikaru fell asleep. She lay on his chest, her mind still whirling. Daylight was not far off. *It's his life or mine, but how can you choose such a thing?* Then a cold chill ran up her spine. Rin sat up in bed. A shadow passed outside the door. She got up and went to the entryway. There was no one there. She looked down at her feet, and at her feet laid the dagger, the same white bone-handled dagger the witch had given her.

Rin scooped it up off the ground. *I have to make a choice. Kill Hikaru and save myself or become a fox.*

She looked down at the dagger once more before turning and heading back inside, where Hikaru slept on unaware. She stood in the doorway for a moment, watching him sleep. He had stretched out, grasping for her in the empty space she left behind. She padded across the room and knelt down beside him. The blade felt warm, as if it had a life of its own. *I must choose.*

She stared down at him, memorizing every line of his face, the curve of his throat, the angle of his cheekbones, and committed all the light and shadow that made up his features to memory. She always wanted to remember the way it felt to kiss him, to feel his heart beat in time with hers, and the way he had loved her. The night had grown lighter; the darkness faded to morning. She sat cross-legged on the futon, staring down at Hikaru, watching the rise and fall of his chest. Her hands trembled so bad she almost dropped the knife. .

I'm sorry, Hikaru...

HE HELD BACK FROM FIGHTING THE OKAMI WITH HIS FULL STRENGTH; not because he did not want to win, but because killing the Dragon's right hand would start a war. And he had sworn above all else to prevent that. No matter how much else he compromised in his quest, he could not do that. But the Okami had no such concerns, he flung himself at Naoki with abandon, teeth snapping and tearing at Naoki's robe. He slashed wide, made superficial cuts, and moved slowly, giving the Okami a chance to dodge, to run. When the Okami spotted Hikaru and Rin fleeing, he tried to pursue them. Naoki launched into the air, flying over the Okami and landing in his path. He brandished his sword, keeping the Okami from advancing. The Okami's red eyes were like bright embers burning in his white fur. His fangs bared, saliva dripped from his jaw onto the ground.

"Let me pass," he growled.

Naoki did not respond, but stared down at the Okami as he tightened his grip on the blade.

"You have no right to interfere," the Okami snarled.

"Do you fear the human?" he taunted. He hated to be reduced to such childish tactics, but he was short on patience and time. If Rin did not kill Hikaru, he would lose his chance to save Tsukiko.

The wolf inched forward. "I will not let Akio have Rin."

"And the human will not take her to him."

"But Akio wants the Hanyou," the wolf corrected.

He had tried to hide Hikaru's identity, but now that word was out, there was no use pretending anymore. He nodded his head.

"Then I cannot leave her with him."

He rushed towards Naoki, and when he prepared to swing and cut him down, the Okami faked right and slipped past him. Naoki gave chase and this time he did not hold back. He sheathed his sword and sprinted after the wolf, catching up in a few strides. He stretched out his energy like a myriad of tentacles wrapping around the wolf's body, tugging him back and slowing him down. He encased the wolf in his energy, freezing him in place. As the Okami lost the use of his limbs, he fell face forward into the dirt, his feet bound up beneath him. Naoki strode over to stand above the Okami, frozen in place, his mouth trapped in a snarl. Naoki hated himself for what he had done to his own kind, the sacrifices he would continue to make to save Tsukiko. He wove his energy around the Okami like a net, binding him in place as he drew from the wolf's energy. It would not hold him for long, just until the next morning. But that would be long enough to let Rin do what she must and fulfill the witch's desires.

"I do not want to do this, believe me, but I have no choice."

Shin's expression could not change, but hatred radiated from his gaze. When the spell was cast, Naoki turned to leave, but when he turned around, the witch was waiting for him. He had been so focused on trapping the Okami he had not sensed her approach.

She smiled at him. "You've done well."

He gave a sidelong glance over his shoulder towards the Okami. He could see the witch and hear everything they were saying.

"Have I?"

"You did everything I asked, betrayed your master and your own kind. You deserve a reward."

His gut clenched. This was it, what he had sacrificed everything for.

"Tell me where she is!" He never raised his voice, but the sound of it was harsh against his own ears. He heard his own desperation, carefully hidden for so long now, break free with his eagerness.

"She is beyond your reach, in a place you cannot tread. She is asleep atop Mount Iwaki."

Rage built inside him like a slow-building fire. It was a lie, it had to be.

"Are you telling me that she sleeps on top of a holy place? One where none but the Kami may tread?"

The witch cackled. "Oh, one other can reach it, though she does not know it yet."

"Who is she?"

She shook her head. "That was not part of the deal."

He unsheathed his blade and rushed for her, but when his blade should have met flesh, instead it ripped through smoke. And the witch was gone. Disappeared like mist. Only the sound of her mocking laughter remained. She had tricked him. He should have known he could not trust her from the start. But he had been blinded by his quest. He turned back to the Okami, intent on silencing him. He had not wanted to kill him, but the witch left him without a choice. But instead he found a jaw full of teeth snapping and tearing. He had no time to defend himself before he was slammed into the ground.

TWENTY-FOUR

They tussled on the ground, Shin snapping and biting while Naoki grabbed onto his shoulders, trying to flip him off him. But he would not relent, he had tried to keep him from Rin, and that had been his mistake, but now he had something even more powerful. He had information. They rolled around on the ground, Naoki tried to draw his blade, but Shin grabbed the hilt in his jaws and tossed it aside. It went flying end over end before landing somewhere in a rice paddy nearby. After a few more minutes of furious fighting, Naoki lay back and ceased fighting. Shin held his jaws over his throat, waiting for him to struggle, to try to reach his sword, but it seemed all the fight had gone out of Naoki.

He growled in his throat. "Will you come quietly?"

Naoki did not meet his gaze but turned his head without speaking. Shin did not back down, in case this was a trap. He waited a few moments before transforming into his man form. He held his hands to Naoki's throat. He felt weak from the energy Naoki had taken, but in his palm was the charm the witch had handed him. He pressed it against Naoki's forehead.

Naoki's back arched upward and he screamed. Shin stared down at him, unfeeling. This bastard would have killed Shin to keep his betrayal secret. Well, too bad for Naoki that the witch was more treacherous than he realized. When Naoki ceased convulsing, Shin stepped back and stared down at his limp form on the ground. His eyes were open and staring at the starry sky above.

"Get up," Shin commanded. As the witch had said, the charm controlled him. Naoki jumped to his feet and did Shin's bidding. Shin turned and Naoki followed. And together they went to the forest and Akio. Considering he had never expected to be able to defeat the guardian's sword arm, he was happy to be alive. Had the witch not come around and given him this charm, he might be dead and Rin in danger. What did the witch want from him? He had seen how she betrayed Naoki, so he knew he could not trust her.

They passed through the forest quickly and without challenge. When they arrived at the bridge to the guardian's palace, they found it unguarded. They crossed the bridge, Shin looking over his shoulder, waiting for the charm to wear off and Naoki to turn on him. When he arrived in the courtyard, with Naoki trussed up, servants appeared and showed him the way through the maze that was the guardian's palace. The guardian waited for them in an informal chamber. He dominated the room, wearing his sleeping robes. The servants announced Shin and then exited. When the three of them were alone, Akio looked Shin up and down, a greedy glint in his eyes.

"I was surprised when they said you had defeated my sword. But it seems it is true." He flickered his gaze towards Naoki, who kept his head bowed. "How did you manage such a feat?"

"I'm a skilled fighter," Shin replied.

The guardian laughed. "Perhaps." He folded his arms over his chest and glowered down at Shin. "What do you want for his return?"

"This is not a ransom. I have information about your man that you may find of interest."

Akio's gaze flickered to Naoki then back to Shin. "Do you now?"

"He planned to betray you to a witch. But she turned on him at the last moment."

"Did he now?" Akio glared at Naoki, a fire in his eyes Shin was glad was not directed at him. "It seems I have kept too slack a leash."

Shin could see why he had betrayed the guardian. No man could serve such a cruel master without some resentment. If he didn't need Akio's favor to save Rin, he would have been more sympathetic.

"Thank you for bringing him to me. I will see he is punished for his crimes," Akio added.

"I did not bring him here out of the goodness of my heart. I came to make a deal."

Akio pressed his hooves together. "I should have suspected as much. What is it that you desire?"

"I want a pardon for Rin."

"Now that is an interesting proposition. But you see, she has broken my laws, consorted with humans, and injured my men. She has to pay for her crimes."

"I could always bring Naoki to the Dragon for his judgment."

A dangerous look sparked in Akio's gaze. Naoki had secrets the Dragon would love to hear. And Shin knew Akio would not let him go so easily. Akio shook his head. "No, you're right, but it will take more than a wayward pet to get out of this."

"What do you have in mind, then?"

"I want the Hanyou. My servant"—he shot a pointed look in Naoki's direction—"was supposed to bring him to me. But if you can bring me him, then I will consider a pardon in exchange for him."

"Done."

WHEN SHIN LEFT, NAOKI KNELT DOWN ON THE GROUND IN FRONT OF Akio. Even pretending to be loyal, which he had done from the beginning, filled him with shame. He had no love for Akio, and only his spell kept him bound to him at all. But still he went through the motions. And his recent failure only filled him with bitterness.

"Master," he said without inflection.

"I'm disappointed, Naoki. I thought you were better than this."

He did not reply. There was nothing he could say in his defense. His only regret was he had not seen Tsukiko one last time. He looked at the ground, preparing for Akio's judgment and his punishment.

"I am not going to kill you. I am not that crude," Akio said.

Naoki did not lift his head, lest he show his shock. "What do you plan on doing with me, then?"

"I have need of you. War is coming and there is yet time for you to prove yourself."

"And the witch?"

"I will deal with her in short order. But I suspect this is just a taste of her meddling." He frowned. "We will need to be even more vigilant than ever."

"Yes, Master."

"Do not disappoint me again, Naoki. I will not be as forgiving next time."

He bowed deep. There was still time, another chance to find this woman who could free Tsukiko. He knew Akio was being generous because he had won, but then and there he swore to himself: This was not the end. He would find Tsukiko and he would end the guardian's life with his bare hands.

What was one Hanyou's life compared to Rin's?

He awoke with the first rays of sunlight pressing against his eyelids. He did not open them at first. He wanted to savor this moment, just Rin and him blissfully tangled together. *She is going to be my wife.* He reached out blindly for her, trying to pull her closer. What he found was empty space. He opened his eyes; Rin knelt next to the futon, a knife in her hand.

"Rin, what are you doing?" His eyes flickered to the knife and then to the desperate expression on her face. Her hands trembled.

She threw the knife aside and tears rolled down her cheeks. He took her hand in his and rubbed his thumb across her knuckles. Her entire body shook; there was a wild desperate energy in her. *She was not doing what I think she was...*

"Let's talk. Why did you have a dagger? Did someone threaten you?"

She shook her head and then she glanced through the open door. Sunlight crept across the room, inching towards her.

Before he could question her, she leaned forward and kissed him. It was hard, fierce, and sad all at the same time. She pulled away from him too suddenly for him to process what was happening. She strode across the room and stood in the sunlight. The beams of light illuminated her as if she were set ablaze. Her body glowed amber, gold, and red. Her hair fell in a coppery cascade over her shoulders, her head topped with red fox ears, and a foxtail swished back and forth behind her.

She smiled. "I'm sorry, Hikaru, this is goodbye."

It was her voice, sweet and sad. He realized then what she was doing, she was leaving him. He jumped up just as her body contorted and she transformed into a fox. The sun had risen and filled the one-room cottage with light. The fox looked around as if in a daze. When her eyes fell on Hikaru, she skittered backwards and headed out into the courtyard. He chased after her, calling out her name. Her ears did not even twitch in his direction. She darted behind trees and rocks to keep from being seen. *She's acting like a real fox.* Then the truth came crashing down upon him. The reason she had said goodbye wasn't because she was leaving him willingly, it was because whatever curse she had been under had turned her into a fox. She was gone. The fox hid in the crawlspace beneath the shrine. She stared out at him with golden eyes that glimmered in the dark. Hikaru fell to his knees, his head in his hands. *I lost her.*

"What have you done?" came a growl from behind him.

Hikaru stood up. The man, the wolf creature who had killed the soldier, stood at the edge of the courtyard. His clothes were torn and bloody and his hands were half formed into claws. Hikaru recognized the threat in his voice and looked for a weapon with which to defend himself. A piece of splintered wood lay on the ground; he darted for it. The wolf rushed towards him, and Hikaru snatched up the board just before the wolf's jaws could clamp down on his arm. He swung it upward, striking him hard across the skull. The wood shattered into a hundred pieces. Hikaru stumbled backwards. The wolf approached him, teeth bared as he loomed over Hikaru, but before he could attack, the fox jumped in front of him and landed on Hikaru's lap. She growled at the wolf.

He glowered at her with golden eyes but slowly backed away. Hikaru's heart pounded in his chest, hard enough to drown out the low rumble of the wolf.

"It was the curse, it turned her into a fox," Hikaru said. The fox was curled up in his lap now, her head facing the wolf.

The wolf's claws retracted and he crossed human arms over his chest. But there remained a dangerous light in his eye. Hikaru was not out of harm's way just yet. The wolf looked down at Hikaru, his eyebrows raised.

"Who are you?" The question came out sounding more intimidating than he thought it would. Hikaru rested a protective hand on Rin's furry head. She pushed against his touch. Her eyes never left the wolf.

The wolf glowered at him; his eyes had a yellow feral cast. He opened his mouth and revealed elongated canines sharp enough to tear him down to the bone. He did not look away, dared not, lest the madman tear out his throat. "I'm a friend of hers."

"Then if you have any love for her, you will not harm me."

The wolf laughed, more like barked without humor. "I love her." There was a bitter taste to his words.

And in that they had something they could agree upon. It wasn't much to start negotiations with, but he'd worked with less. "I swear I will find a way to return her to the way she was."

"She was supposed to kill you," he growled. "I should do what she did not have the heart for."

The fox lifted her head and stared at the wolf. He met her gaze and they looked at one another. Hikaru wondered if they could communicate. *She became this to save me.* He wound his fingers into her fur.

"I would kill you if it wasn't for her," the wolf added.

Hikaru ignored him. If the wolf loved Rin, he would not risk going against her wishes. He had learned in their short time together that she had that sort of effect on people. Rin's will was indisputable. She glanced back at him, golden eyes full of reassurance. *Does she have a human conscious inside the fox body?*

"Who can break this spell?" Hikaru asked.

The wolf scoffed. "As if I would tell you."

Hikaru stood up and displaced the fox. She slid off and wound herself around his legs. The wolf's gaze flickered towards her and a frown pulled down his face.

"Fine. Don't help me if you wish, but I am going to find a way to fix this."

The wolf laughed, a long mocking sound. Rin jumped up and the hairs on her back were standing on end as she stared at the wolf, her teeth bared. Hurt flashed briefly across the wolf's features but was quickly hidden behind his arrogant, intimidating mask.

"What's so funny?" Hikaru asked, arms crossed over his chest.

"Run back to the humans. I will break her curse."

The wolf thought him a fool, easily intimidated and easily dismissed. And for his entire life, he had been. He'd done everything his father asked of him, observed every protocol and every tradition. And what had it gotten him—secrets, lies and betrayal. He was done listening to others; it was about time he did what he wanted for a change. He stomped over to stand toe to toe with the wolf. "I refuse to leave with her like this."

The wolf shook his head. "You are a fool. I have not changed my mind about killing you. It wouldn't take much, just a quick twist of the neck." He held up his clawed hand and flexed it in front of Hikaru's face.

"Just like that guard you murdered and that serving girl at the palace," Hikaru said. He sounded much braver than he felt. His stomach flopped back and forth.

The wolf narrowed his eyes at Hikaru. "What serving girl?"

"A woman at the palace, she died at the hand of some beast. They blamed it on Rin, but I never believed she could do something so vile."

"But you think me capable?"

Hikaru did not answer. Rin came up and rubbed against the wolf's legs. He looked down at her for a moment. Then very slowly he crouched down and stroked her behind the ear. Hikaru stood over him and watched as the wolf petted the fox.

"I did not kill the girl. It was most likely the forest guardian who did."

"Why would he do that?"

"He was looking for her. Some of these messengers he sends are... bloodthirsty. They get distracted easily." He shrugged. "The girl most likely got in the way."

He was trying to scare him, but Hikaru was not so easily deterred.

"Are you going to help me or not?"

The wolf sighed. "There's only one person who can help. You most likely will have to pay a steep price—especially if he wants Rin. You'd be handing her to him on a silver platter." The wolf did not look at him; he continued stroking the fox. Then after a few moments, he gently pushed the fox off his lap and stood up. When the wolf was standing, he was a head taller than Hikaru, better muscled and a Yokai. He could rip Hikaru apart limb from limb without breaking a sweat. Hikaru knew this, but he could also see a comrade, he saw his feelings reflected in the wolf's expression. The wolf loved her as well. This wolf, though violent and arrogant, cared for Rin, and perhaps that was enough to bind them together.

"And you're willing to take it because you love her?" Hikaru asked.

The wolf looked up at him, his golden eyes glowing. "Do not pretend to understand."

"I don't care what the cost is, I have to try. Whatever the guardian wants, I will give it. I cannot let her remain this way." Hikaru pointed to Rin. She wandered around the courtyard, sniffing at trees.

The wolf watched her as well, the expression on his face difficult to read. "She never should have meddled in human affairs," he muttered. "Very well, I will bring you, but if you fall behind or slow me down, I will leave you to the forest's mercy."

"Thank you." Hikaru bowed to the wolf. It only seemed appropriate.

He laughed again. "Don't thank me just yet, human. We're heading into the forest guardian's domain and he is known for his hatred of humans. You'll be lucky if you make it out alive."

Hikaru swallowed past a lump in his throat. "What are we waiting for, then?"

Shin smiled, it was faint and faded quickly, but it was a smile. *At least that's a start.*

TWENTY-FIVE

The forest was quiet. Too quiet for it to be mere coincidence. There was no sound, not even the errant cry of a bird. The absence of the forest creatures, and even the wind in the trees, left the forest feeling empty. *Does Akio plan on double-crossing me?* Shin thought. The only sound was the human's clumsy plodding footsteps.

Shin had run ahead, checking for a trap. He had to protect Rin. Her turning into a fox was an added complication, but once he got her freed from Akio, perhaps the Dragon could return her to normal. He glanced back over his shoulder; the fox sniffed at some nearby bushes. She had followed them without much coaxing. It gave him hope that some of Rin remained locked inside. He stretched out his spiritual energy, searching for other Yokai. Something pricked at his senses like a finger plucking a string. They were not alone. He turned and doubled back to Rin and the human.

"What's wrong?" The human's voice echoed around the forest, amplified by the lack of competing sounds.

Shin ran a finger across his throat to indicate silence. The human clamped his mouth shut so fast he might have swallowed his own tongue. Shin smelled the air, his superior sense of smell detected something nearby, but it was muddled with the scent of earth, decaying plant matter and the human's fear. *If I were alone, then this would not be a problem. I could search out whatever is following us and eliminate it.* He scanned the forest, weighing his options. Dare he abandon the human now and risk the guardian's wrath?

Then a heavy fog rolled in from between the trees. It crept across the ground like a slug and brought with it the scent of decay but not plants this time, this was the sickening sweet smell of decaying flesh. Shin focused the flow of his spiritual energy to his nose and ears; enhancing those senses allowed him to get a better sense of what danger waited in the mist. His fangs elongated and his claws came out. He was prepared to transform into his true form.

"Shin?" the human shouted into the mist. It had swallowed him whole and Rin along with him. The mist carried such an overpowering scent of death and dirt that Shin could not locate them. He growled deep in his throat. *What games are you playing, Akio?* He transformed into a beast, a massive white wolf, big enough that his head brushed against the branches. He bounded through the mist in the direction he had last seen the human. But the fog played tricks on his senses, and instead he ran about in circles. He passed by the same tree for the third time before clawing at it with his massive paw in frustration. He was back where he started. He might as well have been chasing his own tail. Then he heard the human shout, then a screeched followed by the crunch of bones breaking. Silence followed.

Shin howled; his voice echoed back at him from all corners. *Damn it.* If anything happened to Rin, he didn't know what he would do. He rushed forward through the mist again, and at last it let him pass through. He came out into a clearing. A hunched figure holding a blade loomed over a body on the ground. Most likely one of the guardian's warriors had caught the human. *How am I going to explain this to Rin?* Shin growled and lunged at the figure. He pinned him to the ground with massive paws.

The warrior swung his sword covered to the hilt in blood. The fog blocked his features, but it was dissipating and the faceless attacker transformed into the human. Shin leaped backwards off him. He switched from beast to man.

The human knelt on hands and knees, his body shaking as he gasped for air.

When he regained his bearings, he shouted, "You tried to kill me!"

"I was trying to save you. You idiot," Shin said with a sneer.

"From what? I already killed the thing that attacked us!" He swung a bloody hand, gesturing to the gray-green corpse. It was not anyone Shin knew, fortunately, but a ghastly looking creature. It had gray-green skin and long stringy black hair that hardly covered the top of its spotted head. It was twice the size of a man, with large hands with blackened nails. A filthy loincloth was its only clothing. It looked like it had been a human once, but the flesh had started to fall from its body and revealed its rib cage and half of the jaw.

"Was this a test?" Shin wondered aloud as he looked down at the dead thing. He would not admit he was surprised and maybe even a little bit impressed that this tiny human had managed to slay the creature on his own. It had to be a fluke. There were limits to Shin's kindness. "We better get going. The guardian knows we're here; this thing will not be the last."

"You mean there's more?" The human's voice shook and he sounded ready to choke on his own bile.

"Yes, most likely worse," Shin said without looking back over his shoulder. He could not help but smirk at the human's fear. Teasing the human released some of the tension he was feeling.

Rin trotted up and nuzzled the human's hand. The human pulled her close to his chest. Shin looked away before he lost his temper. Rin could not really care for that Hanyou, could she?

They trudged onward. The forest remained silent, as if the inhabitants were watching and waiting to see what happened next.

They found a forest path, and since Akio knew they were coming, Shin decided they might as well use it. There were no more attacks, which felt more suspicious than anything. *What is he doing? Why send one attack? Why leave us in suspense?* The guardian may very well be leading him into a trap designed to start a war with the Dragon. At last they arrived at the bridge that led into the guardian's palace. A canyon separated it from the forest. The swinging rope bridge was their last obstacle, it seemed. Shin looked about, expecting hundreds of slathering simpleminded Yokai to come pouring out of the canyon and attempt to strip their flesh from their bones.

"Is this it?" the human asked.

Shin nodded. He looked at the bridge. It appeared intact and he could not sense any danger, which was suspicious in itself. "It is. But I smell a trap."

The human sniffed the air as if he could scent danger. Shin rolled his eyes—humans were so simple.

"If that's all that lies between me and saving Rin, I am going to cross." Hikaru walked a few steps, but before he could take a step onto the bridge, a puff of smoke billowed in front of him. The smoke parted and revealed a man within. He had red hair that rippled and moved like a flame and black charred skin that crackled like embers in a fire.

Shin scowled; he should have known the guardian would send him.

"Kasai, what are you doing here?" Shin asked.

Kasai laughed. "Shin, what a pleasant surprise. I can assume your master was not the one to send you on this errand?"

"You and Akio both know he was not."

"No, the Dragon has been distracted as of late, has he not?"

Shin gritted his teeth. Was that what these games were about? Getting information on the Dragon?

"Let us cross," the human said. He held his sword out as if he held a threat to the fire Yokai.

Kasai grabbed the tip of the human's sword. It glowed red, spreading from the tip down to the hilt. The human dropped the blade with a curse. He blew on his hands where the sword had burned them.

"I do not play with swords, human. I am man who uses his words." He winked at the human. Sparks flew off of his head and spurted and died.

"I don't have time for games. What do we need to do to pass?" Shin asked. He looked over at Rin. She sat at Hikaru's feet, watching the fire Yokai. There had to be a trace of Rin left inside her if she was not afraid of the creature made of flame. He looked back at Kasai. "If it's information you want, I'll give it to you."

"Though information is tempting, that is not what I desire." He pressed his fingertips together as he studied the two of them. "I have three riddles. If you can answer them, I will let you pass unharmed into the guardian's palace." He raised three fingers and then pointed at the palace behind him with a dramatic flourish. "But." He held up a single finger. "Get one wrong answer and I burn you both to ash."

Shin glowered. He was never good at word games. He was more a man of action. This was all Akio's way of testing him. There was no other arrangement. "Done," Shin said. He had no choice.

"Oh, good." Kasai clapped his hands together and sparks flew where they collided. A few cracks formed along the backs of his hands and flames from beneath the skin licked along the edges. "Let's start with the first, shall we?" He grinned at Shin. His teeth were black as tar, but his tongue was made of flame. "If I have it, I don't share it. If I share it, I don't have it. What is it?"

Shin stared blankly back at him. He hadn't the slightest idea. Was it something you gave away? But that could be anything. He massaged his temple. *I am terrible at these things. What could it be?*

"It's a secret?" the human said tentatively.

Shin spun to face him. If he got it wrong, he could have killed them both.

The creature smiled. "You are clever. I can see you are a wordsmith."

"I am better with words than a sword as well." Hikaru shrugged.

"Then you should answer the riddles," Shin said with certainty. This was their best chance of getting into the palace.

The human stared wide eyed at Shin. "I will, for Rin."

I can see why she fancies him. He is determined, I will give him that.

"For your next." Kasai spun in a circle and then, when he faced Hikaru, smiled deviously. "I will make this one more difficult: They come out at night without being called, and are lost in the day without being stolen. What are they?"

Shin considered for a moment; he had no idea. He hoped he had not made a bad choice in letting the human answer the questions.

"Stars," Hikaru said.

The creature seemed delighted even though they were defeating his game. *I worry what horror waits for us within if Kasai is glad we're winning.*

"I have been too generous. Let's see, what can I use to stump you?" He tapped his chin. "Aha. If I drink, I die. If I eat, I am fine. What am I?"

The human paused for a moment; this one really did seem to stump him. Kasai jumped from foot to foot with glee. The places where his feet landed were scorched black.

"You must answer or pay the price," Kasai said in a singsong voice.

"If I drink, I die..." the human muttered to himself.

Kasai's grin grew wider by the second and Shin feared it would come down to a fight after all. Kasai was not one he ever wanted to tangle with. He claimed to be a man of words, but he was a powerful Yokai. Shin's skin prickled, preparing to transform and fight his way through if it came down to it.

Then the human looked up. He smiled a triumphant smile. "You're fire!"

The creature clapped his hands together. Great flames leapt where his hands collided and Shin could feel the heat radiating off him from a few feet away.

"Oh, that was fun," Kasai said, "but our games have come to an end. Please go inside."

He bowed before stepping aside to let them pass. Hikaru bowed in return and then followed after Shin as they walked across the bridge. Rin jogged along after them. And though Shin and Hikaru were careful to keep the rope bridge from swinging as they walked, she ran across without fear. At the edge of the bridge, a set of stairs led up to a double door, which was open and waiting for them. They climbed the steps, and all the while that feeling of unease clung to Shin's skin. The hairs along his arms stood at attention and his intuition was telling him something wasn't right. *The riddles, the beast a human could kill, those are not typical Akio defenses.* He kept scanning in front of him and routinely looked over his shoulder. When they were inside the palace gates, they were greeted by a servant. One half of her body was that of a beautiful woman, but her head was that of a doe. She wore a long kimono in green with a pattern of red leaves.

"The guardian awaits you," she said in a low sweet voice.

Hikaru's mouth hung partially open. He clamped it shut when he noticed Shin's scornful look. Together they followed after the servant through twisting hallways and up stairs. The guardian's palace was a maze, meant to trap the unwary. Only his servants knew their way around, and anyone who entered left only at the guardian's behest.

At last they arrived in the audience room. It was a long narrow space, lined by red columns. At the far end of the room, the guardian sat on a raised dais. More half-animal women surrounded him. Some of them were deer, like the servant who had greeted them. There were Kitsunes too, with bright red hair and bushy tails. The guardian dominated the space, dwarfing the tiny women beside him. He wore a large hat on top of his head and he was draped in silk, gold and jewels; none of these disguised the fact that he was a boar. He had the head of a boar and the body of a man, but his hands and feet were hooves. He looked like a pig in silk robes. At least that's what Rin always used to say. Now she hid behind Hikaru's legs. Akio set down a glass with a thunk and regarded them as they approached. His tusks gleamed in the flickering candlelight.

"Ah, Shin, I see you've done as I asked." He folded his arms over his enormous gut.

The human shot Shin a curious glance but spoke to the guardian. "We've come to find a way to save the woman I love —" the human began.

"Silence," Akio roared. "I did not give you permission to speak. I know what you seek, but I wonder what madness made you believe I would help you."

"Because you want me," the human protested.

Shin looked at the human from the corner of his eye. *How does he know? He must be bluffing, and if he is, he has some serious guts. I hate to admit it, but he's impressed me.*

Akio grinned, revealing crooked yellowed teeth lining his snout. "That I do. Can I assume you know why I want you?"

"Because I am a Hanyou—half Kitsune. It is said the children of man and Kitsune have special powers," the human said.

Akio tapped his hooves together. "And do you?"

"You will have to reverse Rin's spell to find out."

Akio narrowed his eyes, examining the human. "What if I cannot reverse her spell? You seem very confident I can."

"If you cannot, then I will find someone who can." He turned to leave.

"Wait!" Akio said, half rising from his seat. "I will change her back, but in exchange you must stay here with me forever."

The human did not even hesitate. "I will do it."

TWENTY-SIX

"Your brother is missing, my lord," the warrior said as he knelt before him.

Hotaru exhaled with relief. He never wanted to hurt Hikaru. He just wanted to rule. His uncle and kinsmen had insisted he capture and execute him. Since the order had been given, he had been racking his brain on how to prevent his brother's death. The relief of knowing Hikaru escaped felt like a weight being lifted off his chest. But now was not a time to lose the respect of his men by showing weakness. The clan would look to him for leadership now, with Hikaru fled and Father dead. He was really the elder.

"Stop the search for now." He waved to his man to leave.

The warrior bobbed his head before scurrying out of the room.

Hotaru slumped to the ground. His knees could no longer hold him upright. He rested his head in his upturned palms. The clan's lives rested on his shoulders now. He had dreamed of this moment his entire life, but now that it was within his grasp, he feared he would not be the ruler he needed to be. He had to make difficult decisions, but thinking he had to kill his brother had torn his heart to pieces. They may have had their differences, but Hikaru wasn't a monster. *Even if he is a monster, he is still my blood.* Hikaru mysteriously gone, without trial or official judgment, their neighbors and tenants would suspect foul play, and Lady Fujikawa had disappeared as well. Hikaru might very well have run off with his wife back to her clan house; he might even be plotting to overthrow Hotaru. *I am not safe, not yet. I will need to prepare for him to return and challenge me with his wife's army at his back. How can I keep my place and my brother as well?*

The tinkling of bells interrupted the night's silence. He glanced up and found an old woman in his chamber. She had long white hair in a single braid, which swung behind her back, the only indication she had moved. She stood perfectly still, a smile on her lips.

Hotaru jumped up. "Who are you, and what are you doing in my chamber?"

"I've come to pay my respects to the new elder." She bowed at her waist.

He eyed her suspiciously. He knew enough of the spiritual world to know this woman was not what she appeared. "Normally in these situations, you would wait until daybreak and present yourself properly."

"I'm afraid I won't have much time to linger here."

His eyebrows rose to his hairline. "Who are you?"

"An old friend of your family's. You could say I made it what it is today."

"How—" He stopped himself; of course, she was a Yokai. What else could enter his room unseen, without announcement, and make such cryptic statements? "What do you have to do with my family?"

"Much, I knew you when you were living in holes in the ground." She grinned.

A tight knot formed in his gut. This was dangerous. He had not realized how little he knew about his family's history. Had this Yokai given them the success and wealth they enjoyed? "What do you want from me?"

"Nothing yet, I just wanted to introduce myself to you." She bowed once more.

"Well, I have a few questions for you, then."

She did not move, but her expression shifted from polite to reserved.

"What are you? How can you enter this place without being seen? How could you know my family for so long?"

"All questions that will be answered in time, young lord. For now be secure in knowing you have no challenge to your position. Your brother will not rise against you, and you shall rule for a very long time. I have seen it."

"You have visions?"

"Something like that." And with another bow she disappeared in a puff of smoke.

As the smoke cleared, he noticed something glimmering on the ground. Hotaru stared at the space where she had been, wondering if he was losing his mind, but then he found a staff with bells attached to the top in a triangle shape. He had seen priests and priestesses use this during exorcisms and rituals. He picked it up and they jangled slightly. A note was tied around the base of the shaker. It read *Should you ever need me, ring the bells.*

HIKARU STARED AT THE WALL JUST BEHIND THE GUARDIAN, LEST HE lose his nerve. The gigantic boar creature terrified him. It moved and spoke like a human, but its sharp tusks and crooked evil smiles sent a cold chill down his spine. It reminded him of the one that had attacked him and his men. He'd had no chance against that creature, and if Rin had not interfered, he would not be here. Now it was his turn to save her. Hikaru knew he could not fight it and win. His brother had taken his place as leader of the clan; there was nothing left for him. Saving Rin was all that mattered now. He would have climbed the highest mountain to reach the palace of the Eight to save her.

The guardian leaned forward. He pressed his hooves together and regarded Hikaru over them. His eyes were framed by wiry gray and brown hair that somewhat resembled eyebrows. They were tugged together in the middle, creating a V over his snout. The guardian's beady yellow eyes danced with delight.

"It is good to see someone with some sense for once." The guardian chuckled.

Sweat pooled in the palms of his hands, but he resisted the urge to wipe them against his thighs. He was trying to look formidable. "My good sense cannot be the only reason you wanted me," Hikaru said.

The guardian laughed and his gut jiggled. And the half-human, half-animal creatures that surrounded him tittered along with him. Then with a sharp gesture from the boar they fell silent.

"You are arrogant; that will help you find a place in my palace. Even if you are a half-breed." The guardian snorted in a piglike fashion.

A smile threatened to curl Hikaru's lips, but he thought it would not be welcomed, so he held back. Judging on how the boar dressed, he wanted to be human and probably did not like to be reminded of his boar-like physique. *What does he think I can do for him? That's the real question.*

"You cannot be serious about this, Akio," Shin drawled. "What can this Hanyou possibly do for you?"

Hikaru glared at Shin, willing him silently to hold his tongue. It should have been the ideal solution for Shin. Akio would return Rin to her original form and Shin would protect her. *He would protect her better than I ever could.*

"We made a deal, Shin," the guardian said. He waved a hoof as if to bat Shin away like an annoying pest. "And now I am making a deal with my new friend here."

"And I've changed my mind. You've been trying to get your revenge against the Dragon for centuries, and now I am here, his general, begging you for a favor. What do you want? Information? I'll give you whatever you ask if you'll save Rin." Shin clenched his hands into fists and his jaw snapped shut on the last word. His jaw twitched and the veins in his neck stood out.

The boar laughed. "You think you are wise, wolf, but there are things even you do not know, O master of spies."

They glared at one another for a few moments. Rin weaved in and out of both Shin's and Hikaru's legs. She must have sensed the tension in the room.

"This Hanyou cannot be worth that much to you," Shin replied.

"Oh, but he is." The boar motioned and the doors behind them swung open. Hikaru turned around as a man strode into the chamber.

The man who had saved him from the palace strode into the room. He wore all black, and the painted characters on his forehead stood out against his pale skin and dark hair. Hikaru watched as he marched to the front of the room, where he knelt before Akio.

"Tell me, Naoki, what have you learned about the Hanyou?"

Hikaru's stomach clenched. Naoki would reveal his ruse and with it his chance to save Rin. He had no special powers, other than being able to see Yokai.

"I have performed all the tests, Master. He does not have the gift. His ears and tail were cut when he was young; he is useless to us."

"What!" Akio slammed a hoof onto the table, splitting it in half. The servants who had clung to him jumped backward to avoid falling debris. Only Naoki did not move. He remained with his head bowed to the ground, his back straight.

Akio glared at Hikaru, accusing him with his eyes of being inept. Then he lifted up his hand. A servant rushed forward and cleaned away spilled sake that stained his sleeve.

"Never mind, then." He sighed. "Very well, down to business, I suppose." He stood up amidst much grunting and heaving. He climbed down a few steps towards them. His footsteps shook the ground beneath Hikaru's feet. As he approached, Hikaru had to crane his neck back to see his face. He was four of Shin's size, his legs and arms the size of Hikaru's entire body.

He stopped in front of Shin, Hikaru completely forgotten. "You are lucky, Shin, I am in a bargaining mood," the boar said.

Shin glared at the boar. "Lucky me."

"I want you to swear yourself unto my service. Do that and I will give this half-breed a lotus petal." He flicked his hoof towards Hikaru.

The fox hid behind Hikaru's legs and he could feel her trembling. Shin closed his eyes, inhaled, and when he opened them, he knelt down on the ground in front of the boar.

"I swear my loyalty, my spirit and my blood to you, Akio," Shin said in a monotone voice.

The guardian smiled and the corners of his mouth turned up, revealing the jagged yellow teeth within. "It is done, then." The guardian twirled his hand in the air and a collar manifested in a cloud of leaves. Akio leaned forward and clamped the collar around Shin's neck.

Shin remained kneeling. He stared at the ground as he said, "Now give him the petal."

"Am I not a man of my word?" the boar asked Shin. Then he turned his massive body to Hikaru.

Hikaru took a few steps back. Just being near the boar made him claustrophobic. He nearly tripped over Rin. She yipped, scurried back a few feet, and hid behind a pillar.

The boar sneered at Hikaru. "You are fortunate Shin is a self-sacrificing fool. I would have taken you anyway, truth be told. But in this instance Shin was the greater prize."

Hikaru's mouth felt too dry to speak; he nodded instead. The boar shook his massive head as if disgusted by Hikaru's subservience. He patted his robe, and then dipping a hand into the folds of his kimono, he removed a satchel made of red silk. He tossed it to Hikaru, who fumbled but caught it just the same. "Feed that to her and she will return to the woman she once was."

Hikaru pulled on the drawstrings that kept the bag closed. He poured the contents of the bag into his hand. A red crystallized petal rested in his palm. It was near transparent, shot with golden veins. Before he used it, he had to ask, "Why are you doing this, Shin? You could have been there for her."

Shin did not look up and he did not answer straight away. Hikaru wondered for a moment if some spell had been put upon him. But when he spoke at last, his voice was low and directed to his knees. "She needs you now more than she needs me. I can see that; she was willing to give up her life to spare you. I could not face her knowing that I sacrificed the man she loved."

Hikaru bowed to the wolf. "Thank you, I will never forget this." *I promise, I will find a way to free you.*

Shin shook his head. "There is no reason to thank me. I am not doing it for you, after all. It is for her."

Rin peeked her head out from behind the pillar. Hikaru crouched down and offered the petal to her on the flat of his palm. She regarded him for a moment, her golden eyes blank as an animal's. Then very slowly, she approached him. She sniffed at it at first and then, after a moment's hesitation, snatched it out of his palm. She crunched into it and swallowed. He waited with bated breath. The transformation started with her fur; it grew pale, fading from copper to yellow then to white as snow. Markings appeared around her face and on her paws, whirling red markings that ran up and down her legs and framed her golden eyes. She grew in size as well. When she reached her full height, she was a head taller than him. She had several tails, all whipping back and forth and tipped with licking flames. Hikaru stared at her in wide-eyed wonder. *She is beautiful.* Rin looked around the room, her gaze falling on Hikaru. She leaned forward and nuzzled against his cheek. Her breath was warm against his skin.

She pulled back and then her gaze fell on Shin. He had not lifted his head even once. Hikaru felt the prickle of tension rolling off Rin in waves. She bared long white pointed teeth and moved a step towards the boar.

He held up his hoof to stop her. "Do not get mad at me, Rin. He and I made a deal."

Rin switched from her Kitsune form back to a humanlike form. But unlike the Rin he had come to know, she had coppery red hair and a pair of fox ears on top of her head.

Her tail twitched back and forth as she snarled, "What deal? You cannot hold him, the Dragon's—"

"Enough, Rin," Shin said. His voice was tired.

She looked at him as if pained. "What have you done, you fool?" she whispered.

He turned his head so she could not see his face, only his profile.

"Let him go, Akio. I mean it, let him go, or I will tear this palace to pieces."

Akio laughed. "Who said I was going to let any of you go? Shin traded himself to turn you back to normal. I never said I would let you go."

TWENTY-SEVEN

"You cannot do this. We had a deal!" Hikaru shouted.

Rin clutched her hands into fists. She took a deep breath; flying off the handle would not help this situation. She had learned that the first time she had met the mercurial guardian.

"We don't have a deal, remember? Shin took your place and your chance to break free," Akio said. He yanked on the chain around Shin's neck, slowly bringing him closer to him. Rin watched helplessly as Akio took away everything she loved. He already had Shin, would he take Hikaru away as well?

This is personal. He is trying to pay me back for before.

"What do you want from me, Akio?" she said.

Hikaru swiveled towards her, mouth agape. "No, Rin!"

"Rin!" Shin growled at the same time.

Akio wound the chain around his arm and yanked, bringing Shin to his knees. He glowered at the boar.

"What could you possibly offer me?" Akio said. Though he pretended at indifference, his black beady eyes gleamed.

"Anything you want. If you need a Kitsune, then perhaps I can help you with your problem."

He scoffed. "Only a Hanyou with the right ability could do that."

Rin shrugged. "Fox fire has many healing abilities. I am sure you've heard about the curative power of a Kitsune liver."

"Rin, don't."

She would not face him, could not. She had already come this far to keep him safe, she wouldn't lose him to Akio. Akio paced back and forth, making a great show of considering her offer. Then he came to stand before her. Her knees locked as she looked up at his massive form. She could see his leathery skin beneath the spattering of coarse dark hair.

"Even if your liver could save me, I wouldn't take it. I wouldn't give you the satisfaction." He laughed.

Hikaru stepped in front of her. "Then take me, just let Rin go."

Akio rolled his eyes and then, tugging Shin along behind him, went to sit back down on the raised platform. Shin's gaze was murderous. Rin felt the same. She should have known Akio would play games. She put her hand on Hikaru's shoulder and held back from jumping in front of him to try to protect him from Akio. Though the gesture was appreciated, she could not imagine living knowing he was locked up here while she was free. It was bad enough Shin had made his own deal when she was not able to stop him.

"I am sure if I tried to keep you, she would come back and cause another disturbance. No, I will let you both go, but you must each pay a price," Akio said, gloating all the while.

She stood next to Hikaru and grabbed his hand on reflex. She felt stronger beside him. She considered Akio. Any offer he made was most likely laced with poison. She held onto Hikaru, an anchor for the storm inside her heart. She looked at Shin kneeling beside the guardian, head bowed. It made her heart ache.

Hikaru looked to Rin, and when she nodded, he said, "Name your price."

"From the Hanyou, I want a favor," the guardian said as he leaned back on his cushion. He twirled the length of chain around his arm and the metal rattled, piercing Rin's heart.

"And what sort of favor is that?" Hikaru asked.

He waggled a hoof at him. "I will not tell you, not yet."

She squeezed Hikaru's hand. "You don't have to agree to this."

"I accept," Hikaru replied.

Akio grinned, revealing his crooked yellow teeth. Rin swallowed hard. Now came her price. *Whatever it is, I will do it to protect him.*

"And what would you have my price be?" Rin asked.

"It is simple, I want you to spend one last night with Shin."

Shin growled and looked back at Akio. He bared his teeth; his rage was hardly contained. *What is he getting at?*

"How does this benefit you?" she asked.

He laughed. "When the night is through, I will ask you a question, and your answer will be your price."

Her stomach twisted. Hikaru pulled her closer and wrapped his arm around her shoulder. She inhaled his scent. Now that she was back to her original form, she could pick out the varying notes that made up his own unique signature. She could also sense his worry. Neither of them knew what game Akio was playing, but they could not fight their way out.

"Done," she said.

Akio broke the chain and, with a sweep of his hoof, set Shin free. At least in part, the collar remained around his neck like a beacon highlighting his servitude to the boar.

Rin looked to Hikaru.

He nodded his head. "Go to him. I'll meet you in the morning."

She squeezed Hikaru's hand one more time before running to Shin. She wrapped her arms around his shoulders and buried her head into his chest. "You idiot, why did you do this?"

"Maybe we should talk in private?" he asked. Akio grinned at them deviously. He would love for them to play out their tragic drama in front of him—she was sure. She would not give him the satisfaction.

She nodded. A servant came and escorted Hikaru out one door, and then another led Shin and Rin out another. She did not want to be parted from Hikaru. She watched as he disappeared out the opposite door. He kept his eyes locked on her until the door closed between them. *I just have to hope Akio will stay true to his word and he will let us go come morning.*

THE DOE-HEADED SERVANT SHOWED HIM INTO AN ADJOINING ROOM that was separated from the main audience room. Hikaru was feeling restless, so he picked at his already tattered sleeve and paced back and forth. He listened to the receding footsteps of Shin and Rin. Worry twisted his gut; why did he get the feeling he would never see her again after tonight? The door at the back of the room slid open. He turned around to see the guardian ducking through the doorway. He clenched his hands into fists to hide his anger. It was his fault; if he had just accepted Hikaru's offer, then Rin would have been set free.

"My lord guardian." Hikaru bowed to the vile creature.

The boar grinned. His yellow teeth looked even more rotten up close and the stench of his breath was putrid.

"I've come for my favor."

Hikaru held his breath, waiting. "And what is that?"

"I want you to see something." He waved his hoof and a mirror appeared out of a cloud of leaves. At first he saw his own face reflected there. Seeing his image was startling. He hardly recognized himself—the dark shadows under his eyes, his torn and battered skin, and his topknot had come undone, his hair falling forward.

"You want me to see my own reflection?"

"No, look closer."

And so Hikaru did as he was bid, he peered into the mirror. His image disappeared and in its place he saw Rin and Shin alone in a small chamber with a single bed. *Does he expect them to sleep together?* His gut twisted with jealousy. He had no reason to believe Rin was his. Though he had asked her to be his wife, he had never gotten her answer. Had he misinterpreted her intentions? But if she did not care for him, why sacrifice herself for him?

Shin had his back to Rin, and she seemed to be saying something, but Hikaru could not hear what they were saying. From the way she gazed at him, captured by Shin's every word, Hikaru knew it was serious. Shin turned to face Rin, and tears rolled down her cheeks. Hikaru's stomach sank. *Has he confessed how he feels? Does she feel the same?* Shin had given up everything to save Rin, how could she not love him in return? Hikaru could not turn away as

Rin fell to her knees and Shin wiped away her tears. She grabbed onto Shin's robe and buried her face into his chest. Shin wrapped his arms around her. And Hikaru could not look any longer.

"Do you know what he asked?" the boar taunted.

"What?" Hikaru asked, though he feared the answer.

"He asked her to choose between the two of you. Who do you think she chose?"

His head said Shin, it only made sense, but his heart thought differently. They loved one another, he was certain of that much. But the guardian had filled him with a fragment of doubt and that was what held his tongue.

"I'll wait for your answer until morning. If you're right, you both go free; if you are wrong, then you both belong to me."

THE ROOM THEY WERE GIVEN WAS TINY WITH A SINGLE FUTON FOR them to share. They had slept side by side more times than she could count, but when they entered the room and the sliding doors were closed, the air felt charged. Shin stood with his back to her and his hand pulled at his new collar.

She went to his side and took his free hand in hers. He tensed; all his muscles corded in his back and arms like an animal poised to take flight. They stood like that for a moment, not speaking. *This cannot be the last time I see him. I will not let it be. I will find a way to free him from Akio.*

Shin dropped her hand suddenly and then stepped away. She could read the unease in every line of his body.

"Shin...?"

He did not answer.

"You know what question Akio is going to ask me, don't you?"

He would not look at her. He was not acting like himself. In fact, he had been acting strangely since the witch cursed her. *He said there was something he wanted to ask me when I could speak again.*

"Answer me, Shin!" she shouted. After everything that had happened, she was on edge. Was he still mad from when she slapped him? She knew he could hold a grudge but never against her.

He flinched. He never flinched unless he felt guilty. *What is there to feel guilty about?*

"You love him?" His voice held no inflection; it was like he was reading rehearsed lines.

"I do." She crossed her hands over her chest.

He ran his hands through his hair. "Then the question does not matter."

She walked around to face him. She peered up into his eyes. "What possessed you to make a deal? What were you thinking?" She reached out to shake him, but he stepped back before she could touch him.

He looked up at her at last. His gaze pinned her in place. "We do things for those we love that we never imagined."

She clutched at the silk of her kimono just above her heart. "Shin..."

"It was my own fault for not telling you sooner."

She did not know what to say. So she asked, "How long have you been in love with me?"

He looked at her; his dark eyes pierced her through. "Always."

She gasped. She felt as if her world had tilted sideways. "And the question?"

"Akio wants you to choose between Hikaru and me."

She sank to her knees. Her legs could no longer support her weight. Shin hovered over her. His expression was guarded, closed off. She had never seen him that way before.

"Why didn't you say anything?"

He sighed. "I wanted to, but it never seemed like the right time. I thought I could be happy just being by your side. But then you had that affair with the Dragon..."

Her hands were shaking. "I never loved the Dragon. It never meant anything to either of us."

He nodded. "I can see that now."

"Oh, Shin."

His face hid much of his emotion, but she could see his disappointment beneath the cracks in his facade. She wanted to reach out to him to comfort him. But it felt tainted now. She did not want her actions to be misinterpreted. *Nothing has changed; it's still Shin.* They had always been one another's rocks, but she never imagined she would be the one to cause him pain. *Had I known, would things have been different? Could things be different?*

"I'll find a way to break you free of Akio. I promise," she said.

He shook his head. "I am content to know you are happy. Live your life with the hu—Hikaru." His mouth twisted wryly. "Bear his children. Forget about me."

Tears pushed the back of her lids. He knelt down in front of her and wiped an errant tear from her eye. She tried to hold herself back, but she could not any longer. She grabbed his shirt front and held on tight. She buried her face into his chest.

"You're an idiot," she said.

He stroked her hair. "If I'm an idiot, what does that make you?"

She laughed despite herself. "I'm not going to give up. You know that, don't you?"

"Stubborn to the end."

"Always," she replied as he pressed a kiss to her brow.

Twenty-Eight

Hikaru paced the length of the chamber they had allotted him. He had not slept the night through, he was too busy thinking about Rin. He kept going back and forth on his answer. He wanted to believe she would choose him, but a lifetime of self-doubt left him questioning his worth. Could he really be worthy of her? He stopped pacing when the door at the far end of the room slid open. The half-deer woman stood just outside.

"My master will see you now," she said.

He stared at her a moment before registering her words. From her feet to her neck she looked human, only her head was that of a deer. Her clothes were not dissimilar to what he would expect from a servant in his own house. Plain and easy to move in. She stared at him with large black eyes, blinking and waiting patiently for a response. He clamped his mouth shut, realizing too late he had been staring. He nodded to let her know he had heard. He could not force words out of his mouth. *This is Rin's world,* he realized. *The things that are strange to me are probably common fare for her.* How could he bridge this gap between their two realities? Was she willing to leave her life behind? Was he willing to leave his life behind? But this was his world too. His mother's world. No matter her answer, it was time he learned more about it.

He followed the servant through the twisting corridors of the palace. The doors popped up at random and some pathways seemed to end at blank walls. And when he turned around to look where he had been, the pathways changed, and where there had been rooms, now a garden appeared, with butterflies flitting among the jasmine bushes.

He hurried to keep up with the servant, fearing what would happen if he fell behind. The servant led him to a chamber, different than the one he had been to before. This one reminded him of the morning room back at the palace. It was a large open space that faced out onto a garden. The guardian sat behind a table that looked miniature in comparison to the guardian. He held a large bowl in his hooves and he used a pair of chopsticks to sloppily shovel rice into his mouth. A few stray white granules clung to the coarse hairs on his snout. When they entered the room, he did not stop or acknowledge their presence but continued making loud slurping noises. Hikaru fidgeted with the hem of his robe as he waited for the boar to finish his meal. The guardian finally set his bowl aside and smacked his mouth. Then he finally turned beady black eyes on Hikaru.

"Do you have an answer?" the guardian said.

Hikaru bowed, as he deemed appropriate. If he read this beast right, and he thought he was, he appreciated the respect. "My lord, before I answer, I would ask you a favor in return."

Akio sputtered and laughed, shaking the ground beneath him. The vibrations reached all the way to Hikaru, but he did not break for a moment. He had done enough negotiating for his father and the clan to know when someone was trying to intimidate him. Hikaru was not one to back down so easily.

"Well, I underestimated you. I am hoping you answer incorrectly so I can better utilize you," he said.

"But if I am correct, you will hold to our deal?" he asked.

The boar narrowed his eyes at Hikaru. "I never go back on my word."

Hikaru shrugged. The guardian liked to play with words and manipulate to his own ends. But he was partially true, he had not gone against any of his promises, not in word anyway. "Then I would add this to our deal, if I win, you will pardon Rin and allow us to live near your forest."

The boar laughed again. "Why would you stay here? Your brother will be out for your head, and Rin will never find friends here."

He was shocked it had been this easy. Perhaps the guardian

was in a good mood, or perhaps he had his own motives for hearing him out.

"My brother doesn't know it yet, but he'll need my help. And I would like to rebuild the shrine at the edge of the forest and dedicate it to your worship," Hikaru said.

The boar sat up straighter; now he was paying attention. "Do you now?"

"I have been turned out from my home, and seeing as the shrine is abandoned and the Kami vacated, I thought it an appropriate tribute. It is your domain."

He tapped his hoof on the table, rattling the dishes, which clanked together like the tinkling of bells.

"It is a good trade. And in exchange I pardon Rin?"

"Yes."

The boar stopped tapping. "Ah, there we have it. I suppose you think she chose you?"

"I do."

"And what will you do when the witch comes back for her?"

The question caught him off guard. He knew Rin was under a spell, but there had never been much time to explain how the spell had been cast.

The boar leaned forward. "You didn't know, did you? She was under a witch's spell; that's how she became human."

"And where is this witch now?" Hikaru tightened his hands into fists. He did not have much power, but he would do whatever it took to protect Rin.

"Gone, if she has any sense. Her plan failed. I suppose she's off licking her wounds."

"You sound as if you know her."

The boar sat back, and though he appeared relaxed, Hikaru could sense a tension in him. "Yes, I know her very well."

"We will be careful."

The boar snorted as if he did not believe it. "What makes you think she will choose to live with you?" he asked.

Hikaru opened his mouth to answer that he was certain she would want to spend her life with him, because she had to feel what he did. A sense of completion when they were together, it felt right. No matter how he tried to think about it, he could not imagine her choosing Shin. She had given up her life for him, why would she abandon him now?

"Well, you shall see, I suppose. If you are right, you have my leave to build your temple, and if she chose you, she will meet you at the bridge. If you're not, Naoki will come fetch you back. And don't think about running away, I will find you."

Hikaru bowed again. "Thank you."

The servant waited for him outside. She led him back through the palace at a sedate pace. Once more they meandered through the maze of passageways. Every moment they delayed, he felt that his heart might burst. What would he do if she was not there waiting for him? But he feared if he rushed, he might never find his way out again. He kept close to the servant, the closest he dared without touching the creature. When they reached the outer courtyard, he gave a sigh of relief. He could see the bridge beyond at the bottom of the steps.

The servant stood aside and he rushed out the gate and went to the bridge. She was not there. He spun in place, expecting her to appear. Even the servant had left. He was alone with the creaking of the bridge as the wind pushed it to and fro. The wind rustled through the trees and pricked the hairs on the back of his neck. He sensed someone watching him. He spun in place and found Naoki standing in the center of the bridge. His chest clenched as his stomach sank. She had not chosen him?

"She chose Shin?" Hikaru asked.

Naoki shook his head. "No, I came here on my own."

Hikaru stared at him for a moment. Everything about him seemed ordinary but for the markings on his forehead and his strange-colored eyes.

"Why are you here?" Hikaru asked; the words just tumbled out.

Naoki did not answer right away. He looked over the canyon and the wind tangled in his hair. He wore it long and loose. He was a different man than the stern captain at the palace yet very similar. There was a wild energy that hung about him, like a caged animal.

"To warn you, the deal you've made with the guardian is a double-edged blade."

"I gathered as much." He scrutinized Naoki's face, hoping his intentions would be written there. He was unreadable as always. "Why risk his wrath to warn me?" "

"It's the honorable thing to do."

"But you're the guardian's man."

"Doing what we are told and doing what we know is right are two different things. He may hold me, but I am still my own."

Hikaru chewed on this for a moment. He opened his mouth to ask another question, but Naoki had disappeared like a wisp of smoke. He had looked away for just a second and he was gone. Hikaru spun around, wondering where he had gone to, when he saw her standing at the top of the steps that led into the palace. He let go the breath he had been holding. Despite it all, for a moment he had still feared she would not choose him.

Her auburn hair hung in a curtain down her back. She wore a bright red robe with a pattern of white flowers. She smiled at him and it was the same mischievous grin he had come to love. She leaped down the steps and then ran the distance to him. She threw herself into his arms and they nearly toppled over to the ground. He laughed as he touched her face. *She is real and she is mine.* She was even more beautiful than he remembered. He ran his hands along her auburn hair, marveling at the color. This was the real Rin. She smiled down at him and then captured his lips in a kiss. The very essence took his breath away. There was power in her, a fire that burned, and he could feel a similar fire burning in his chest, calling out to hers. For the first time in his life he felt complete.

They broke apart.

"Say my name," he whispered.

She stroked his cheek. "Hikaru."

He grabbed her tighter, pulling her legs around his waist. "Now give me your answer, will you be my bride?"

"Yes," she said and punctuated it with a kiss.

When he thought he would be dizzy from kissing, he set her down on her feet and they crossed the bridge together, hand in hand.

"Where are we going?" she asked.

He thought he would never get tired of hearing the sound of her voice.

"To start our lives."

Once they were across the bridge, she looked over her shoulder. He squeezed her hand. He knew her thoughts were with Shin imprisoned in the guardian's castle. He thought he should be jealous, but he could only pity the other man. He had given up everything so Rin could be happy. Hikaru owed his happiness to Shin.

"I promise we'll find a way to free him," he whispered in Rin's ear.

She pecked him on the cheek. "I know we will."

EPILOGUE

Winter had a firm grip upon the shrine. Banks of white snow clung to the sides of the buildings and weighed upon the rooftops. Bright patches of crimson peeked out beneath the white as Rin ran along the rooftop, melting snow with her fox fire. Hikaru, down on the ground, hurried to hang the last of the streamers. It was possible none of the local farmers would show up; it had only been a few months since they established the shrine. The cleanup had been tedious, and had it not been for Hikaru, Rin would have given up and run off into the woods for a romp on more than one occasion.

She melted the last of the snow on the roof, and rivers of clear water ran down the top, forming into long dangling icicles along the eaves. They sparkled in the sun, casting multicolored lights on the banks of snow below.

"Finished up there?" Hikaru called from on the ground.

Rin launched off the roof and sailed through the air towards Hikaru. He opened his arms to receive her as she fell into his arms once more in a human form. He spun her around.

"I rather like you in your fox form," he said as he nibbled her neck.

She purred. "Do you now?"

"You look very powerful."

She laughed, tossing back her head. Life had been good. The shrine restoration was coming along, and Akio's blessing had allowed them a measure of protection. Hikaru was not the only reason she decided to stay behind. Akio was up to something, and being close would help her find out what. In the wake of her affair with the Dragon and her being turned into a human, she could not return to the palace. Not that she wanted to. She was happy with Hikaru.

She had seen nothing of the witch. Though she still woke with panic at night, thinking she heard her whispering in her ear. As Rin's laughter died away, she heard the tinkling of bells—someone had walked beneath the tori arch in the courtyard. Rin turned, ears tilted towards the sound. She lifted her nose in the air. It was a human—not the witch. She exhaled. Would the fear ever go away? she wondered.

Hikaru brushed his fingertips across her cheek. "We're safe here. There's no need to worry."

She leaned her forehead against his, inhaling his scent and indulging in their private moment just a bit longer.

The footsteps drew closer, and from the sound of them, they had a crowd. Hikaru pulled away, although hesitantly, and went to greet the worshipers. She followed him around the corner of the building into the courtyard, which she had cleaned of snow earlier that morning. A small group hovered near the bright red tori arch. Their coats were well made and lined with fur, and she could see from a distance the jewelry and trappings that set them apart from mere farmers.

"Welcome," Hikaru started to say, but he stopped in his tracks.

Rin peered around his shoulder. Her lips pulled back into a growl and she felt the fire in her gut churning. She considered transforming, not that these humans could see her if she did. "What are you doing here?" She tried to move around Hikaru, but he put up his hand to stop her. The humans could not see her if she did not reveal herself.

"Brother," Hikaru said.

Hotaru bowed low, much lower than was required. For the sake of appearances he was treating Hikaru like a proper priest.

What does he want? She stood at Hikaru's side, glaring at the unaware Hotaru.

"We've come to leave our offerings and ask the Kami for their blessing for the new year," Hotaru said. There was none of his usual haughty arrogance. His voice seem tempered. There were bags beneath his eyes and a certain weight to his expression that was not there before.

Rin recognized the members of the Kaedemori clan that joined him, all those that were close to Hotaru and surprisingly no guards. They could not see her, so she was free to scrutinize them at her leisure. She wondered what brought them this far out. They could have performed the new year's rituals at the family temple just as easily.

Hikaru approached his brother, his hands folded in front of him.

"I suspect you seek more than the blessing of the Kami," Hikaru said. His voice was not angry, nor cold, more like curious.

Rin's chest swelled with pride. Hikaru was more generous than she would have been with his forgiveness. His brother had betrayed him and would have had him killed, given the chance. If Hikaru was willing to listen to him, however, then Rin would be patient. One wrong move, and she would strike without mercy.

Hotaru knelt down on the ground, and his household followed. The people of the Kaedemori clan one by one fell to their knees and bowed before Hikaru, their heads nearly brushing the ground. Rin gasped and covered her hand with her mouth.

"I have betrayed you, brother, I conspired against you, but you have received the blessing of the Kami. I have learned the error of my deeds and I seek your forgiveness."

Hikaru bent down and placed his hand on his brother's head. "I forgive you. Because I was never the right man to lead the clan and you knew it. This is where I belong."

Hotaru looked up at his brother. It may have been Rin's imagination, but it looked like there were tears in his eyes. He stood up and embraced Hikaru. Rin wiped away an errant tear that escaped from her eye. It was good to know they could live here in peace without the interference of the human world. While the witch remained at large, they would never be truly safe. She took a step in their direction, intent on revealing herself to the humans, when a voice called out to her.

"Wait a moment, Rin."

She spun in place to see the Dragon leaning against the shrine building, with the careless smirk that she loved. Today was a day for surprises.

"Master." She fell to the ground at his feet in a bow. *He came. Why now when I no longer need his help?*

He waved his hand. "There is no need for that. Stand, please."

She got to her feet, her stomach in knots. "Master, why have you come?"

"Why are you so formal, Rin? I have told you thousands of times to address me as your equal."

She laced her fingers in front of her. "This feels more natural; I am your servant." *I never thought myself worthy of you, so I put myself beneath you. Even when we were lovers I thought myself beneath you.*

He shook his head. "I suppose there has been little to serve, which has led you and the others to distraction." It was not a chastisement, not really. It wasn't an apology either. She had no doubt that no matter how humble he pretended to be or how human he acted, he was still a proud creature.

He did not move closer and Rin felt more comfortable at a distance. She had not forgotten the fear she'd felt when he tried to kill her. But he seemed unaware. When they had last parted, it had been as lovers, and now their lives had changed drastically. She never thought her life would have taken this path and she was sure the Dragon felt much the same. She still could not believe he had taken a human lover.

"I have heard rumors that you and Shin are serving Akio now." He frowned. "Akio is rather proud of his acquisition of Shin." He crossed his arms and Rin knew it was taking all of his self-control to not go stomping back to Akio's palace and demand the release of his right-hand man.

"Yes," she said, not daring to say more. Lying to the Dragon would keep him safe until she could stop Akio and get Shin his happy ending after all.

The Dragon shook his head. "I'd say I'm disappointed, but..." He sighed. "I cannot blame you. I should have shielded you from the others. I knew rumors would start, but I let you suffer alone."

She bowed her head. "Do not blame yourself; it was my choice as well."

"You've done well for yourself, it seems. You have chosen this Hanyou?"

"Yes, Hikaru and I are wed, and we are caretakers to this shrine."

"You love him, this Hikaru?" the Dragon asked.

She looked at him without answering. Even now, after everything they had been through, she found it difficult to express her feelings to the Dragon.

The dragon petted her on top of her head. She lowered her eyes. "They have a way of creeping into your heart, do they not?"

"This one did," she replied.

The Dragon sighed. "We live so long, Rin, and they live only a moment. It is difficult to love them, they are fragile, but they love more fiercely because of it." He looked down at her. "If you have found someone who makes you happy, I want you to stay here with him."

"Are you sure? I swore fealty to you..."

"And I release you from your promises. I have made my own decisions, and I will not bind you to me as I chase what makes me happy."

"Then I suppose this is goodbye?" Rin ventured.

He smiled at her. "For now. I am sure we shall see one another again. We do live long lives."

She bowed to him again as he transformed into his dragon form. His body filled the small space between the buildings and his back end coiled around the top of the shrine. He grinned down at her, revealing his long white teeth.

"Goodbye, Dragon," Rin said.

He bowed his head before taking off into the sky. She watched him go, closing that chapter of her life.

Hikaru came running around the corner. He craned his head back. "Who was that?" His question was more curious than accusatory.

"An old friend," she said as she threaded her fingers with his.

They held onto one another for a moment, staring up at the blue sky, not even a cloud to mar its perfection. The dragon's serpentine body was like a smudge of paint against a blue canvas, growing smaller as he flew into the distance.

She leaned her head against his shoulder and he put his arm around her, bringing her closer. "You know I will live forever," she said.

He pressed his lips to her hair. "I've been thinking about that, actually. I know I will not live forever as you will, but I swear I will always find you. No matter how many lifetimes it takes."

The fear of his death was real and palpable. It clutched at her heart for a moment. She tightened her grip on his hand. She saw their years stretched out in front of them. For her endless and for him, in the scope of her existence, it was finite. True, he would have a much longer lifespan than most humans. If they were lucky, they would have centuries, but not forever. *I have to believe we will find one another again. I know because he was meant for me.* She turned and kissed him. "I know you will, and I will be waiting for you each time."

Also by Nicolette Andrews

Moonlight Dragon

Empress Ascending (Newsletter Exclusive)

Dragon's Deception

Dragon's Temptation

Thornwood Series

Fairy Ring (Free)

Pricked by Thorns (Free)

Heart of Thorns

Tangled in Thorns

Blood and Thorns

World of Akatsuki

The Dragon Saga

The Priestess and the Dragon (Free)

The Sea Stone

The Song of the Wind

The Fractured Soul

The Immortal Vow

Tales of Akatsuki

Kitsune: A Little Mermaid Retelling (Free)

Yuki: A Snow White Retelling

Okami: A Little Red Riding Hood Retelling

Diviner's World

Duchess (Free)

Sorcerer (Free)

Diviner's Prophecy

Diviner's Curse

Diviner's Fate

Princess

Witch of the Lake Series

Feast of the Mother

Fate of the Demon

Fall of the Reaper

ABOUT THE AUTHOR

Nicolette Andrews lives in San Diego with her husband, youngest child, cat and dog. A lover of rom-com K-Dramas, stabby heroines, and brooding heroes. She's best known for twisty-turny romantic fantasy and angsty plots. When she's not torturing her creations, she enjoys cooking, camping, and cozy videos games.

You can visit her at her website: www.nicoletteandrews.com or at these places:

- facebook.com/nicandfantasy
- twitter.com/nicandfantasy
- instagram.com/nicolette_andrews
- amazon.com/author/nicoletteandrews
- bookbub.com/authors/nicolette-andrews
- goodreads.com/nicolette_andrews
- pinterest.com/Nicandfantasy
- tiktok.com/@nicandfantasy